THE CARRIER

SOLOMON CHURCH
BOOK 4

MORGAN GREENE

MERCURY BOOKS

ALSO BY MORGAN GREENE

The Last Light Of Day
The Mark Of The Dead
The Hiss Of The Snake
The Devil In The Dark
The First Snow Of Winter
The Deepest Grave Of All

Standalone Titles

Savage Ridge
A Place Called Hope
The Blood We Share
The Trade

THE CARRIER

ONE

2010, NOBILSK, RUSSIA

A LATE WINTER storm was raging beyond the walls, the gusts of eighty miles an hour carrying frozen shards across the surface of the endless tundra.

The nearest civilisation was 500 miles away, making Nobilsk the perfect location to house one of Russia's most dangerous secrets. No one was on the streets. The city was completely deserted, everyone hiding from a cold so vicious it would kill without mercy. But it wasn't the only deadly thing hiding there.

Two hundred feet below the surface of the frozen earth, in a bio-security level 4 lab, Dr Anatoly Zorin was putting the finishing touches on his life's greatest and most terrible work. He'd been awake and in the lab for more than twenty-six hours, and his assistant next to him, Alexei, clad in the same oversized, cumbersome and sweat-filled hazmat suit, was barely on his feet, his movements sluggish and imprecise. But they were so close—so close to finishing, so close to going home—that Anatoly would not let him rest. Or himself.

They hadn't spoken in more than five hours, both of them sick of the other, forced to work together, live together for more than a year with no outside contact with their families. Though Anatoly knew that his were long gone. His wife had promised that she wouldn't wait for him, and Anatoly had begged her not to reconsider. Had pushed her away to ensure she didn't. Had said that the reality of the situation was that even if he did as instructed, even if he managed what they asked, he knew—knowing what he knew, knowing how to do what he knew how to do—they would never let him walk free again.

He looked up, staring through the corner of the visor of his hazmat suit, breathing stale air fed through a filtration system in the small of his back, watching as Alexei pushed himself to a weary stance, turning away from his open notebook—the meticulous notation that they'd been instructed to keep as tall a task as their main objective—and turned towards the incubation chamber to his left.

Anatoly glanced forward now, catching his reflection in the two-way mirror in front of him, wondering whether anyone was standing beyond it. The clock said that it was three in the morning, so he guessed there was probably no one physically standing there—but that there was always someone watching through the camera in the corner of the room. Beyond the glass to his right, outside of their fish tank lab, he could see his and Alexei's cots next to the small bookcase filled with paperbacks—their only relief from the boredom and the endlessness of their task.

He screwed his eyes closed, dreading what came next.

He'd prayed for so long for this task to be over, and now that they were at the precipice, he wished that it would carry on forever. The uncertainty of his fate carried a heavier weight than even the moral implications of their project and their work there in that lab. He'd been racking his brain for months, trying to figure a way out, knowing that there was none—that here, locked in this place, he could be murdered, and no one would ever know, no one would ever hear the shot or find the body.

He'd ceased to exist to the outside world the moment he climbed into the back of that car in St Petersburg fourteen months ago, sealed his fate, put it in the hands of men he couldn't ever trust. Alexei's laboured steps and heavy breathing dragged him back to the moment, and he turned, watching as the man opened the incubation chamber and pulled out a tray of test tubes—all labelled, all sealed—and turned back towards the steel workstation in the middle of the room.

But Anatoly had begun focusing on something else.

He turned on his swivelling stool and stared down at the corner of the table, a tiny piece of white fabric snagged on the very end. He reached out for it curiously with his thick rubber-gloved hand and closed two fat fingers around it, pulling it free of just the tiniest sharp burr of metal, holding it up before his visor in the harsh halogen lighting.

There was a rattle of glass as Alexei put the tray of test tubes down on the table and leaned in to inspect the piece for himself.

'What is it?' Alexei asked in his native Russian.

Anatoly's mind was as tired as his body, seemingly unwilling to work at full capacity.

He lifted his eyes to his assistant, ready to say that he didn't know.

And then it struck him, his gaze falling slowly down the length of Alexei's body to his right hip. And then to his right thigh. Searching for it.

There.

He could see two flaps of the inflated plastic hazmat suits they were wearing gently billowing, the air circulating within Alexei's suit now streaming through the tear on his leg.

Anatoly's blood pulsed quickly and heavily in his temples, his throat choked. He knew that he was at no risk of breathing what might have been in that room, but he could no longer say the same for Alexei.

The man's suit was compromised. And what happened next was of the utmost importance.

Anatoly rose slowly from his chair and lowered the piece of fabric, wondering what he should say—what he *could* say—seeing the panic already rising in his assistant's eyes. A thousand possibilities whirled through his mind, ranging from very bad to globally catastrophic, and he knew they had to act quickly and decisively if they were going to limit—or perhaps even prevent—the worst of them from coming true.

'Alexei,' Anatoly said, lifting his hands. 'You must remain calm.'

Alexei's eyes fell on the fabric once more and realisation flooded through him.

He looked down at himself, groping at his body, at his legs, until his finger hooked into the tiny slit in his suit and he froze, feeling it there—the touch of the rubber glove against his bare leg. Inside the sweltering suit, the pair of them wore only their underwear, a vest and socks beneath the airtight plastic.

Alexei gasped—one long, sharp inhale that he held reflexively, determined not to breathe anything else in the room.

'Alexei,' Anatoly said firmly. 'You must remain calm.'

But he was deaf to everything except the truth—that there was a breach in his suit, and if infected, he was as good as dead.

Anatoly reached out, trying to calm him, trying to get him to sit down. There was a puncture kit less than five feet from them, secured to the wall. They could still do this—there were no leaks, no spills in the lab. There hadn't been for weeks.

But Alexei knew, as well as Anatoly, that it likely didn't matter—that the people running this operation would take no chances. And that only meant one thing.

'Don't do it,' Anatoly urged him.

But before he could even lay a hand on his assistant, Alexei sprang forward, shoving Anatoly in the chest. He sprawled backwards into the table, searching for grip, only succeeding in pulling it over with him as he went down.

It tilted, spilling the tray of test tubes onto the ground and—though Anatoly's vision was obscured by his hood—the sound of shattering glass was as clear as day. And he knew what it meant.

'Alexei!' he screamed, his voice echoing in his own head. 'Alexei!'

But the man didn't respond, and by the time Anatoly managed to pull himself to a stance, he was alone in the room.

He looked up towards the door, just in time to hear it hiss closed, Alexei already inside the airlock. The man had his hands up at the sides of his head, turning slowly as he was bathed in high-pressured CO_2 and UV light designed to kill any bacteria or viruses that might be lingering on the outside of his suit.

But it wasn't what was on the outside that mattered now.

Anatoly got up and lumbered forward, hurling himself against the locked door, the decontamination process sealing him inside the lab. He pounded on the reinforced, bulletproof plexiglass with his fist, knowing it was pointless.

'Alexei!' he screamed. 'Don't do this, you can't do this! You know what will happen!'

The man completed his about-turn to face his mentor, his expression grave, eyes wide, face flushed.

'My family…' was all he said, and Anatoly knew exactly what he meant. That someone would have been watching what happened in the lab. Someone would have already made a call—and the men ordered to keep the peace and keep the order in this place would already be on their way, with only one intention.

The only thing Alexei could do if he hoped to survive the night was run.

And that's exactly what he intended.

Behind him, the outer door to the airlock opened and he turned, sprinting through it in his oversized suit, reaching down, fumbling for the duct tape covering the front zip as he circled around the lab, past their cots and towards the outer door.

'No, Alexei!' Anatoly called, raking his visor across the glass viewing window. 'Don't! You'll kill us all!'

But the warning was too little, too late.

Alexei knew what he was doing. And he didn't care.

The man's self-preservation instinct—the desire to get back to his family, to try to save them from the powers that would put him in the ground and kill them just to tie up loose ends—was too great for his tired mind to comprehend.

And though Anatoly knew, as he stepped back from the glass, watching Alexei disappear deeper into the complex, that despite his intentions to do right by the people he loved…

The only thing he succeeded in was dooming them to a death that could hardly be imagined.

TWO

PRESENT DAY

CHURCH WAS REPOINTING Mitch's chimney when he heard his name.

It echoed across the farmyard and over the roof of Mitch's house. Church turned his head, searching for the source, and heard the din of an engine in the distance. A vehicle was idling behind the gate at the tree line at the bottom of the field in front of the house. At the same moment he picked out Mitch to his left in the vegetable garden. He was tilling the earth in the early spring, readying it for planting, determined to grow as much of his own food as possible to limit his need to leave the place. He'd become a hermit since his death ten years ago, and Church didn't blame him. The farm was as close to a paradise as he could really imagine. Sealed off from the rest of the world. Hidden. Except from a few choice people. All of whom seemed to be arriving more frequently these days.

Much to both of their chagrin.

Who knew coming back to life came with so many challenges and unannounced visits?

Church peered over the chimney, his hands grey with cement, and looked down at Mitch below, leaning on his garden fork, squinting at the entry road and the gate there, trying to figure out who was coming.

Church's eyes were still as sharp as they'd ever been, and he could see who it was immediately.

Julia Hallberg.

Of Interpol.

Confidante.

Sometimes boss.

But mostly the person that kept his head attached to his shoulders.

They got by on a mutual *exchange of services.* In the loosest possible terms, of course. He did things for her, and she did things for him. Things that weren't within the confines of the law, and things that couldn't be sanctioned by her station or her agency. And yet, it was a relationship that worked. A professional one, but also one that Church didn't mind maintaining out of office hours. He didn't like many people, but he liked Hallberg. And despite being unhappy to see her opening Mitch's gate and rolling up the driveway, of the people that did know where they lived, she was the most agreeable, he thought.

Though, he'd never voiced that out loud.

Church slid down the slate roof of Mitch's farm-house and teased his way back onto the ladder, climbing down onto the patio. Mitch walked out of the vegetable patch, wiping the dirt from his hands on his old, ill-fitting jeans. He'd grown slight with the years, his belt now cinched into homemade holes, the end lopped off so it didn't dangle.

'You weren't expecting her, were you?' Mitch asked.

Church just shook his head, watching as Hallberg's black SUV crunched up the gravel roadway towards them.

The two men exchanged a glance, knowing that if she was dropping in like this, it meant nothing good.

Church sighed and cleaned his own hands, clapping them together gently to loosen the dried cement dust, wondering why everyone couldn't just leave them in peace.

'Would have been easier,' Mitch said, as though reading Church's mind, 'if we'd just stayed dead.'

'I'm beginning to think that myself,' Church grumbled, walking out to the edge of the patio to greet Hallberg.

She pulled up and killed the engine, not waving or smiling as she climbed out, carrying a brown paper folder.

Church's eyes leapt to it, the unmarked file making him stiffen a little.

'Afternoon,' he said, almost tentatively.

She stayed where she was, in front of the SUV, the apprehension clear in her posture. She was a full head shorter than Church, her dark hair pinned back behind her head, her large eyes staring up at him. Almost hopefully.

Yeah, she was definitely here to ask for something, Church surmised.

'Is this going to be a casual *chat by the car* sort of visit? Or do we need to go inside?'

'We need to go inside,' Hallberg replied, moving her weight from foot to foot.

She had a naturally tanned complexion. But whether it was the gloomy British winter, or perhaps just the stress of her job, or what was weighing on her right now, she seemed to have grown pale over the last few months.

As much as he wanted to turn her away, though, he couldn't. She'd done too much for him. And even if she hadn't, he doubted he could refuse her anyway.

He stepped aside, beckoning her towards the front door, listening to Mitch tut as he did.

'You know you live in the shepherd's hut up in the fucking woods, don't you? That this is my house.'

Church lifted an eyebrow at his friend.

'Well then climb on the roof and fix your own bloody chimney.'

'You must be joking,' Mitch laughed. 'With all that moss up there? It's a damn ice rink. I'm not going to risk breaking my neck.'

'But you'll risk mine?' Church replied.

'Well yours is a lot fatter than mine is. More padding.' Mitch grinned at him.

Church grumbled and shook his head, breezing past his friend and into the house, looking around the living room, seeing that Hallberg had already stepped through into the kitchen. By the time he joined her there, the folder was open, a set of what looked like crime scene photos spread out across the table.

Mitch entered a second later and stopped, looking down at them.

He sighed loudly. 'I'll pop the kettle on then.'

'Best had,' Church mumbled, folding his arms, eyes already scanning the scene laid out in front of him.

Blood. And lots of it.

Dead bodies. Multiple.

Church's eyes lifted to Hallberg then. He could see her sitting there, hands clamped around the edge of the table, chewing on her bottom lip, staring down at them, eyes flitting back and forth over the pictures.

Church's heart beat a little harder. At first it had struck him as any crime scene. There was nothing, at first glance, to separate it from your run-of-the-mill shootout. And considering Hallberg's position in Interpol, it could have been anywhere in the UK or Europe. She specialised in trafficking operations, and this scene wouldn't be out of place in any of her investigations. But she wasn't easily rattled. The opposite, in fact. She was tough and focused. So to see her like this worried Church more than anything.

'What exactly are we looking at here?' Church asked, pulling out a chair and easing down into it with a little sigh.

Mitch put the kettle on the stove behind them, the whine of the heat conducting through the metal bursting the heavy silence.

Hallberg took what seemed like a long time to answer and then she reached out, putting her finger on one of the corpses displayed in the photo. 'Chinese,' she said, and then moved it to another photo, another body. Both bullet-riddled. 'Albanian.' She opened her hand then and swept it across the photos, and Church could see that it was nail-bitten, something he'd never noticed before. She didn't chew on her fingers. But this, whatever it was, had got her rattled.

Church surveyed the scene with the new information. Surmising there was only one reason that a group of Chinese would meet with a group of Albanians—for some kind of sale. The Chinese nationals, he saw, were a mix of casual and well-dressed. The Albanians, less so.

'This on UK soil?' Church said, half question, half statement.

Hallberg nodded.

Church was the one biting his lip now.

'And the Chinese flew in for this?'

Hallberg nodded again.

Church reached out, spreading the photos, rotating a few towards him, spotting one and stopping, bringing it closer.

He could see in one of the crime scene photos, among the evidence markers that had been laid out by the SOCOs, that there was an open metal briefcase. A foam-moulded insert visible. The depression a long, thin space. Five or six inches in length. An inch wide at most. And empty.

'The Chinese—were they selling or buying?' Church asked, looking up at Hallberg, his hand still on the photograph.

'Selling,' she said.

'And what is it?'

Hallberg let out a long, shaking breath now.

'Unknown substance. The sample was degraded,' she replied, almost robotically, a regurgitated statement.

She reached for a photo in the far corner, one that Church hadn't looked at twice, and picked it up, laying it on top of the one under Church's nose. It was of a man's body. He was lying on his back, blood streaming from his nose. It looked like he'd been shot in the throat, his eyes lolled at odd angles, but Church could see now that there was something next to his head. What looked like a broken glass tube, secured at both ends with rubberised bumpers and a sealed screw-on top. But it was smashed in the middle, a dark liquid having leaked out and soaked into the carpet it was lying on.

It was the right size and shape to fit in the insert.

Church, looking at it, stiffened in his chair, his breath stopping in his throat.

'Unknown substance. Degraded sample,' he parroted back to her.

'That's what the techs say,' Hallberg muttered, shaking her head. 'They're running further tests, but they could take days. And I don't know if we have that.

We intercepted chatter a few days ago...' She began, Church knowing what she was going to say before the words even came out of her mouth. 'Through a monitoring investigation we have running on an Albanian smuggling ring operating across Europe. It said that the Chinese were bringing an agent into the country.'

Mitch loomed behind them then.

'Like a spy?' he asked.

'Like a biological agent,' Church cut in, studying the photo. The broken ampoule.

'Could be a virus,' Hallberg said, 'or a toxin of some kind. We don't know. But surveillance confirms that eight Chinese nationals passed through passport control at a private airfield outside London yesterday evening. And there's only seven here.' She lifted her chin, scanning her eyes across the bodies. 'One is still unaccounted for.'

'Jesus,' Church muttered.

Mitch stepped away to tend to the tea, his silence signifying his unease at the news too. It was a nightmare that they'd both already lived once and weren't keen to revisit.

Hallberg rested her elbows on the table and put her head in her hands now.

'The house where this happened,' she said, 'is 20 minutes outside London city limits. Home Office want this buried. No panic, no pursuit, no manhunt, nothing.'

Church sucked on his teeth.

'They're risking nine million lives to save face.'

Church swallowed the lump in his throat.

'It's not surprising, considering recent history.' His voice sounded strange, strained in his own ears. 'But they're right, it is probably nothing,' he forced out.

'Nothing?'

Hallberg snapped, looking up at him. 'What do you mean nothing? You think eight Chinese nationals are going to risk smuggling an unknown biological agent into the UK, meet up with a bunch of Albanian smugglers, get into a fucking shootout outside the most densely populated city in the country, all for nothing? I doubt this is the common fucking cold, Church.' She snapped, slamming her fingers down onto the photo in front of him so hard that the whole table shook a little.

When he lifted his eyes, she was staring right at him.

Pleading, almost.

Church stared back.

'What do you want from me?'

'I want you to fucking help,' Hallberg said. 'The higher-ups have told me to leave it alone. And I think that's a huge fucking mistake.'

'Maybe you're wrong,' Church told her.

She blinked in astonishment at him.

'If your superiors are telling you to leave it alone, that it's nothing... Maybe it is. Maybe you should.'

She scoffed, incredulous. 'Seriously? Coming from you? Mister *never followed an order in his fucking life*?'

'I've followed plenty of orders,' Church told her. 'For better, and for worse.'

'Right. So, when you feel like breaking the rules, that's totally fine. But when I ask you for one little fucking favour, you just spit in my face? After everything.'

Church sank backwards in his chair, knowing that it was one of those times where anything he said would only make it worse.

Silence was the least painful way to get through this now.

For him, at least.

'You're unbelievable,' Hallberg practically spat, reaching out and dragging the photos towards her, reshuffling them angrily and loading them back into the file. She shoved herself to a stance then, the chair almost falling over behind her.

'You understand what could be at risk here, don't you? Of course you do,' she said, answering for him before he could get a word out.

Or perhaps knowing he wasn't going to try.

'You just don't give a shit when it doesn't concern you, right? That's it, isn't it? Unless it's all about Solomon Church. It doesn't matter.' She laughed, shaking her head. 'You know, I was really starting to think that I could count on you.'

He winced inwardly at the comment, forcing himself to keep his eyes open, to keep looking at her.

She stared at him for a moment longer, the kettle reaching boiling point on the stove, whistling shrilly. The sound piercing. Almost as sharp as Hallberg's words.

And then she just stormed out, breezing past him and through the door.

Her footsteps receded quickly, the front door opening and then slamming shut.

Behind Church, Mitch pulled the kettle off the flame and filled just two of the three cups he'd set up.

'I'm surprised,' he said.

'About the Chinese?' Church asked almost absently, still staring into space in front of him.

'No, that you're going to let her do this alone. You know she's going to do it anyway. She's going to go after this guy. Probably get herself killed doing it.' Mitch shrugged, lifted the tea to his lips, blew on it and slurped a little of the red-hot liquid.

Church's eyes drifted down to the now empty table, thinking about that. Thinking about her.

'Fucking hell,' he grumbled, pushing himself to his feet now.

'There we go,' Mitch said, chuckling. 'For a second there, I thought you were going to abandon your girlfriend.'

Church paused at the threshold of the kitchen door and looked back.

'She's not my girlfriend,' he said grumpily.

Mitch just smirked, taking another sip. 'Yeah, maybe. But does she know that?'

THREE

2010, NOBILSK

LESS THAN SIXTEEN hours later and almost three thousand miles from the walled city of Nobilsk in Russia, Solomon Church, along with three of his closest squadmates, was led down a staircase in Stirling Lines, Hereford—the seat of the SAS in the UK—and on to the basement level in the main building.

Church exchanged a glance with Mitch, the man at his right, his wiry frame and fair hair shaded by the man in front of him. A step below but at the same height, Foster's huge bulk echoed through the stairwell as he took each step, his heavy boots clunking on the concrete.

Church stared clean over the head of the man to his left—the captain of their team, Cole—his dark buzzcut resembling the bristles of a toilet brush more than a normal head of hair. His pointed features and stern expression made him easy to pick out of a crowd, but Church rarely needed to. In fact, he would have known the faces of the men around him among any in the world—not just his friends or his teammates, but his brothers.

And Church knew, in the back of his mind, that those bonds would be tested once again.

They didn't currently have a mission they were gearing up for, but you weren't told to report to a windowless classroom in the basement of a building unless something had just landed at your feet. And not the usual kind, either. This kind of secrecy—the four of them approached individually by their squadron commander, Neil Calder, told to report to that room at that time, not given any other details other than to not be late and to not tell anybody else? Church knew it wouldn't be the kind of mission any of them were excited for, but it would be the kind that required all the skills and fortitude they'd developed over the course of their careers.

They stepped into the long corridor and paced along it in silence—Cole at the head of their train, Church at the rear—checking over his shoulder instinctively, searching for anyone that might be coming up behind them. Not an enemy combatant, but perhaps someone who might give him some idea of what they were walking into.

Cole pushed open the door to the room—a nondescript square box filled with rows of tables and chairs, a projector screen, laptop, and a desk set up at the front.

Church had been in rooms like this before, for countless briefings, but this one felt different.

It was proving to be a very wet winter, and that dampness—the endless drizzle that had been falling over Hereford in sheets—seemed to have pervaded every inch of the building, including this room. The air, thick and moist, choked him as he filed in and sat in the front row, leaning forward on his forearms, waiting for the other shoe to drop.

And as if on cue, the door opened and three people filed in.

The first man Church knew well—their squadron leader, Neil Calder. A man he'd come to know since his selection. A man he'd come to trust with his life—the same as all his other brothers. But he wasn't wearing his usual stony expression. The one that was unreadable.

He was usually a man you couldn't tell whether he was happy or sad—whether his mother had just died, or his wife had just given birth. He was in his late fifties, tall, with a shock of grey and white hair, and the kind of lined face that made him look like his skin was made of tanned leather. But today, he looked stricken. Frustrated. A tinge of anger creeping in at the edges—even, Church thought—as he moved through the room, his eyes turning to the man walking in behind him. A man, at first, he didn't recognise. But his posture, his clothing— a tailored suit, draped over the shoulders of a man who looked like he'd seen combat himself... Church put the pieces together, recalling his name and matching it to his face. He'd seen him before. The man was Hugh

Haddon, current DSF of the UK—the Director Special Forces.

And at the sight of him, Church's blood ran a little colder. The stakes suddenly higher for the DSF to be out in person to make this trip. To do what Church assumed was a brief face-to-face. It must be serious.

And that was backed up by the presence of the third person.

A woman, close to Calder's age. She had pale blonde hair pulled back in a tight bun behind her head. Her thin lips were painted a dark red. She wore a grey pantsuit with a white shirt done up to her throat. Her expression was the same as the others—stern, unhappy —but with an unmistakable worry buried below the surface. She was not in the service. And nor did Church know her from any pictures, meetings, briefings or ceremonies he'd attended. No. She was a stranger to him. Completely anonymous. And that frightened him more than anything else. Because if he didn't know her and she was here, that meant she was from somewhere else. And when combined with Haddon's presence—and Calder's clear apprehension—the only logical explanation was that she'd been called in by SIS to relay the kind of information no one else had access to.

Calder cleared his throat loudly and leaned on the desk, spreading his hands to brace his large frame.

'Gentlemen, thank you for coming and for being on time,' he said evenly, his words a little stilted, as though difficult to say. 'I'm here with DSF Hugh Haddon, and Rosalind Kerr.'

No rank, Church thought. Further confirmation of her station.

'As I'm sure you've gleaned by now,' Calder went on, 'we've got a mission on deck, and it's not the kind that's exactly public knowledge. It's of the utmost importance and secrecy. So much so that I don't even know where it is they're shipping you off to. I've just been brought here to make the introductions. So with that, I'm going to hand you over.'

He gave a nod to the men in front of him and stood straight, glancing towards Haddon as though offering a final plea for him to stay. Not because he wanted to know for his own curiosity, but because he wanted to know what he was signing his soldiers up for. It was as though he knew there was a good chance they wouldn't come back—and as he cast his eyes along each one of them in turn, Church figured that he'd probably been asked who his four best were.

And in answering that question, he'd probably resigned all of them to their deaths.

There was the pain, Church thought, as Haddon met him with silence and Calder walked out, shoulders slumped, pulling the door closed sharply behind him.

When his footsteps had faded down the corridor beyond, Haddon stepped forward and folded his arms, his suit wrinkling at the shoulders.

'You're being assigned to a covert operation. Completely deniable. Deep behind foreign lines, deep in territory that we have no business being in. To a place where, if you're discovered, you cannot—I repeat:

cannot—be caught. Do you understand me?' He looked around at the men, waiting for verbal confirmation.

'Yes,' they all answered, almost in unison.

'You either extract on the arranged transport or you don't extract at all,' Haddon said. 'We're not in the business of leaving men behind, but we expect you to face extreme resistance when you arrive at the DZ. They're not going to want to let you leave alive, and it's important that you know that before you go in.'

'In where, exactly?' Cole asked first. Fearless, as always.

Rosalind Kerr stepped forward now, not missing a beat.

'Russia,' she said. 'Siberia, to be precise.'

'In the middle of fucking winter?' Cole clapped back, eyebrows creasing.

'Technically, it's early spring,' Rosalind replied, unfazed by the pointedness of his retort. 'But I'd suggest wrapping up warm.'

Cole huffed a little and sat back in his chair, crossing his arms.

Haddon reasserted himself as the man in charge, speaking up once more.

'Insertion will be via HALO jump. And once you're on the ground, you're on your own. Exfil is two hundred miles away from the AO, and you need to find your way there under your own steam and signal for extraction twelve hours before arrival. We fully expect that you'll face extreme prejudice from enemy combatants. All cards on the table—we don't know what you're going to be walking into. But this one is not going to be a stroll in the park. So if any of that frightens you, tap out now and you can walk away before it's too late.'

Silence rang in the room.

Haddon inspected each of their faces one at a time, looking for any hint of a crack—but none showed any. Church, Mitch, Foster and Cole all stood stalwart in the face of what came next.

'Good,' Haddon said after a moment, nodding firmly. 'Then I'll hand you over to Roz for the specifics.'

He stepped back and the woman came forward, still not offering a formal introduction.

Typical of SIS, Church thought, wondering if Roz Kerr was even her real name—and knowing that even if it was, he'd have no way to check. She wouldn't appear in any search of any kind.

She slipped a USB stick from her pocket and leaned down to the laptop positioned on the desk, inserting it. A moment later, the projector screen burst to life, showing a grainy satellite image of a vast white sheet. A group of black squares huddled in the middle in a loose, circular shape, a faint ring running around the outside.

Church wasn't sure where he was looking at, but he knew what it was—some kind of walled settlement.

'This is Nobilsk,' she said. 'Siberian Peninsula. The northernmost major settlement in the country, five hundred miles from the nearest town that isn't just a group of tents and natives roasting reindeer on sticks. And twelve hours ago, it went completely dark.'

'Dark?' Church couldn't help but ask himself now, reading the emphasis she put on the word. 'What does that mean?'

'That twelve hours ago, any radio or satellite communications going in or out stopped completely. There's been no communication to or from Nobilsk during that time. They are completely cut off from the outside world.'

'And what's in Nobilsk,' Cole asked before Ros could get there on her own, 'that requires us to get dropped out of a plane at thirty thousand feet and shot at by what I assume is going to be Russian special forces the moment we touch down?'

Roz straightened a little, glancing back at Haddon.

He looked back at her, his face unreadable.

This was the secret part, Church thought—the reason they were all there, underground, hidden away from the world. To hear what came next.

'Nobilsk is home to a level four bioresearch facility,' she said, the words almost strained as they came out. 'The current project, our intelligence tells us, is being led by one of Russia's top virologists—a man named Anatoly Zorin.' She clicked a button on the laptop and the face of a man in his early sixties popped up: a thick moustache covering his mouth, his large eyes lined, the top of his head bald, a ring of hair above his ears.

'Zorin went missing over a year ago,' she said. 'He was researching communicable diseases, cataloguing the ones that pose the largest risks to humans—and then, suddenly, he was gone. Left behind a wife and three children. Dropped off the face of the earth. No trace of him. That was until this morning. We received an encrypted communication sent to the Home Office in Moscow, supposedly from Zorin, claiming that there'd been a breach in the level four lab. That a deadly pathogen had escaped containment.'

She paused a beat, letting that land.

'He transmitted his location—both inside the city of Nobilsk and inside the lab itself—and he offered, in exchange for his rescue, access to not just the project he was working on, but also everything he knows about the Russians' bioweapons programme. To which he promises he's privy.'

She looked up at them now, her expression flat.

'I don't have to explain to you the importance of this. If this man is working on something dangerous and he's seen fit to reach out to us, asking for extraction, saying that his pet project might be on the loose—then it's not just Nobilsk that could be in danger. The Russians will be keen to contain and complete the project. We have no doubt of that. Their prize pony, Novichok, is getting a little long in the tooth now, so we're not surprised they've been cooking up a sequel. The Geneva Convention be damned. They seem to think that because they've got six million square miles of uninhabited ice and snow to play with, they can do whatever the hell they bloody like out there. Nuclear testing, weapons development, viral research... They may not have an intention to deploy it, but they're still trying to make it all the same. And that's a big problem.

For us—and the rest of the world. And now we've got the chance to strangle it in the crib. And we're not passing it up.'

'So what's the mission?' Cole asked.

'You drop into Nobilsk. Locate Dr Zorin. Destroy his research on site—all traces of whatever he's working on—and get him to the extraction zone.'

'Oh,' Cole laughed, 'well, it sounds easy when you say it like that.'

'That couldn't be further from the truth,' Ros replied. 'This isn't the kind of mission we expect to work,' she said. 'But it's the only option we have. Zorin is too valuable a potential asset to pass up. And if Nobilsk has gone dark, that can only mean one thing— that they're scrambling to contain whatever he was working on. And we hope, in that confusion, there'll be a small window where we can get this done.'

'You hope...' Cole repeated back to her, his voice hard—and as cold as the Siberian tundra itself.

'We hope,' Ros said back. She sighed, easing down into the chair behind the desk. 'When it comes to a mission like this... it's all we can do.'

FOUR

PRESENT DAY

CHURCH JOGGED through the house and out into the afternoon sun, a bite of winter still in the air.

Hallberg was already pulling away down the driveway when he reached the gravel, lifting his hand and waving at her as she trundled down the hill.

He thought sprinting after the car was a bit much. That she'd see him in the rear-view. And when the brake lights flared and the car squeaked to a stop, he knew that she had.

It sat there on the brakes for a few seconds and Church lowered his hand, wondering whether or not she might just drive off after all. But then the reverse light came on and the car began backing up slowly until it drew level with him.

Hallberg wound down the passenger window and leaned across the centre console, scowling.

Church rested on the window sill, hoping that would prevent her from speeding off again.

'I'm sorry,' he said. 'I didn't mean to shut you down like that.'

'No? So what did you mean to do?' Hallberg pushed him, still scowling, not letting him off easily.

'I just didn't want you to rush into anything... dangerous,' Church managed to get out, trying to choose his words carefully. It had never been his strong suit.

'But then you had a change of heart,' she said. 'And now you want to join me in saving London?'

'*Want* is a strong word,' Church said, 'but I knew that you'd do it anyway. Alone. And I couldn't let that happen.'

'You knew I'd do it anyway,' she said, raising an eyebrow. 'Or Mitch pointed that out to you after I walked out the door?'

Church wasn't quick enough to hide the surprise in his face.

He was often reminded just how perceptive she was —uncannily so. He thought he did a good job of hiding most of himself from everyone. But whenever he was talking to Hallberg, he always got the sense that she saw right through him, saw all sides of him. And if she could still stand to be around him, that meant he shouldn't squander whatever relationship they did have. People Church could trust were in short supply. And the feeling didn't come easily to him—and oftentimes not at all.

'Well, pushed or not,' Hallberg said with a sigh, tinged with relief, 'I'm glad you came to your senses.'

'Yeah, something like that,' Church muttered with a shrug, pushing himself back from the door. 'Maybe I just wanted to make you sweat.'

She laughed.

'What?' he said. 'I'm not a trained dog. I don't just leap to heel at the snap of your fingers.'

She smiled at him, lifted her hand, and snapped her fingers right in front of his face for effect.

'Oh, look, and there you are,' she said, almost smugly now.

'Don't make me change my mind,' Church told her.

'Couldn't if you tried,' she said.

He found himself grinning then too, but quickly gained control of himself, turning his head away, Mitch's last quip ringing in his ears.

Was there something between them?

No, there was.

He'd been around long enough to know that feeling, to know what it felt like coming from another.

But there were a thousand reasons they couldn't, shouldn't, go further than a professional relationship.

Least of all, the fact that he was the best part of twenty years older than her.

And perhaps most of all, how important she was becoming to him.

He knew his pattern. He knew the cycle. He knew that letting someone in was hard and that pushing them away was easy, and that he wouldn't be able to resist doing that if it got too real.

He had to stop this before it began, cut off the infected limb before it spread.

He cleared his throat, still not looking at her.

'Give me a second,' he said, pulling away from the car and jogging towards his Land Rover Defender parked at the side of the house. He left it open, always, in case he needed a quick exit, and opened the back door, reaching under the bench seat there for a duffel bag he kept specifically for those quick exits.

He pulled it out and shouldered it, feeling the weight of spare clothes and boots, of a roll of petty cash, a Glock 19, and a trio of loaded magazines filled with nine-millimetre hollow point ammunition, along with a ballistic vest and a few other choice items.

He walked quickly back towards Hallberg's SUV and climbed up into the passenger seat wordlessly. But she didn't drive away, despite the seeming urgency, as though waiting for him to look over.

When he did, he noticed she was holding something in her hand.

A smartphone.

'I got you a present,' she said, waving it gently at him. 'So I can keep track of you.'

'So you can keep track of me,' Church repeated, taking it reluctantly.

'Yeah, well, after Stuttgart, Prague, and then, oh, that's right, Oxford University—where you got into a gunfight in the middle of the library there and killed one of the lecturers—I thought it best that I know where you are. Just in case, you know, I need to bail you out again, for what, the hundredth time?'

She smiled coyly and Church resisted the urge to say something charming.

To say anything at all.

'I don't think this is necessary,' he replied quietly, offering the phone back to her. 'You always seem to know where I am anyway.'

'Keep it,' she told him, lifting her palm and pushing the device towards him once more. 'This makes my life easier, and who knows, it might make yours easier too. Hell, you might even start to like it, if you give it a chance.'

Church knew that that was a truer statement than she realised. That if he did give it a chance, he would definitely like it. And not just the phone, either.

He waited for the moment to pass, for it to become awkward even, before he risked speaking again.

'Why me?' he said, after an age of silence.

She blinked at the question, caught off guard by it.

'What do you mean?'

'Why ask me to come?' he said. 'Why come here and petition me? Interpol won't back you. The Home Office say leave it alone. This isn't you, Julia. You're not a rule breaker. You're not a rogue. You're risking everything.'

'I asked you,' she said measuredly, 'because you're the most capable man I know. Because you can do things that I can't, that no one can. And,' she said, leaning closer to catch his eye, 'because you owe me.'

He could have argued, could have said a lot of things to dissuade her of that fact—that he was capable of anything. To remind her of what she was risking, of what the consequences would be if she was wrong. But he didn't think anything would have swayed her in that moment—least of all a speech from him.

Satisfied that her point was made, the discussion won and ended definitively, she eased the car into drive and pulled away, crunching over the gravel towards the gate and then onto the smooth tarmac of the lane leading away from Mitch's farm, Church's eyes drifting out of the window, back, over all the times it had been proven to him how incapable he was. How he could certainly fail. How he could certainly get things wrong. Drifting back over all his missteps and bad decisions. Over all his missions. And most of all, back to that walled city in Siberia.

He reached down and scratched his forearm absently, his body itching all over all of a sudden, his skin alight and tingling.

He waited with steady breaths for the feeling to abate.

But it didn't.

It lingered.

And as they ate up the miles towards the city, towards whatever was in store...

It only seemed to worsen.

FIVE

2010, NOBILSK

IT WAS 6 p.m. when they walked out of the damp basement classroom in Stirling Lines.

And exactly twenty-four hours later, they were standing on the tarmac at Helsinki Airport outside the cargo depot, staring at a Boeing 747-8F—a modified jumbo jet designed to carry freight across the longest flight paths in the world.

Finland had always been an ally of the UK, and the route this particular Polar Air Cargo plane was taking flew directly over Siberia on its way to Tokyo. And with a slight northern diversion due to inclement weather, it would take them almost directly over the top of Nobilsk.

Church, Mitch, Foster and Cole stared up at the flying behemoth, its nose propped open, cargo being loaded into its mouth via forklift trucks and telehandlers, huge rolling pallets sliding down its four hundred feet of length, its four massive engines already spooling up.

This plane was built to fly far and fast. But what it wasn't built for was HALO insertions—probably the reason all four men had fallen silent as they looked at it. They'd been briefed on how this was going to go, and none of them were looking forward to it. A standard HALO jump required a few things. Firstly, a maximum flight speed of around 200 miles per hour—and even then, it was like jumping straight into a blender. The Boeing 747-8F, however, had a minimum stall speed of 265 knots—304 miles per hour—far above the recommended safe threshold.

Second, there was no rear ramp. Jumping from the back of a plane was one thing—you could catch the wash, control the rotation and pull yourself into the right fall position without too much trouble. Jumping from a 747-8F meant using the side exit, which at low speeds wouldn't be too problematic. But at 300 miles an hour, Church didn't know what to expect. He'd made hundreds of jumps—but never out of something like this, never at that altitude, and never at that speed.

And though none of them said it aloud, Church guessed they were all imagining it was going to feel like getting hit by a truck the second they stepped out of the plane.

Their liaison—and the man who'd made this happen—a ranking member of Finland's intelligence service, pulled away from his conversation with the pilot. He was no doubt explaining that this needed to happen for the safety and security of Finland as much as for the UK. He walked towards Church and the others, giving them a nod: all had been arranged, the pilot had his instructions, and they were cleared to board.

He approached the men, looking at each of them in turn. Barely a word had been exchanged since they'd arrived at the airport nearly an hour earlier when he'd first greeted them. Church figured he knew about as much as he needed to—and that Supo, the Suojelupoli-isi, Finland's intelligence service, were happy to bank a favour from the SIS. One they'd no doubt call in at some point.

The man, who'd never given his name, extended a hand to Cole, and he shook it.

'Good luck,' he said, offering the smallest polite—but professional—smile that Church thought was possible. Then he turned and walked back into the terminal building.

'Come on then, lads,' Cole said with a little sigh. 'Let's get this done.'

He leaned down and picked up the two hulking duffel bags at his feet and began lumbering off towards the plane.

Church picked up his own and followed, feeling the weight and heft. The one in his left hand contained everything needed for the HALO jump itself. The one in his right contained everything they'd need after. Their gear was unmarked—black, tactical wear bearing no insignia. Their weaponry was non-standard for the SAS too. Even without flags on their shoulders, if they were killed and their gear was recovered and it was all standard issue, it wouldn't matter a lick. The Russians would know—and it would be an international incident before lunch.

They climbed the passenger staircase into the front of the plane and bypassed the steps leading to the upper deck and cockpit, instead moving towards the back, taking up residence in a row of jump seats opposite their exit door.

They'd been briefed heavily on how this would work, and Church didn't like it one bit. In order to slow down to a speed that wouldn't kill them instantly, the aircraft needed to climb to a ceiling of 38,000 feet. Then the pilot would pull the nose up and throttle back, easing them into a slow descent on the edge of a stall. At 32,000 feet, they'd been assured the aircraft would be flying at something close to 300 miles per hour. At that point, they'd be given the go-ahead to jump. The plane would bank left sharply, giving them a small window— ten seconds—for all four men to make their exit. After that, the pilot would point the nose down, regain speed with a dive to 30,000 feet, and pull back up to cruising altitude—never deviating far enough from the flight path to tip off the Russians or anyone else as to what crimes had just been committed.

And when it was all laid out on paper by Ros Kerr, it somehow seemed not only doable, but almost trivial.

Church figured that was a skill she'd acquired over a long career in intelligence work: making the impossible not only seem possible, but easy.

He eased himself down into the seat and buckled in, kicking his duffel bag under the seat, laying his HALO suit at his feet. He was sandwiched between Foster and Mitch. The wiry man on his right leaned off his seat to give Church space to move his arms. Foster couldn't do the same—far too large for the seat. He spilled over the sides, a slab of muscle and flesh so big that Church couldn't even see Cole on his other side.

A thunderous whirring rang out down the length of the plane as the nose began to close up, the pilots appearing in the far distance wearing their Polar Air Cargo shirts. They paused at the metal staircase leading to the upper deck and looked at the four men at the far end. They were far too distant for Church to make out their expressions, but he suspected their apprehension was clear. They said something to each other and then ascended—and less than a minute later, they were pushing back.

The engines grew in intensity, deafening them inside the cargo hold, which lacked the soundproofing their commercial counterparts came with. Just a bellowing roar of burning kerosene and churning jet turbines, loud enough to make Church's teeth chatter in his head.

Cole reached up above him and pulled a headset—complete with sound-cancelling earpieces and an old-fashioned microphone on a boom—from a hook on the wall. He slipped his on and Church and the others did the same, the scream of the turbines fading, replaced by the dim, somehow comforting hum of static. A sharp click rang out and the pilot's voice came over the airwaves, tinged with a Finnish accent.

'Good evening, passengers,' it said, almost stiltedly. 'We don't usually get ride-alongs on this route, but I don't suspect anything about this trip is usual. I've got my orders, and I assume you have yours too. We're only going to get one pass at this—one chance. We'll be flying over your...' He cleared his throat, the words not coming easily—everything in his training telling him how unsafe this all was. 'Your *drop zone* at around 12:15 a.m. local time. Will be a few hours yet, but I don't suspect that's news to you. Unfortunately, there'll be no drink service on this flight. Our stewardesses are out sick today.'

Church curled a small smile, appreciating the strained attempt at humour—but he could hear the fear clear in the pilot's voice. No doubt they were used to many hours of uneventful flying with no passengers, no deviations from their standard route, and certainly no rapid decompressions mid-air—especially not ones that risked pissing off the Russians.

A lot of airlines and carriers weren't allowed to fly over Russian airspace for national security reasons, but Finland was one of the few that could. Their relationship with Russia was historically fraught but currently on tentatively good terms. That still didn't mean any perceived slight would be well received.

'Strap in, gentlemen. If you want to get some sleep, I would recommend doing it now. We're about five hours from your destination. If you need to pee, too bad. There's no bathroom on the lower deck and I don't want to see you up here. As far as I'm concerned, you don't exist—and if anybody asks me about it later, that's what I'll be saying too. So if you need to go, do it in a bottle and take it with you. I don't want to find any piss in my plane when I land in Tokyo tomorrow morning.'

And with that, his voice faded, the static returning.

They completed their about-face on the runway, and without warning, began to accelerate.

Church and the others slid sideways in their seats, the belts digging into their hips, the endless string of crates in front of them rattling and shuddering, cargo netting flapping. Whatever they were carrying, Church didn't know—but nor did it matter. This was a means to an end. He just hoped they weren't headed towards theirs.

When the plane lurched, dropping a few hundred feet— his stomach going with it before levelling out—Church woke, opening his eyes and looking around the dark interior of the plane.

Mitch had his arms folded next to him, still asleep, leaning slightly against Church's shoulder. Foster sat like a monolith, bolt upright, eyes shut. Church couldn't tell if he was sleeping or not—he never could.

Cole was leaning forward, elbows on knees, staring aimlessly at a massive metal box in front of him, a black stencil across its side reading simply: *CARGO.* He seemed to become aware that Church was awake and turned his head, lifting his watch.

'About an hour to go,' he whispered, his voice clear in Church's ears through the headset.

'Should we start gearing up?' Church whispered back.

Cole considered it, then shook his head. 'Nah. Let the boy sleep a few minutes more.'

'You get any shut-eye?' Church asked.

He shook his head. And Church knew he wouldn't elaborate further.

They sat in darkness and silence for a while longer, and then the pilot's voice kicked up again, rousing the other two.

'Good morning, stowaways. We're nearing your destination, and I'm going start our climb "to avoid some bad weather" momentarily. I radioed ahead and let base know we're making a slight deviation for a high-pressure system and some bumpy air, cruising a little north of the planned flight path to avoid the worst of the storm. And you know what? It's not a lie. Weather's not looking great. It's okay up here, but below 25,000 feet... well, let's just say you guys are in for a rough ride.'

'Great,' Mitch muttered.

'I'll let you know once we reach thirty-eight and start to back off our speed. We'll speed up gradually to make up the time, and then the deceleration will be quick. We can't lose too much time or they'll know something's off. You guys need to be ready or you're going to miss your stop.'

'Copy that,' Cole replied. Then the pilot was gone once more, and Cole signalled for the boys to get up and begin their preparations.

There was dim security lighting down the length of the plane—an orange glow that gave them just enough illumination to unzip their duffels and start dressing.

A regular HALO insertion required a full jumpsuit—but one from this altitude, at this speed, in these temperatures... they were wearing full thermal suits, thick neoprene and heavy gloves, rubberised boots that fit over their shoes, a full-face rebreather along with a thermal hood. Their combat gear was fixed to a harness that slipped over their legs and around their shoulders, securing it down the entire length of their chests and between their knees. When you were wearing it, you had to waddle with your legs splayed to accommodate the weight pulling down on your entire skeleton. And that wasn't even counting the parachute itself or the HALO gear.

One full chute, one reserve, along with two oxygen tanks, a reinforced harness and webbing, and a mask—totalling over thirty kilogrammes all said and done. They began dressing themselves, the cold interior of the plane quickly disappearing as Church began to layer up, sweat building inside his suit.

They were already in their combat gear—fatigues and thermal long sleeves—but their arctic equipment was securely stowed in their duffels, and they'd need to change into it quickly on the ground before frostbite was able to set in. Church could hear the rattling of his weapons in the bag as he began checking his chutes and oxygen: a suppressed Heckler & Koch MP5, which, while used by the British military, was also used extensively by different forces around the world and was one of the most easily acquired black-market submachine guns. They were carrying Beretta M9s as sidearms, a cumbersome pistol Church never liked much, but again —something any arms dealer in the world could get hold of. The only weapon more ubiquitous was the AK-47. But it meant that if their bodies were recovered with their equipment, there'd be no telling who they belonged to. Similarly, their HALO suits and all the other equipment they were using was off-brand—army surplus, acquired by the intelligence services over the years, exactly for missions like this where deniability was key.

Church tried not to think about how old the suit and chute were as he zipped up and got ready, pulling out the third and final tank of oxygen from his duffel and slipping a breathing mask over his face. He opened the tap and began taking slow, steady breaths, suddenly awake and alert—the flood of pure oxygen entering his bloodstream immediately.

Pre-breathing like this was imperative when it came to a HALO jump, to avoid hypoxia and the bends by purging nitrogen from the body. Cruising at this altitude for a long time allowed nitrogen bubbles to build up in the blood, and as soon as the door was opened and the hull depressurised, those bubbles would rapidly expand inside the blood vessels, muscles, soft tissues—even the brain. Best-case scenario would be a terrible case of the bends. Worst case would be death—and not a pleasant one either. Something he was keen to avoid, especially as he jumped from 30,000 feet. He'd heard horror stories of that exact thing happening. Rapid hypoxia onset during a freefall. Dead before the jumper even hit the ground.

None of them had to be told what the risks were, and as Church secured the last of his HALO suit and looked around, he saw the others had all begun their pre-jump routine too. The engines strained around them as they continued to climb, and then the pilot came back on to say they were at 38,000 feet, that it was two minutes to deceleration and less than five minutes to drop.

Cole gave him a hard copy. And that was it.

The pilot had to trust that they'd get the job done—and they had to trust that the pilot would slow down enough not to kill them.

When he started to bank hard, that would be the cue: door open, jump.

And as they seemed to level off, the engines cooling before the pilot hit the brakes, they all waddled forward, dragging their huge bags between their legs towards the exit—weapons strapped to their chests—squeezing awkwardly between the pallets of cargo as they made for the door that read 'DO NOT OPEN UNDER ANY CIRCUMSTANCES. EMERGENCY EXIT ONLY.'

Cole hooked his hand into the webbing on the crate next to him to steady himself, waiting for the slowdown, and the others did the same. Church found a solid grip just a second before the engines quelled, the flaps lifting along with them, the tail of the plane seeming to sink. The cargo all hopped forward, then began pulling backwards, straining at its restraints as it tried to slide towards the rear of the hold.

Cole lifted a hand and gave a two-minute warning. The men all nodded back. Church continued to breathe in the oxygen, taking deep breaths, trying to steady his heart.

His full-face jump rebreather was sitting on top of his head. Cole, staring at his watch, pulled one finger down, telling them it was a minute to jump.

Church ditched his auxiliary oxygen tank, pulling down the rebreather instead, reaching to his side and opening the taps on the two smaller tanks there.

He felt the gas flood once more into his lungs, the condensation inside his visor disappearing in a second. He looked at his wrist—the altimeter showing that they were rapidly falling down through the 30,000s, approaching their target altitude.

And then, just as they dipped below 33,000, the plane tilted to the right and then banked sharply to the left.

The engines howled.

And Church watched—clinging to the cargo netting —as Cole reached for the emergency handle and pulled it.

He didn't need to tell the boys to hold tight. They all tensed, waiting for the suck.

And the moment the seal broke, they felt it instantly.

All of the pressure inside the plane rushed towards the open door. Cole heaved it inwards and slid it to the side, and even through all the layers of thermal protection, Church could immediately feel the cold air slicing right through his suit and into his skin.

'You reading me, lads?' Cole asked into the mic inside his suit, relaying his words to the others.

Everybody made the OK sign with their hands, and Cole gave one back. They were already in a full bank, and there was no green light to wait for.

'On me,' Cole said then, releasing the webbing and stepping towards the doorway.

Church glanced at Mitch and Foster—the order given—and then Cole was gone, plunging into darkness.

Mitch stepped after him, swearing under his breath as he entered the nothingness.

Foster went next, stumbling forward awkwardly and ducking under the door, folding his arms as he disappeared out of sight.

And then it was just Church.

He could already feel under his feet that the plane was beginning to pull out of the bank, and he knew they'd be back on the throttle in a moment, accelerating hard. Each knot they gained in speed would intensify what he was about to experience.

There was nothing to do but go.

He consciously willed himself to move, drawing one deep breath, hardening the muscles in his trunk ready for the impact—and then he strode towards the opening, folding his arms across his chest, clamping the bag between his knees as he tumbled forward out of the plane.

The impact was instant—and despite his best effort—knocked the wind clean out of him. He was right: it was like being hit by a truck. By the time the stars faded from his vision, the only thing he knew was that he was in freefall. He didn't know which way was up, and which was down. He couldn't feel the air passing over him in any one direction. He was just careening, flipping wildly through the sky, 30-odd thousand feet above the Siberian tundra. They were in pure darkness, none of them carrying any lights or beacons. And though, for a second, Church thought he made out the lights on the corners of the wings on the plane above, as quick as he spotted it, it was already gone—swallowed by the high clouds.

Breathe steady, he told himself, knowing he had a full two minutes of freefall. *Take your time*. Inside his suit he was protected, and he had plenty of altitude to re-centre himself, to right himself, and to control his fall. He let the air wash over him, opening his arms as he slowed his speed, letting the air itself guide him towards the ground.

He spread his fingers, feeling through the gloves as the air rushed between them, adopting the full spread-eagle position. All around him he saw nothing—just streaks of thick cloud. The air was reasonably calm.

But he was quickly approaching the 25,000-foot ceiling of the storm the pilot had mentioned. And he could just make it out below. Like a false earth. A turbulent sheet of black, waiting to swallow him whole.

He didn't know what to expect.

Jumping into blizzards wasn't something that was recommended or done—except as a last resort. And when Church hit the cloud bank, it was like being pierced by a thousand needles. Tiny shards of ice exploded across his visor, pricking at him, even through the suit, numbing his fingers almost immediately.

He screwed them into fists, tightened his body, falling even faster as he pulled himself into a dive. The longer he was up here, the longer it would last. The wind rush climbed in his ears as he approached terminal velocity—around 180 miles an hour—in a full tuck position, glancing down through his visor every few seconds to measure the altitude on his watch. He was buffeted and thrown around by the wind like a rag doll, unable to discern where the others were—or what kind of state they were in. He could hear nothing in his ears except strained breathing, and he wasn't sure if it was his or someone else's.

He was down now to 10,000 feet and still falling— the optimum altitude to open between 2,500 and 3,500 —just a few seconds from death at this speed. He heard a grunt ring out through the comms, and knew that was Cole pulling his chute. Mitch came next. Then Foster. And then suddenly Church was at 3,500 and reaching for the loop on his chest.

He dragged in a hard breath and held it, bracing for the jolt, and ripped on the fabric strap. For a moment nothing happened, his suit unfurling above him, buffeting and clapping loudly before it filled with air—expanding rapidly, compressing his spine under the weight of both his own body, the sudden resistance, and the gear strung between his legs.

He reached up, looking for the guide handles to control his descent, the snow still blowing, whipping in circles around him.

As his altimeter dropped under a thousand feet, he still couldn't make out the floor below. But he knew it was coming up fast.

The vast, open tundra was drenched in night—featureless, covered in snow. He couldn't see the others. Couldn't see anything.

All he could do was pull hard on the guide handles, lift his heels, and wait for the crash.

SIX

PRESENT DAY

THEY MADE small talk on the road, heading towards the city until Hallberg pulled off the main road and guided them back into the countryside.

Church watched small, cutesy hamlets roll by until Hallberg turned them off a B road and up a long track towards a lone house standing in the middle of an open field. It looked old, a little run down, the pebbledash walls browned with algae and dirt. Church hadn't known what to expect—whether there'd be a sea of police cars littered around.

But there wasn't.

The place was completely empty except for the yellow tape strung across the entrance road, reading: POLICE LINE, DO NOT CROSS.

Otherwise, he wouldn't have known that anything untoward had happened here at all.

Hallberg climbed out of the vehicle, went over, and unpinned the tape from one side, tossing it on the ground before she got back into the car and drove them up towards the building. Church inspected it as they closed in.

'Let me guess,' he said with a sigh. 'This place is owned by some shell corporation that's part of a holding company, registered out of Luxembourg or the Cayman Islands.' He lifted an eyebrow, glancing over to her, looking for confirmation.

She chuckled a little. 'Not quite,' she said. 'Airbnb, if you can believe it.'

Church's brow furrowed. 'What the hell's Airbnb?'

She laughed out loud then, the same sweet dulcet notes that always seemed to escape her before she could quell them.

'I forget you live under a rock sometimes,' she said when the laughter had faded, 'and that you've been dead for ten years.' With a gentle sigh, she explained it as though she might have to a child. 'It's a website that— wait—you do know what a website is, don't you?'

'Ha-ha,' he said emphatically, 'yes, I know what a website is. It's one of those internet things.'

'Right... one of those internet things,' she repeated back, unsure if he was joking or really that technologically lame. 'Anyway, Airbnb is a site where people can list their homes for short-term rent. You just go on there, find a property that you like, and you can rent it for a day, a week, a month—however long you like. Some people rent out flats to uni students, others rent out spare bedrooms in their house and do the whole classic bed-and-breakfast thing. Some list villas on the Costa del Sol—'

'And some just rent dilapidated run-down shitholes in the middle of the English countryside,' Church finished for her with a sigh.

'Exactly,' she said. 'Marvels of the technological age.' She pulled them to a stop on the driveway and killed the engine. 'What a wonder, hey?'

'Yeah,' Church muttered. 'I'm still pissed off they got rid of fax machines.'

She looked at him quizzically again. 'You know, I really can't tell if you're joking or not.'

'Would it be such a bad thing?' he replied, grinning despite his best efforts not to.

'Come on, let's just get this over with.'

She exited the car and walked towards the building, towards the X of police tape across the front door.

Church watched her, reluctant to follow. The banter hadn't just been for his own pleasure. Church knew in the back of his mind that he was stalling, not wanting to go in there, not wanting to risk it.

And yet, he couldn't hesitate for too long. That would beg more questions. What's wrong with you? What's happened? What are you not telling me? All the things that he didn't want to talk about.

He eased himself from the car and headed after Hallberg, willing his legs to move.

She'd already removed the tape by the time he caught up and was proffering him the living room.

The scent of blood was what hit Church first, before he'd even stepped over the threshold.

This was where it all went down. He could tell from the pictures.

Hallberg was carrying the file that she'd brought to Mitch's house under her arm, ready to offer it to him for comparisons. What she hoped he might glean from the scene that the police investigators who'd already been through here hadn't, he wasn't quite sure. But they were here now, and the least he could do was look it over.

'SOCOs have already been through,' Hallberg said, sweeping her arm around the room like she was an estate agent showing it to a potential buyer. 'Coroners have taken the bodies. Police removed the vehicles that they all arrived in.'

She caught him looking then at the spot on the floor where the broken cylinder had been. A curious dark brown stain on the carpet. A few tiny fragments of glass left behind.

'Don't worry,' she said. 'The scene has been cleared. There's no contamination. No risk of catching anything.'

He just tried to muster words, but just sort of grunted instead.

'Are you okay?' she asked then, seeing right through him as always.

He lifted his head, adopting his best poker face. 'Fine. Why?'

'You don't seem yourself.'

'No? And how do I seem?'

'More sullen than usual. More withdrawn than usual. Which, honestly, I didn't think was possible.'

'I'm a man of many layers,' he reminded her.

'Are you now?' She stood back, putting her hands on her hips. 'And what hides beneath these layers? And more importantly—why are you doing everything you can to hide it from me?'

'If I told you that,' he quipped, 'I'd have to kill you.'

'Try me.'

They stared at each other for a moment longer. Hallberg, trying at playful but a sharp undertone to her line of questioning. Church, feigning the same thing, an unshakeable angst festering beneath.

'What are we doing here?' he asked her then, keen to shift attention back to the matter at hand.

'We're looking for a lead,' Hallberg said. 'The only reason Interpol were involved in this was because of the Albanians and the overlap with one of our investigations. But when I pushed to have more of a hand in it, to get things moving, to get a manhunt going, that's where I started facing pushback.'

Church could tell she was the one hiding something now. 'You pushed too hard and they booted you off the investigation, you mean?'

She didn't answer, but her silence was all the confirmation Church needed.

'Right, so this isn't even your crime scene,' he replied, looking around with more interest now.

'NCA investigators cleared it,' she said, 'and went away. They're reviewing the evidence, building the case, but like I said, the Home Office want this quashed. So I have no idea what kind of resources, if any, they're dedicating to it. They've shut me out and warned me off doing anything on my own.'

'Right, and like with a kid, when you tell them not to touch something because it's hot...'

She harrumphed a little and looked over at him.

'That's why you're here. You never follow rules. If anyone asks, I'm just babysitting you on another one of your crusades.'

'Scapegoating me, by the sounds of it,' Church said.

'Hey, if we track this guy down and we find him before the NCA even get off their arses, they'll be hanging laurel wreaths off our necks.'

'And if we don't...?'

'Then we risk interference and obstruction charges.'

'Great,' Church replied.

'So you know,' Hallberg went on, clapping her hands, 'chop chop.'

Church let out a breath and scanned the room once more, seeing bullet holes in the walls now. Blood splatters, blood stains on the carpet. Shell casings had all been removed, but there was still enough evidence ingrained in the bones of the house to tell what had happened.

'Which side were the Chinese on?' Church asked.

'By the door,' Hallberg said.

Church backed up a little and stepped into the room once more like he was entering for the first time.

Looking at the red marks on the carpet... 'They lined

up here,' he said, shoulder to shoulder. 'The Albanians were over there, behind the sofa.' He pointed to the far end of the living room, towards the back wall.

There was a door behind where Church said they were standing, and one to the left. The sofa, hammered and marked with bullet holes, its ancient white stuffing spilling out.

'They took up a defensive position before the sellers even arrived,' Church said, reading it like a book.

'Expecting things to go wrong,' Hallberg muttered.

'Just good sense,' Church told her. 'Going into a buy like this, I guess there was no mutual trust. I don't know how much you know about Albanians, but in my experience, quite often they like to renegotiate in the moment. And I suspect they weren't happy to let the Chinese leave with their prize. That big spray on the wall behind you,' he said, gesturing to the blood splatter on the wall next to the kitchen door. 'I bet that was first. Chinese started this. That kind of spray comes from someone getting shot in the head, probably a hollow point. I'd say 9mm, just because that's what's easiest to get. And I'm assuming they didn't want to risk bringing weapons into the country with them.'

Hallberg smirked. 'You're right. We don't know how they got the weapons but they didn't have them with them when they arrived. And the slugs retrieved from the bodies were 9mm hollow points, just like you said.'

Church stuck out his bottom lip, nodding. 'The guy that got the first shot off, he was trained. You can see the blood spray is high up—starting at six feet, going up the wall. The shot came from low down,' Church said, making his hand into a gun and holding it at his side. 'The guy is shot practically from the hip. That's no mean feat. That's military precision.'

'The PLA,' Hallberg said back. 'The People's Liberation Army? You think that the Chinese government might have had a hand in this?' She seemed surprised, the thought not occurring to her.

Church shrugged. 'Hard to say. Could be the PLA, or the MSS. Could be former military PMCs. Hell, could be somebody just moonlighting, who knows. What I do know is that the guy standing here shot first, and then all hell broke loose. You can see the spray on the wall behind me here,' Church said, hooking a thumb over his shoulder. 'That's just firing blindly. And I'd say, with automatic weapons. 9-mil or... .32 ACP if it was a Skorpion. Depends what the Albanians got hold of. I know they like the Skorps.'

Hallberg smirked again, shaking her head this time, as though Church was right on the money—but she didn't want to continue to inflate his ego. Church continued to look around the room, pointing out how it had progressed.

'The door frame behind you is destroyed. I reckon somebody ducked into the kitchen to try to get out of the line of fire.'

'They did,' Hallberg said. 'One of them took three shots in the back, made a mess of the tiles.'

Church nodded. 'I'd say the remaining two got

down behind the sofa, but I doubt it afforded much protection.'

'You're right. One of them was found behind it.'

'And the last one,' Church said. 'I bet he tried to scramble for the bathroom door there, and that big bloodstain next to the threshold tells me he didn't make it.'

'Jesus,' Hallberg practically scoffed. 'Were you here or something?'

Church shook his head. 'No, I've just seen a lot of scenes like this. And been in one too many myself.'

'And what about the sellers? The Chinese?' Hallberg said.

'Well,' Church drew a slow breath, 'considering the case was open, and the product on the floor, I'd say that they were just about to make the deal. That the Chinese showed the Albanians what they were buying, and then decided to walk away when the price suddenly started going down. You said there were four of them, right?'

Hallberg nodded.

Church stood right above where the dark brown stain was and looked back towards the front door, just a few feet to his left and behind him.

'The case,' he said. 'It take a couple of hits?'

Hallberg nodded. 'Yeah. It was aero-grade aluminium. Stopped the bullets, two of them.'

'Well, that's how he survived,' Church replied. 'The guy showing off the product went to close it up, and all hell broke loose. He got the case up in front of him, deflected two shots, dropped his shield, sprung for the door, got tagged on the way out,' Church muttered, turning and walking back outside, scanning the few blood drops he could see on the outer steps leading down into the driveway.

Ten feet out, he stopped, seeing a heavier spray.

'This,' Church said, pointing down at it. 'That's blood flicking off a hand. So I reckon he got hit in the arm, maybe the leg. Though I'd put money on the arm. The drops are too far apart.'

Hallberg was behind him now, hands on hips. 'Alright then, Sherlock. And where'd he go from there?'

Church stepped back a little, lining up the drops he could see.

'Back down across the field, towards the road, but not via the driveway. There's a copse of trees inside the fence, and it's the closest natural cover,' Church said, pointing towards a group of gently swaying pines in the distance. 'I'm guessing they brought dogs in but didn't find a body?'

'They didn't,' Hallberg said.

'Then he did get away.' Church let out a sigh, turning back towards the house, a sinking feeling in the pit of his stomach. 'We're not getting ahead of this,' he said. 'In fact, I got a feeling we're already a long way behind.'

'And what does that mean?' Hallberg pressed him, as though waiting for some kind of revelation.

He didn't have one for her, just the truth.

'I don't know,' he went on, swallowing and looking down into Hallberg's big dark eyes. 'But I'm sure it's nothing good.'

SEVEN

2010, NOBILSK

'EVERYONE ALIVE?' Cole asked, his voice ringing in the darkness.

Church pulled himself out of the snow and stood, the soft upper layer reaching to his knees, and steadied his breath.

'Still in one piece,' he said back.

'I'm here,' Foster replied.

'Just about,' Mitch added.

Cole sighed with relief. He was far from a sentimental man, and that was about as warm and caring as he got.

'Fun as that was,' he said, 'let's not do it again. Get your beacons on, lads. Just for a minute. I can't see shit out here.'

Church reached to his shoulder and flicked on a

small red light there, turning a full 360, trying to pick the others out of the darkness.

He was still being battered by the wind—gusts up to 80 miles an hour, they'd been told—and he was feeling it. He picked out the first red light swimming in the storm, unsure who it was, and began hauling himself towards it, his hips screaming as he lifted his knees, feet kicking out to the sides, churning through the deep snow, his pack dragging between them.

It was exhausting work, but he could see the red light getting closer and closer.

And when he saw it rise above him, he knew it was Foster.

The big man lifted his hand in the darkness.

'Welcome to Russia,' he said, chuckling a little under his breath.

Church clapped him on the shoulder—like hitting a bull—and side by side, they turned to see another red dot floating towards them.

Mitch, they guessed—and they were right.

And then finally, Cole rejoined them too.

He hadn't flicked his beacon on, but had zeroed in on the others, and when they were all in one spot, they killed their lights, just able to pick each other's outlines out in the Siberian night.

'Let's get changed, lads, quick as you like,' Cole told them. 'Eyes on a swivel, yeah? We don't know what we're walking into here.'

'Copy that,' everyone said back as they began unzipping their packs, shedding layers, hissing and swearing against the cold as it found the tiny patches of open skin.

Church opened his duffel—his thick winter jacket on top—and he shed his HALO suit as quickly as he could, donning the coat in its place. A few seconds between shedding one layer and adding another— enough to chill him to the bone. He kept his thick gloves, pulling on a pair of waterproof over-trousers before he slid a merino wool balaclava over his head, pulling his helmet—equipped with night vision goggles —on tightly above it, scarf around his neck, mask pulled up to the eyes.

He flicked the NVGs on—everything lighting up ahead of him—Mitch, Cole and Foster painted ghostly white in front of him. And though the ability to see did little to quell his anxiety, he had to admit that it felt a lot better to have vision restored. He lifted and shouldered his weapon next, checking it was loaded, and he chambered a round just in case, throwing the strap over his neck.

The body armour was last—a thick Kevlar vest that settled over the top of his jacket and pulled the loose fabric in tightly to his body. And once he'd strapped on the spare magazines—nine-millimetre Parabellum rounds, stacked thirty in each, five extras slotted along the front of his vest—he affixed his thigh holster and secured both his combat knife and Beretta, and reached for the last item in the duffel bag: a full-face filtration respirator.

'Fucking bargain basement bullshit,' he heard Cole

mutter behind him, securing his own gear and weaponry.

A couple of chuckles rang through their comms, the boys appreciating the momentary lightening of the mood.

'We all good to go?' Cole asked them.

Church hummed a reply, nods coming from Foster and Mitch.

'Single file then, boys.' Cole snapped a magazine into his MP5, banging it into place with the heel of his hand before glancing down at the watch he'd fixed to his wrist, the GPS showing on the screen, giving them a path towards their objective.

He set off as quickly as the snow would allow and Church fell in behind him, watching over his shoulder through the reticle affixed to the top rail of the MP5—an old dot scope. Difficult to sight with night vision goggles, but this was the exact kind of scenario they'd been trained for—and the whole reason the four of them were there.

Because they could do things that others couldn't.

But Church couldn't help but wonder whether or not the task that was set out for them was even possible.

Ahead, their objective finally swam into view—a black slab of concrete topped with tiny blinking lights doing all they could to cut through the swirling blizzard. Church laid eyes on Nobilsk—a walled city completely cut off from the outside world, the only way in and out via secure militarised checkpoints—one of which they were about to go through.

They had no idea whether it would be manned by a few guys or by an entire battalion. And though they had other options—routes through the drainage system or over the wall, laid out for them by Ros Kerr during the briefing—this was the quickest and easiest way inside.

And Church just hoped that a few bullets would be their price of entry.

Cole crept up low to the snow, and Church crouched behind him, the surface brushing the backs of his thighs. They moved in silence, stopping every twenty feet or so for Cole to pull out his night vision telescopic monocular and sight the area. He would hold up a fist to signal that they stop, and then motion them forward again when he was satisfied.

They moved carefully, the cold biting through Church's boots and into the soles of his feet. He figured no amount of insulation or thermal reflective foil would stop Siberia from robbing him of what little body heat he possessed. When they were just a hundred feet away and staring right through the mouth of the gate, Cole paused them once more and took a final look, lowering the monocular for a second before lifting it back up.

'What is it?' Church whispered behind him.

'What the fuck?' Cole muttered back, turning to look at Church, brow creasing. He motioned with his hand for them to spread out then, and they did—fanning into a wide line, each of them approaching on their own.

While being single file made them much harder to see, moving in a line like this made them much harder to hit. If they were standing behind each other, a single well-placed high-calibre round could punch through two or three of them at once. A single grenade or rocket could take them all out in one blast. At least this way, they would have a chance to shoot back.

Church didn't know what had Cole rattled, but as they drew closer and closer to the gate—Church seeing no movement ahead—he began to realise that the steel slabs meant to secure Nobilsk from the outside world were lying open, the thick wooden barrier laid across the entrance smashed through the middle, lying in pieces on the ground. The guard station just to its right was unmanned, windows open, interior dark.

Church's boot crunched on something solid, and he looked down, seeing tyre treads underfoot. Who had driven into this place in this weather? And then it struck him. He turned slowly, bringing his rifle scope up to his eye, facing away from Nobilsk. In the distance, he could see just the faintest outline. He moved towards it, picking up pace as he walked in the tyre marks, now almost blotted out by the storm.

He had no way to know how old they were, but he guessed it was hours.

He picked up pace and the sound of breathing in the comms told him the others had begun to follow. Church pulled his weapon tight to his shoulder, bracing to fire, and approached what he saw now was a 4x4, front left wheel sunk into the deep snow. It had rammed through the gate at speed, trying to get out of the city, but the snow had made it hard, and it had snaked, slowing until the momentum had run out, and it had simply nosedived into the powder.

Church approached the rear quarter, breathing slow, steadying his aim, and waited, searching the interior for any hint of movement.

The doors were all closed, the side windows intact, and as he skirted around the side, the fate of the occupant became apparent. The driver—the only one in the car—was slumped forward against the wheel, head turned towards the glass. Church could see now there were bullet holes through the windscreen, spiderweb cracks radiating out from them. Three distinct shots that would have hit the driver square in the chest.

Whoever had been guarding the gate had made sure that this escape would be unsuccessful.

The others caught up with him as he reached the driver's window and he glanced back. Cole was tapping the top of his helmet with his hand—the signal to regroup on him. Church waited as he came forward to do the final inspection, turning alongside his captain to look at the driver, the pair of them freezing in place, their blood running colder than the endless sheet of ice around them.

Church stared inwards, at the man who'd given his life to escape, and realised all at once that there probably wasn't much life to give.

The bullets had dealt the final blow, but there was something deeply wrong with the man before he'd even climbed behind that wheel. His lips were purple, his eyes swollen and bleeding, streaks of red running down his cheeks, the veins in the backs of his hands still locked around the wheel, dark and bulging.

'Jesus Christ,' Cole said, pulling back from the glass, giving himself space from the driver and the car.

He looked around him, unable to hide the fear in his eyes.

'Masks on. Now, boys,' he said, 'and make sure they're tight.'

'What is it?' Mitch asked, his eyes drifting from the driver to his captain.

Cole just shook his head, fishing his full-face respirator from the position hanging at his hip and pulling it over his head.

'I don't know, Mitchie,' he said, voice cracking, 'but I know none of us want to fucking catch it.'

EIGHT

PRESENT DAY

THEY CLIMBED BACK into the car and sat in silence for a few seconds, Church staring out at the now-cold crime scene.

'If you start poking around,' Church said, 'is that going to set off alarm bells?'

'Depends how hard I poke,' Hallberg replied. 'What are you thinking?'

'Chinese national,' Church said. 'In the UK, alone, shot. I'm guessing that the NCA will have covered the obvious bases whether they're under orders to keep this quiet or not. They would have checked local hospitals for anyone matching that description coming in, looked at CCTV in the area... But guys like this—if they managed to get into the country with this thing, if they managed to secure vehicles and weapons the second they landed, if they managed to get a first shot off like that in there—they're trained, they're connected, they're financed. They came in on a private plane, you said?'

'That's right.'

'And they would have been met at the airport. There were four of them in to do the drop. But they already had people here, in the country, helping them. I'm going to take a wild stab at this and say they didn't rent the car they used to get here from Enterprise?'

'What are you saying?' Hallberg said, shaking her head.

Church was just thinking out loud, trying to align his thoughts as he voiced them. 'What I'm saying is, wherever this guy is, I don't think he ran there. They would have wanted to ensure they weren't being tracked coming to a meet like this. But who doesn't have one of these in their pockets these days?' He fished out the smartphone and showed it to Hallberg. 'If you can, check for any devices that were powered up around the time of the incident in this area. Because I bet that guy called for help. And I bet it came running.'

Hallberg chewed her bottom lip.

'That's good thinking,' she said, turning on the engine and fishing out her own phone. She made a phone call that lasted no more than ten seconds, giving clear, concise instructions to someone on the other end as she drove away from the crime scene, heading slowly but steadily towards the city.

Church wasn't sure if she had a destination in mind or if she was just trying to keep them moving. But either way, they didn't make it very far before her phone rang and they had the answer they needed.

A voice came over the Bluetooth system and echoed in the cabin. It sounded like a young man—English, with a hint of a West Country accent. He dispensed with all the introductions, plunging straight in.

'A phone did power up around the time of the meet,' he said. 'SIM card has an out-of-country number. Plus 86.'

'China,' Church muttered under his breath.

'And did it make any outgoing calls?' Hallberg asked hastily.

'Not that I can see,' the technician said. 'But I do see some app activity here with an outbound signal.'

'What was the app?' Hallberg said.

'Uber,' he replied.

Hallberg slammed on the brakes and wrestled the car into the side of the road.

Church strained against the belt as she did, his hand on the dashboard.

'Uber,' she said. 'Fucking Uber?'

'Yeah,' the technician repeated, almost nervously. 'Is that a problem?'

'Well, not a problem,' she said sharply. 'I just can't believe that a Chinese national here to sell a potential fucking bioweapon called a fucking... Uber.'

'Well, they're everywhere now,' the tech said back. 'It was probably the quickest way out of there for him.'

Hallberg let out a long sigh, pinching the bridge of

her nose. 'Okay,' she said. 'And where's the phone now?'

'I don't know,' the technician replied. 'It only came online for a few minutes, and then went dead again. They're probably carrying foil bags to make sure they can't be tracked.'

'Right,' she replied. 'Well, get in touch with the company—I want to know where they went.'

'That'll be hard to do without a court order.'

'Fucking hell,' Hallberg muttered to herself. 'You're right. And if I petition a judge, that definitely will raise alarm bells.'

Church was surprised that she was speaking so freely considering what was at stake. But he suspected she must have built a good team around her at Interpol. A team that trusted her, that was loyal to her even in the face of losing their jobs. He wasn't shocked at that, though. She was the exact kind of person that he'd follow straight into the line of fire. The kind of leader that inspired loyalty.

'But...' the technician came back, 'what I can do is pull local traffic camera footage from around the time of the incident. Cross-check licence plates with the Uber registry and see whether or not any drivers were in the area at the right time.'

'And then you can pull their information straight from the DVLA,' she said, harrumphing, impressed.

'Already working it,' the technician said back. 'Give me five minutes.'

'You've got two,' Hallberg replied, hanging up.

She sighed and looked over at Church, shaking her head.

'Fucking Uber. Can you believe that?'

Church arched an eyebrow. 'I hate to ask, but... what's Uber?'

Hallberg had barely got done explaining it by the time the technician called back again.

'I've got something,' the tech said. 'An Uber Black was caught at a traffic light two miles from your location and the footage shows someone in the back seat. It's the only one that could have conceivably been anywhere close to the property at the time. It's registered to a guy named Jake Smalls. I've got his number here, if you want it?'

'Send it through,' Hallberg said. 'Thanks.'

'You got it.' The technician was the one who hung up now, Hallberg's phone beeping a second later.

She opened the message and dialled the number with surgical efficiency, and it started ringing all around Church. He watched Hallberg work, impressed. And after a moment, the driver picked up.

'Hello?' he said, the North London accent apparent from the first word.

'Mr Smalls,' she said back. 'My name is Julia Hallberg. I'm calling from Interpol. You picked up a Chinese national yesterday from the roadside twenty miles outside the city.'

There was silence on the line.

'You've done nothing wrong, but this man poses a

risk to national security and I need to know exactly where you dropped him off.'

There was further silence on the line as though Mr Smalls was weighing up whether this was some kind of prank. And if it wasn't, what kind of jeopardy he might have put his position as a driver in. Slowly, he found his voice.

'I'm not supposed to share information like that with... Who did you say you were again?'

'Julia Hallberg,' she repeated, voice hardening. 'Interpol. The man that you picked up is involved in an ongoing investigation and is potentially very dangerous. If you don't tell me where you dropped him off immediately, then I'll assume you're intentionally trying to obstruct justice. And I will come after you with an assisting an offender charge, and if you really make things difficult, then it'll very quickly escalate to a perverting the course of justice charge, which carries a maximum penalty of life imprisonment. Do you understand what I'm telling you?'

'Whoa, whoa, whoa,' Mr Smalls said back. 'No need for that—'

'There is a need for that,' Hallberg snapped at him. 'This is extremely important. Tell me where you dropped him off and you'll never hear from me again. Refuse and there'll be police at your door in ten minutes and we'll continue this conversation in a police station instead. Your choice, Mr Smalls.'

More silence.

'Don't make me count to three, Jake,' she said.

'Alright, alright,' he came back after a second, letting out a long breath. 'Fucking hell. I didn't tell you this, alright? But... I took him into the city.'

'The city,' she said. 'To the hospital? He was bleeding. Injured, wasn't he?'

'Yeah,' Mr Smalls said. 'He was. From the arm. But he said it wasn't anything serious. That he'd just... fallen off his bike.'

'And did he have a bike with him?' Hallberg asked sharply.

'Well... no. But you know. I'm paid to drive, not ask questions. People say all sorts of stupid things. But he tipped well, and asked me to get him there fast. And, well, I was happy to oblige. I've got a five-star rating.'

'I'm sure you have, Mr Smalls,' Hallberg said, screwing her eyes closed. 'Now continue to be a five-star Uber driver and tell me where you fucking dropped him off.'

'Oh, right. Yeah,' he said. 'Tower Hamlets.'

'Tower Hamlets?' Hallberg replied, her brow creasing.

'Yeah. He said he was headed home. Dropped him at the Westferry rail station.'

He barely got the words out before Hallberg reached out and hung up the phone on Mr Smalls, turning her head to look at Church, her graven expression making the skin on the back of his neck prickle.

'What is it?' Church asked, reading the frightened look in her eye.

'Westferry rail station,' Hallberg repeated back, almost in disbelief. 'That's Canary fucking Wharf.'

Church didn't need to be told why that was a problem. Canary Wharf was an extremely densely populated area. A huge tourist attraction. Tens of thousands of people flowed through it every day. Tourists and locals alike, flooding in from all over London and the wider country, from all corners of the globe. And leaving in just as great numbers. If there was one place that would make it impossible to contain some kind of outbreak, it would be there.

And Hallberg came to the same conclusion, stomping on the accelerator, the car surging forward, the tyres scrabbling for grip on the loose verge before biting on the tarmac and hurling them forward. They burst from the trees and onto a main road, the distant outline of London rising in the distance, swimming out of the afternoon haze.

Neither of them said another word as they drove, the weight of what had just been laid on them all but crushing the air out of their lungs.

Church felt his throat tighten, his heart beat harder, his palms grow sweaty as they ate up the miles, Hallberg weaving between cars as she hammered down the motorway, overtaking dangerously, desperate to make up some of the time they'd lost.

But Church knew—no matter how fast she drove— that if this thing was one tenth as bad as he was fearing it would be, then it didn't matter how much time they gained.

Because it was already too late.

NINE

2010, NOBILSK

THEY APPROACHED the gate to Nobilsk slowly.

It was impossible to tell how long that man in the car had been dead. The bullets had ended him, but he'd been infected with whatever pathogen Doctor Anatoly Zorin had been working on—that much was clear. But when did he catch it? Who was he? And what was his goal?

The closest settlement was five hundred miles away. There was no way that vehicle was going to make it more than a few miles outside the city—at best—before it got caught up in a snowdrift, even if the driver hadn't been shot. Which meant that risking getting out, blowing through the barrier, and getting shot was better than whatever was waiting for them inside.

They split into two pairs, Church and Cole approaching from the left-hand side of the gate, Mitch and Foster from the right, keeping their eyes peeled, night vision glasses focused on the street leading into the city visible beyond the gate. A wide road ran around the perimeter, separating the first line of buildings from the wall itself, making it impossible for anybody to climb out or in without being spotted, Church guessed.

He'd seen similar designs in other enemy fortifications. It was a choice that builders had been making for millennia. Simple and effective, making the guards' lives easier. But where they were now, Church couldn't say. The checkpoint next to the broken gate was abandoned, the door open. And once Cole was satisfied that was definitely the case, he motioned for the lads to form back up and head into Nobilsk proper. They stepped over the remnants of the wooden barrier, boots crunching on the snow, and breathed their first still breath—the wind, all at once, extinguished behind the shelter of the walls.

Church shivered and rolled his shoulders back, scanning the empty streets ahead of them. No lights were burning inside the buildings. No hints of life.

The streetlights were on, illuminating empty roads with almost completely snow-covered tyre tracks, one set leading directly towards the gate and through it. Their mystery escapee, Church thought—but otherwise all of the cars parked on the kerbs were still. And had been for some time.

Pale halos ringed the streetlights above, filled with swirling snow, hanging just above the level of the wall, still hammered by the wind. But down here, at street level, things were eerily still and their footsteps rang out, echoing between the buildings. They paused for just a moment, looking around before Cole motioned them forward, keen to make up the kilometre or so to the bio-research lab, positioned right in the centre of the city—in as difficult a position to get to as possible for enemy combatants looking to make any kind of attack.

They pushed deeper into Nobilsk, sticking closer to the buildings, the brutalist architecture prevalent here. Huge slabs of poured concrete, grey cubes with small windows to ward off the cold, quickly constructed between the Russian winters. But despite this being a city to hold tens of thousands, it didn't seem that anybody was moving, let alone on the streets.

'I don't like this,' Mitch muttered as they neared the halfway point. 'This is fucking weird. Where is everyone?'

'Shut it,' Cole ordered. More of a growl than a polite request. 'Doesn't fucking matter where anybody is. We've got a job to do. Stay sharp.'

Foster grunted, and Church couldn't tell whether it was one of agreement or dissent. But either way, they had to keep moving. Out here in the open, they were easy targets.

They paused at a corner and then hurried across an open intersection, the traffic lights above blinking orange constantly—not switching to green or red—as though someone behind a computer somewhere had set it that way, knowing no traffic would be passing by that night.

It was thirty-six hours since the SIS had gotten the message from the doctor, and it seemed like far too short a time for an entire city to collapse in on itself. Church wondered how much the denizens of this place knew about what was going on here, how many of them were involved with the Russian military and their research projects, and if it wasn't a large number, what possessed the others to remain in a place like this, cut off from the rest of the world?

Mitch was dead right. It was weird. Eerie. Frightening, even, as they crept along, heels crunching on the grit-lined pavements.

Something rattled behind them then—a clang of metal dustbins—and all four of the men turned, dropping to a knee, weapons to their shoulders, looking for the source. All four, on edge, fingers twitching on the triggers. Cole put his left fist up next to his head, signalling them to hold fast while he moved forward to inspect, turning the corner on the intersection and scanning the area with the suppressed muzzle of his MP5.

He motioned the others forward once it was confirmed clear and pointed to what was ahead of them.

Church looked at it, could see that one of the cars parked just ahead wasn't parallel to the kerb. The front tyre was mounting the pavement, the front door ajar.

He edged towards it, Cole covering the mouth of the alleyway opposite, and scanned the interior. Empty. Abandoned. But unlike the others that had snow built up on their bonnets, this one was clear, enough residual warmth lingering in the engine that the ice hadn't yet been able to settle.

Cole made a low whistling sound and pulled Church's attention away, and they both turned to face the mouth of the alley, still looking for the source of the noise—perhaps one of the inhabitants hiding for their life. Foster and Mitch formed up with them now and they stepped into the alleyway together, out of the glow of the streetlight and into shadow, reticles all fixed on a pair of huge metal bins sitting against the wall on their right.

Cole motioned for them to stop once more and touched the side of his head next to his ear: *listen* was the silent order, and they did, hearing an almost inaudible champing, slurping noise rising from the darkness. And then it stopped and they all froze, each of them, Church was sure, putting as much pressure on their triggers as he was. And when the trash can threw itself over, spilling rubbish across the floor, and a dog darted out from behind it, they all nearly pulled and obliterated the thing.

It took two steps and skidded to a halt, scarpering in a circle upon seeing the four of them standing there before it dropped what was in its mouth and charged away down the alley, claws scratching on the snowy ground. Each man breathed a sigh of relief and a little chuckle rang out among them, each of them terrified of what had just been a stray dog.

Foster went forward, inspecting what it was the dog

had been chewing on and leant down, picking up an old leather boot, holding it up for the rest to see.

'It was just a shoe,' he laughed, lifting it up higher for them.

But the laughter was extinguished in an instant when the tongue flopped open and a severed human foot fell out.

It landed on the ground and bounced, settling upright, a gnarled piece of bone sticking out of the half-frozen flesh. Foster dropped the boot and jumped backwards, staring at the thing, swearing and wringing out his hand as though it were covered in blood. He wiped the slobber hastily on the leg of his trousers as Church, Cole and Mitch crowded forward.

Questions raced through Church's mind as he looked at the thing. Where had it come from? Whose was it? And generally... what the fuck? Church could see the foot had taken on a ghostly white colour, that the ends of the toes had begun to turn black, the nails darkened, dying almost—but not from frostbite either. He'd seen enough of that up close to know the difference.

This was something else. Something far more frightening.

Cole was the first to regain himself, stepping back, grabbing Mitch by the shoulder strap and pulling him away, shoving him back towards the street before reaching out and touching Church's arm.

'Come on,' he said. 'We've got to keep moving. We've got to get to the lab, now.'

Church held fast, meeting his captain's eyes.

'The lab,' he said back. 'Ground zero.'

Cole's grip tightened on Church's arm. 'It's the job,' he said, expression obscured behind his full-face rebreather. 'I don't like it any more than you, but it's what we signed up for.'

And with that, he turned and strode back towards the street, following Mitch, Foster going after him. But as Church stood there, alone in the alley, looking down at the rotting, infected foot once more, his brain reeling with possibilities for how exactly the dog had got hold of it and how exactly it had gotten detached from its owner, he couldn't help but question—was this what they'd signed up for?

Or was it a whole lot worse?

TEN

HALLBERG THREADED her way through the city like a native.

Church knew that she was Swedish by birth, had worked in the Swedish police before being snapped up by Interpol, and that she'd been stationed in the UK for a few years now. But she seemed to have hit the ground running and knew London like the back of her hand, heading for Canary Wharf as quickly as the oozing London traffic would allow.

She pulled up on a kerb outside Westferry station and threw her Interpol credentials on the dashboard. Church doubted it would be enough to ward off traffic wardens—but there was always hope.

She killed the engine and they stared out across the busy street towards the entrance of the station; Hallberg scowling, thinking, Church scanning the crowd. People moved in and out. Canary Wharf loomed above them to their right, the high-rises casting long shadows across the city.

There was no way to know where their carrier would be.

But they did have the location that he was dropped off as well as a time frame. And that was enough.

Hallberg's phone buzzed then, and she looked down at it, receiving an email. She clicked it open and read the text quickly.

'Update from Fred,' she said.

'Fred?' Church asked.

'Fred at the office,' she answered, not even looking up, still parsing the information.

Church assumed that was the West Country lad. The computer savant that had fed Hallberg the information over the phone earlier. And the one who was feeding it to her now.

'Fred says that the phone came back online for a few minutes during the journey into London. And that it placed a short call that pinged off a tower east of here. It was outgoing to a blocked number. One we won't be able to get without another court order,' Hallberg mused. 'But I'm guessing it was made to whoever was the liaison on the ground here. The Chinese had to have help getting in and out of the country, getting their weapons... And that means there's likely someone—or a group of someones—that are well connected and stocked, operating out of London,' Hallberg said. 'And we know nothing about them. The Chinese government or MSS, or hell, just some kind of organised syndicate... I don't know which would be worse.'

'You don't sound surprised,' Church remarked, reading her tone.

'Nothing surprises me anymore,' Hallberg said. 'Happens after you work in intelligence. And if you're asking me if I'm shocked that foreign forces are working on British soil without authorisation... then no, I'm not shocked. If anything, I'd be shocked if they weren't.' Hallberg let out a long breath, the email seemingly filled with information, none of which was particularly useful.

She elected to call Fred instead, and his Cornish accent filled the cabin once more.

'Boss?' he asked.

'We're outside Westferry station where the Uber driver dropped our target,' Hallberg said. 'It took us about forty minutes to get here. I'd assume it would have been an hour for the Uber, so we've got a loose time frame. I need you to pull CCTV from the station and surrounding buildings. Look for the Uber pulling up, run NPR and find this guy. I need to know where he went and where he is now.'

'On it,' Fred said. 'Anything else?'

'Yeah,' Hallberg said, biting her lip. 'Pull CCTV from Pennyfields too. If he was being dropped at the station, I doubt he got on a train. There are plenty of stations closer to where they met the Albanians. If he came here, that meant he was going somewhere close by. And Pennyfields has one of the densest Chinese populations in the city. If he's got a contact in London, there's a good chance they could be there. Oh, and if there's any satellites flying over that you can piggyback on without an official requisition, do that too. I want coverage of the area if we can get it.'

Fred drew air in through his teeth. 'That last one might be tough.'

'That's why I'm asking you, Fred, and not Katie.'

Fred chuckled at that. 'I won't tell her that you said it.'

'Thanks.'

Hallberg hung up and Church arched an eyebrow, looking over at her.

'We don't like Katie?'

'She makes a brilliant cup of tea,' Hallberg said. 'As a digital intelligence officer...' She let out a sigh. 'Well, let's just say there's a reason that I call Fred.'

Church drummed his fingers on the tops of his knees. 'So what do we do now?'

'Now,' Hallberg said, clearly frustrated by the prospect. 'We wait.'

'Alright,' Church muttered. 'We wait.'

He reached out for the door, rolling the window down a little, listening as the sounds of the city flooded in. The smells, too. He grimaced a little at it.

Though London wasn't the worst-smelling city he'd ever been to—and he'd been to some pretty terrible-smelling places—he didn't like it. The air wasn't fresh. It was stale. And now somehow it felt tinged, tainted by something worse. The breath of a million people. A quickly spreading infection. The thought of that made him queasy. And after a second he rolled the window up and rested his head back, calming his breathing, his heart. Trying not to think about Siberia. But even in the warm interior of Hallberg's car he couldn't help but shiver, the bite of the snow-swept streets of Nobilsk still sharp on his skin. He resisted the walk down memory lane but failed, the events of that night playing over and over in his head on repeat. The muzzle flash still dancing behind his closed lids. The rattle of his breath inside his rebreather echoing in his ears. How long he was inside his own head he didn't know, but the buzz of Hallberg's phone, the squeeze of her fingers around his knee, shocked him back to the moment.

He drew in a short breath and looked over at her— grinning now, holding her phone up.

'Told you Fred was good,' she said. 'We got him.'

'Already?' Church asked, glancing down at his watch, realising that at least twenty minutes had passed.

Hallberg cranked the engine and pulled off into traffic, a shriek of horns behind her as she cut someone off. She filed diagonally across two lanes and then pulled under the overland rail, past the station and in towards Pennyfields, taking a right between the park and a long stretch of apartments. She slowed, looking up at them and pulled in at the kerb, pushing the car into park.

'Fred said CCTV had him walking past the station

and up towards Pennyfields. He cut in through a door here and then we lose him.'

She leaned forward on the wheel, practically resting her chin on it, staring up at the hundreds of possibilities.

'Jesus, how do we find him?'

Church thought on that for a second.

'Are we operating on the assumption that he's here to meet the person on the other end of the number he called?' he asked, wondering if what he was thinking would even work.

'Probably. He's shot, injured, not going to a hospital. He'd need to link up with someone. It makes sense he'd be coming to whoever he called.'

'And the number was blocked, wasn't it?'

'Yeah,' Hallberg replied. 'It was—we can't trace it without a court order. Can't even get the number. And especially not the address it's registered to if that's what you're thinking.'

'I was thinking...' Church said slowly, 'that all of these apartments in this block are occupied, right? And every single person living in them probably has a phone.'

'Yeah...' Hallberg said, not following him just yet.

'And the vast majority of those phones are unblocked. The vast majority registered... to one of these apartments.'

The light bulb went off behind her eyes. 'So we don't look for the blocked number. We look at all the ones that *aren't* blocked,' she said. 'Cross-reference them to all the flats here. And when we find the flats that don't have numbers registered to them...'

Church nodded. 'Exactly. We don't find the needle in the haystack. We just toss out all the hay.'

She smirked a little and shook her head. 'You know when we first met, I thought you were just this big dumb soldier that bumbled into the middle of my operation in the DRC.'

'And now,' Church said, 'you've changed your mind?'

'No. I still think you're a big dumb soldier... who gets a good idea every now and then.'

'Yeah,' Church laughed. 'Tell that to Fred, go on. He seems to be doing all the heavy lifting here anyway.'

She scowled—and then grinned—reaching out and socking him playfully in the arm.

And though Church was sucked in by her charm momentarily, his eyes drifted back up to the flats overhead and he realised that his idea—if it worked—was bringing them into direct contact with the man they were chasing. With a man infected with a potentially lethal pathogen.

And he had a good head start on them. A day, at least. And who knew what the incubation period was. Whether he'd be contagious. And if so, how contagious.

And as Church looked around, he realised that he didn't have any kind of mask, gloves, nothing. He was ill-prepared. But he reminded himself that only mattered if he got close. And he'd learned that lesson before. He didn't have any intention of getting anywhere near this guy. And though he was sure Hallberg was planning on bringing him in alive...

Church was under no such illusions.

And the first chance he got, he was going to put this guy down.

For good.

ELEVEN

2010, NOBILSK

THEY MOVED MORE QUICKLY NOW, but with no less care.

Cole was at the front of the train and tracking fast, desperate to close the distance to the lab and get this over with. En route, they exchanged theories about where the hell everyone was—whether there'd been an evacuation order and people had been airlifted out, whether people were just holed up inside their homes, barricading themselves in against whatever had escaped the lab, or, perhaps most terrifyingly of all, whether everyone was already dead.

Cole stamped out the conversation as quickly as it started, telling them to focus up as they turned a corner, the lab coming into view in the far distance. It was unmistakable: a wide-set building, low-slung and entirely concrete except for a glass entryway, the outside floodlit, rows of cars parked along its front.

They paused, Cole motioning them to tuck tight to the building they were skirting, pulling out his monocular once more to lens the front, checking for the resistance they were supposedly yet to meet. Church didn't think he saw anything, but going in the front of a place like this was never the best idea. So when Cole said that they were doubling back, going to find the back entrance, he was relieved. They all were.

The team streaked through the city at even greater pace now, sticking to narrow streets and alleyways as they made a wide loop of the building and approached from the rear, breaking cover from the buildings that seemed to be positioned the best part of a hundred yards back from the lab itself. A huge swathe of open tarmac separated them, that Church suspected would have usually been empty—but now instead was filled with a grim sight. And they all stumbled to a halt when they saw it.

They were coming up on a loading bay, a series of large roller doors, four feet off the ground so the trucks could back up to them to deliver goods. Church expected them to be all locked up, but they weren't. The four of them stood open to the elements and the city, and it was clear as to the reason why.

Piled up in a mountain in front of them was a heap of long yellow sacks with stark black zips running down one edge. They were printed with text in Cyrillic—Russian—a language Church couldn't read, but he didn't need to be able to identify that these were body bags, the biohazard symbol emblazoned on the front a clue as to what they were looking at.

It wasn't tens of thousands, but dozens at least, Church guessed—the workers from the facility. This was the source. Where the pathogen would have first gotten out, would have first begun to spread. These were the first infected—and perhaps not infected as well—rounded up, executed, Church surmised, bundled into biohazard bags and piled on the street, ready to be incinerated.

The four men looked on in horror, grips tightening reflexively on their weapons.

Cole let out a shaking breath and turned to them, gesturing to their masks.

'Make sure your seals are tight, boys,' he said. 'No skin on show.' They all nodded back, checking that their sleeves were down over their gloves, that their water-proof over-trousers were secured on the tongues of their boots.

The masks they were wearing were rated for both bacterial and viral pathogens. But could you ever completely trust a piece of equipment when it came to a situation like this? That was the exact question Church found himself asking as Cole motioned them forward.

'Eyes up,' he said. 'Weapons tight.'

The men nodded back, advancing on the open doors.

Weapons tight meant to not engage unless you had to. To not shoot unless you were shot at first. The main objective was still to slip in and out undetected. To recover the virologist, destroy the research, and bug out to the exfil without firing a single bullet. But as they got closer, the smell of blood pervading the masks' filtration systems and climbed up into the loading bay, that seemed more and more like a pipe dream.

All around them was evidence that when things had gone wrong here, they'd gone very wrong. Church could see empty shell casings, blood splatters, pools that had frozen over, drag marks as bodies had been hauled away.

They canvassed the scene, taking it in, each of them homing in on something different. Church visualised it —people running for the exit, getting gunned down. He followed a trail of splatters leading to a pool. Bloodied handprints and drag marks. He crouched. Someone shot in the back. They fell. Landed hard. Bleeding out, they tried to crawl towards the door.

Church lifted his eyes to the loading dock exit, staring into the darkened city.

They'd got so close.

Mitch snapped his fingers, grabbing Church's attention, and he looked up to where the man was standing, right under a loading door. He was pointing down at the metal eyelet in the floor, and as Church looked over, he could see it was half out of the concrete, the metal cut through with an angle grinder.

Church stepped over the bloodstain and walked towards him.

'They did everything they could to get out,' Mitch muttered, shaking his head.

Church's brow furrowed as he looked around them,

seeing bootprints in the blood, dried now on the concrete, but a window into what had happened.

'I don't think they were cutting their way out,' he said. 'I think someone was trying to get in.' He pointed to the prints. 'Not civilian issue,' he muttered, looking around him. He made out a few sets at least.

Cole stepped towards them now. 'Russian military,' he confirmed with a nod. 'I'm guessing they were called in to *clean up the mess*.'

Mitch understood then. 'Cut their way inside, hunted down the workers...'

'A few got past them,' Cole said, voice even, 'almost made it out.'

'Got caught here,' Church finished.

'Then they bagged and tagged them,' Mitch sighed, looking out towards the pile of bodies outside the loading dock.

Foster stared into the darkness solemnly. He was a man of few words, but his silence spoke volumes. Whatever had gone down here, it was bad.

Wholesale extermination was the phrase that came to Church's mind.

He grimaced inside his mask and turned away, feeling Cole's eyes on him.

He reached out, taking Church by the elbow. 'You good?' he asked.

Church gave him a nod. 'I'm good.'

'If you're not, you tell me now, Sol.'

Church pulled his arm free. 'I'm good.'

'Alright then,' Cole said, holding up a hand and

making a circular motion with his index finger. 'Let's wrap it up. We got a long night ahead of us.'

They all left the bloody scene behind and filed towards the door in front of them that led deeper into the facility, none keen to be first through. There was no denying that Russian military was on site. That they were armed. That they were killing without warning or conscience. But backing out wasn't an option, and Cole was keeping them on track, the door already open, the man already disappearing through it.

Mitch and Foster went next, Church at the back, checking their six, keeping their formation tight. And then the door was hissing closed behind them, sealing them inside with who really knew what.

A long white corridor stretched out ahead, halogen lights burning brightly overhead.

Church lifted his night vision glasses, hinging them back on top of his helmet so they were out of his eyes. There'd be no need for them now. The whole place, he figured, would be lit up like Oxford Street on Christmas.

They pressed on to the end of the hallway, coming to a set of heavy double doors.

The sign above them, in both Russian and English now, read *Biohazard Level 1*. That was the lowest risk—required minimal PPE. Basic research, petri dishes. Nothing serious. Nothing deadly. But Church knew as the levels increased, so did the risk.

Cole laid his hand on the handle and paused, looking back at them.

'Everyone ready?' he asked. The nods seemed slow, unsure, Church included.

'Alright then,' he said. 'When we get through here, it's radio silence. The facility is four floors going down. We're on the ground floor, which is BSL-1. The lockdown was triggered on Level Four, sealing it off from the rest of the facility. Intel says the lifts won't go down, the doors down there won't open. So we got to change that. Plan's simple: we find the central control room, we get inside, lift the lockdown, descend to Level Four, find the doc—Zorin—and then we're out of here, alright?' He checked his watch. 'I reckon twenty minutes is plenty, but if we can do it in fifteen, that'd make me very fucking happy—and you do want to make me happy, don't you, lads?'

They all smiled wanly, faces ghostly behind the rebreathers.

Church appreciated the attempted humour, but he didn't think any amount of jokes could lighten the mood just then.

They all knew what they were walking into.

And it was tantamount to hell.

TWELVE

PRESENT DAY

HALLBERG RELAYED the order to Fred and they waited once more, but this time Church stepped away from the car.

His anxiety was building, a tingling taking root in the tips of his fingers. He'd waded through all manner of terrible situations—he'd been pinned down by gunfire in the depths of Pakistan, had crawled through the muddy swamps in Bolivia avoiding drug cartels, and faced off against Somali terrorists in the jungles outside Mogadishu. There wasn't a corner of this world that he didn't feel like he'd faced down some shit in. But here, on home soil, against one man? He was rattled.

He took to pacing to try to calm himself and Hallberg fell into step with him.

'What are you doing?' she asked.

'Looking,' Church said, lying, his eyes roving up and down the exterior of the block of flats.

'For what?' Hallberg said.

'You think he's just going to be standing in the open? No. I'm looking for ingress routes. Egress routes,' he hedged. 'This guy makes a run for it... we need to know where he's going to pop out if we've got any hope of catching him.'

Hallberg seemed to buy it, nodding, taking it upon herself to do the same thing.

It wasn't a bad idea in situations like this and Church hoped that reverting to his training would supplant the dread building in his guts. But luckily, Fred came to the rescue once more, working fast, and gave Hallberg the update she wanted.

She answered the phone, pulling it to her ear.

'There's only a handful of apartments with no mobile phone registered to them,' he told her. 'Three of them are listed as unoccupied on the council's register. The other three of them are listed as occupied.'

'That's great,' Hallberg said. 'Three makes our life a lot easier.'

'It gets better,' Fred told her. 'One of those apartments that's listed as unoccupied has a landline registered to it. And mysteriously, miraculously, considering nobody lives there, a call was placed thirty seconds after our escapee finished up his call with our blocked number.'

Hallberg relayed it out loud for Church.

'So an unoccupied apartment managed to place a

landline call just after our carrier called the block number. Do we know where to?'

'We do,' Fred said. 'It's a veterinary clinic on Saltwell Street. Just around the corner, a couple of hundred metres from where you are.'

'Saltwell Street,' Hallberg confirmed, looking around and then taking off at a brisk walk.

It seemed like she'd memorised every street in London by the way she was striding confidently, Church thought, jogging across the road and into the park opposite the flats to catch her up. She cut a diagonal path across it, making a beeline for the other end, seemingly blind to everything Church was seeing. Mothers with strollers, children laughing and playing, people walking dogs, an old man breaking up crackers and tossing them on the ground for pigeons. Innocence, Church thought, in every conceivable sense. And an unknown man carrying an unknown disease had walked the same route they had, past these same people, he thought. Hell, they could already be infected. They could already be dead.

'Hey,' Hallberg called out to him, turning back, snapping her fingers to grab his attention. Church realised then he'd lagged behind, had come to almost a complete stop.

Hallberg ran back to him, reaching up and putting her hand on his shoulder, squeezing hard as though to focus him.

'What's with you today? I need you focused, I need you dialled in, I need you strong, alright?'

Church swallowed, choked a little and then looked

down at her, nodding. He wanted to lie, wanted to tell her that he was good, that it was nothing, but he couldn't. He could barely breathe, his throat tightened through a pinhole.

Hallberg stared up at him, inspecting him once more, seeing right through him, Church thought. But she didn't stop, didn't give him any quarter.

'Come on,' she said, pulling him along with her, keeping him now at her side. 'We need to move.'

They swept out of the park and followed the road around on the other side until they turned onto Saltwell Street, zeroing in on the vet's clinic ahead of them, the sign above the door reading *Saltwell Animal Clinic*. But despite the hour and the fact it was midweek, all the blinds had been drawn, the door was closed, a sign in the window displaying the message: *Sorry! We're closed.*

Hallberg slowed as she neared it, Church too, instinctively reaching to his hip, resting his hand on the grip of his Glock 19, tucked in a concealed holster inside his waistband. He didn't draw it, not in broad daylight in the middle of London. But something wasn't sitting right.

They closed in on the front door and he and Hallberg seemed to sense it at the same moment. Or maybe smell it. A coppery tinge in the air. Blood. Faint through the closed door, but disturbingly familiar to Church.

Instinct took over and he stepped ahead of Hallberg, motioning her back behind him as he came up on the glass, pressing his ear to the frame, listening in lieu of

seeing. A blackout blind was drawn on the other side—
he couldn't make the interior out except through a tiny
gap if he held his cheek to the door. Inside was
completely dark, the place empty, despite the opening
hours clearly inscribed six inches from his nose.

'What can you see?' Hallberg asked him.

Church just glanced at her and shook his head,
reaching out for the handle, turning it.

It was locked and he let out a little sigh. Nothing
was ever that easy.

Without waiting for Hallberg to suggest how they
were going to get in, he took a step back, glanced
around the street to make sure that it was empty, and
threw his elbow into the pane of glass.

It bounced off, the double glazing too thick, pain
lancing through his forearm.

Church grumbled, looking back at Hallberg who had
her eyebrows raised.

'That hurt, didn't it?'

'Fucking double glazing,' he muttered. 'That used to
be so much easier.'

'Yeah, I bet,' she said. 'Or maybe you're just losing
your touch.'

He hummed unhappily and motioned her back now,
turning and launching his heel into the wood instead,
right below the handle.

This time it gave and the door blew open, Church's
Glock flying from its holster, reflexively.

He swept inside, sweeping the nose of the pistol
around the reception, the entire room empty and quiet.

He motioned Hallberg inside and she closed the door behind them, her own pistol drawn now too.

They moved in single file, Church in front, stepping around the welcome desk and through the waiting room, pausing to look down at a semi-dried pool of blood next to an overturned office chair. He stepped backwards, seeing the drag marks along the tiles around the corner and down a corridor towards the treatment rooms, and signalled Hallberg to look at the puddle as well. But she'd already seen it, the colour draining from her face a little.

Protected inside a car or just chasing down leads was one thing, but this had suddenly got very real, very fast. Church didn't know what kind of operational experience she had, but this was now his world, and she let him lead without question.

Church moved along the corridor, coming up on a room with number one on it. He paused at the wood, listening, and hearing nothing, pushed it open, revealing the source of the puddle of blood. A young Asian woman was lying on her side on the tiles, a pair of bullet holes through her chest, punching right through the sternum into the heart, a double tap. Military style, Church thought immediately, remembering the crime scene of the house in the country.

Had the carrier done this? Walked into the vet's office and executed her?

No. That didn't make sense.

He began piecing it together as he backpedalled into

the corridor once more, leaving Hallberg staring down at the woman's body.

If the carrier made contact with someone here in the city, if he risked coming into the most heavily surveilled city in the world, that meant he was looking for help. Help with his wound, help to get out of the country, help with whatever he'd been infected with.

His contact had called the veterinary clinic, likely made arrangements for him to come by to be treated, so it would make no sense for him to come here and execute the people that were going to help him.

And if he was cleaning up after himself he would have had to come back out from the procedure rooms to see the receptionist. And why risk gunshots when he could take it silently from behind with no noise?

Church didn't voice any of this as he continued to push forward, checking the second examination room and finding it empty before pressing on to the third at the end of the corridor, opening it to see not just one, but two bodies, both of them wearing polo shirts bearing the logo of the clinic.

One of the men was Chinese, probably in his 50s, the other white, maybe early 40s. But that wasn't all that was here. Both of them had been executed in the same way as the receptionist, but whoever had done the killing hadn't stuck around to clean up.

A large steel table dominated the centre of the procedure room and on it were wads of bloodied gauze, forceps and scalpels caked in blood too, discarded latex gloves and a little metal tray on which

Church could see a stitching needle and thread hanging out of it.

This was definitely where the carrier had come and, by the look of it, had been patched up before the gunman had arrived.

There were other pieces on the board, then, he surmised. The Albanians seeking retribution? Or someone else? Either way, he and Hallberg weren't the only ones chasing him.

Church scanned the room for further signs of what had happened, took stock of where the bodies were, what positions. The receptionist had been dragged into a procedure room to hide her body from anyone peeking in the door. But these two had been left where they'd fallen.

Church could see that the Chinese vet had been interrupted in his work, dead next to the metal table, and that the younger one had come in afterwards, his body slumped almost at the threshold. Church was standing between them now and guessed this was just about where the shooter had been when the second vet had run in.

Church turned back to the door, lifting his pistol in re-enactment, seeing a blood spray on the wall next to it. Yeah. The second vet had burst into the room at the sound of the noise, surprised the gunman. He turned, fired, put him down.

But what about patient zero? Church turned in place once more, could see bullet holes in the back wall, around chest height, sweeping from right to left. Three in a line, the last one taking a gouge out of another door frame.

Church surged towards it, Hallberg only now entering the room behind him. He opened it, seeing that it led to a small rear car park and back out into the city. Church looked up at buildings in the distance, the biggest maze on earth, and then slowly eased the door closed, stepping back inside, letting out a long breath.

This scene was as cold as the one in the country, both the carrier and the mystery shooter long gone.

But who was the new player? Church found himself asking, and how was this all going to shake out?

He lifted his eyes to see Hallberg drawn, nauseated. Church approached her, filled her field of vision. Forced her to look at him, not the bodies.

'Hey,' he said. 'You good?'

She swallowed and looked up at him and he thought she might shake her head. But she mustered the strength to nod instead.

He was sure this wasn't the first grisly scene she'd walked into. He was impressed, if anything, she'd retained enough of her humanity to still be shaken by this stuff.

He hadn't. His had left him a long time ago.

'We're a few steps behind here,' he said, 'but it looks like we beat the NCA to the punch, at least.'

He glanced around the room and then up towards the corner of the ceiling, a CCTV camera hanging there, a little red light under the lens.

'And that,' Church went on, pointing up at it, 'might

just be exactly what we need. Our target was being chased and I bet that the shooter went after him and didn't stick around to wipe his tracks. We need to get into that system, find the footage and figure out our next move.'

Hallberg's expression hardened as she continued to regain herself.

'Is that something you can handle?' Church asked her, smiling a little, looking to elicit one from her in response. 'Or do I need to call Fred?'

THIRTEEN

2010, NOBILSK

THE BIOLAB REEKED of death as they pressed inwards, the gravity of what they were coming up against finally sinking in.

A flatbed trolley lay abandoned in the hallway, its wheels caked with blood, a few flies buzzing in lazy circles above the stained wooden bed, bloodied hand-prints littering the steel bar used to push it.

This was what they'd used to cart the bodies out, Church thought, and as the other men looked down at it, he suspected they'd come to the same conclusion— though nobody voiced it. Beyond the trolley was a scene from a nightmare. It seemed like whoever had been assigned the job of evacuating the bodies had given up, the task perhaps too large, and had instead resorted to a quicker, more efficient, more barbaric method.

Ahead of them, the clean white walls were scorched

black. Trails of fire led across the floor and up the brick-work—the kind that came from spraying flammable liquid out of the nose of a flamethrower. And there, in the wake of fire, Church could see them: charred bodies, littering the ground like rubbish. Discarded *things*. Not humans. No. Just gunned down and then torched like they were nothing.

And as they crept along the length of the corridor, stepping over shell casings, inspecting the fallen, all Church could do was hope that they'd already been dead when there was a light put to them.

'Jesus Christ,' Mitch muttered, crouching to inspect one of the corpses less burned up than the others. Church could make out the sleeve of what looked like a police or military jacket, a star sewn to the shoulder, the remains of a pistol holster at the hip, the weapon nowhere to be seen.

Cole took one glance at it and made his decision.

'Security guard,' he said. 'Probably worked at the lab.'

They agreed and moved on, pressing through another set of double doors, stopping the moment they did. There, in the middle of the corridor, was a fully clothed and unburned body, lying face down—this one in tactical gear. Flak vest, full-face respirator, duct tape around the cuffs of his jacket and trousers.

Cole approached first, motioning the men to stop, and scanned the length of the hallway with his weapon, confirming it empty before stepping to the man, digging his toe under his belly and rolling him over. He still had a rifle hanging around his neck and Church identified it quickly: an AKS-74U equipped with a tactical stock and suppressor.

Russian special forces standard issue.

The man, by the looks of it, had taken a shot to the head, and it took a moment for Church to piece together what had happened. More bodies lay further down the line, these ones, too, burnt up. Church closed his eyes, visualising it—the whole thing.

It was clear that Russian special forces had been dispatched here to clean up the mess, or even just clean house entirely. They'd come in force, cut their way through the outer door, swept through with extreme prejudice, executing both lab staff and security alike. But it looked like one of the guards had got off a lucky shot—took down one of the Spetsnaz operators. Russians versus Russians. A merciless story, Church thought, as Cole let out a low whistle and motioned them onwards. Church continued to lay it out in his head as they moved. The Spetsnaz had burned up the men and women who might have been infected, but had left their comrade here, ready to take his body home when their mission was finished. Just, Church thought, as he or any of the others would do for one of their own.

But if this body was still lying here, that could only mean one thing: the job *wasn't* done. The Spetsnaz was still on site, still clearing through. They hadn't left.

Cole came to this realisation just as quickly as Church, looking back at the men.

'Eyes up, weapons tight,' he reiterated, giving a firm

nod to show just how serious the situation was. 'Let's keep moving.'

They pressed through corridor after corridor—long stretches of brightly lit hallway lined with labs working on who knew what.

Church suspected it was all nasty enough, though. Five hundred miles from the nearest civilisation, in the middle of Siberia, inside a walled city... what else would they be working on? They checked off the rooms one by one for any sign of survivors or special forces, Cole guiding them towards the centre of the building— towards where Church assumed they would gain access to the lower floors, to the more secure labs, and to the control room that Cole was directing them to.

Church opened a door into one lab, a large square room with a sprawling work surface in the middle, replete with microscopes, centrifuges, beakers, incubators lining the back wall, along with a line of workstations and computers. He swept it briefly, called out that it was clear, and began to pull back—stopping only at the sound of something at the far end.

He froze, turning his head towards the room once more, listening for it again. Silence for a second, and there it was—just the faintest shuffling noise. Something scraping, scratching—he couldn't tell what. He looked back into the corridor, locking eyes with Cole, and lifted his chin, moving his head towards the room to show that he was giving it another pass. Cole took a step towards him, watching Church work, covering his back.

Church moved in steadily, weapon to his shoulder,

muzzle trained on the ground six feet in front of him. He could see nobody above the counters, but that didn't mean someone wasn't cowering behind them. He made a loop of the room, finding nothing—and no one. No trace of anything alive. But he hadn't imagined it. He knew that much. He was in the vicinity of the noise, he thought, and he waited now, lowering himself a little, listening for any hint of what he'd heard before.

Then—there again. A little scrape, like a heel being pulled across wood.

He turned his attention to one of the cabinets under the central workstation—large enough, he thought, for someone to climb inside and hide if they were desperate enough. He pulled his rifle tight against his shoulder with his right hand on the grip, finger on the trigger, and reached out with his left, taking the handle and pulling it wide, ready to fire.

But he didn't see the violent eyes of a soldier—just the frightened face of a woman.

She was in her mid-twenties, with angular features, her face slim, cheeks sunken. How long had she been in there? Church wondered, backing up, keeping his rifle on her. She had her knees to her chest, her arms locked around them, hiding her face, cowering away from him in his respirator and black gear. To her, he was no different from the Russians—just another man with a gun, here to kill her.

Church's Russian was almost non-existent, but he knew a few words—the same ones he knew in half a dozen languages. The ones most often used on missions. This time, it was a simple order.

'*Viydi,*' he said. Simply: *come out.*

The woman looked up at him, perhaps noting the poor accent or pronunciation, knowing he wasn't a native speaker.

Her brow creased quizzically and she leaned forward to get a better look at Church, her face edging into the light of the lab now, out of the shadow. He recoiled a little, holding his breath instinctively as he laid eyes on her—her eyes bloodshot and ringed with blood, droplets having run down from her cheeks like tears; her lips purpled and cracked; the fingertips still locked around her knees, blackening.

They were both still for just a moment, her eyes roving up and down Church, as though searching for something. And then, before he could react, she lunged —springing out of the cabinet with more speed than he'd given her credit for.

But she wasn't making an attempt to run.

No—she threw herself straight at him, hands outstretched, scrabbling at his mask, pulling at it. Trying to get it off for herself, no doubt, to protect herself from whatever she already had. Her weight bowled him backwards, off his heels, and he sprawled onto the ground, driving his knee into her stomach, pushing her back— not wanting to wrestle his weapon in between them, not wanting to execute her like that. But she was clawing at him, climbing up him furiously, desperately, trying to save her own life. All thoughts of sense and logic gone from her mind. Watching all of your colleagues executed, hearing them scream, listening, and smelling as they burned would do that to you. There was nothing she wouldn't do to survive in that moment, Church thought.

But she was infected—with what, he didn't know—but it wasn't anything good. And he knew if he allowed her to keep going, if he allowed her to take his mask, he would be too. He dug his knee into her ribs again, and shunted her backwards, lifting his weapon this time.

'Stoy!' he called. *'Stoy!'*

The Russian word for *stop*.

She understood.

He knew she did.

And for a brief moment she followed the order, standing over him, staring down at him, staring right into the barrel of his gun. *Don't do it*, he pleaded silently. *Don't make me do it.*

But she knew she was already dead. And she came at him again, drawing her hands back, bending her knees, ready to pounce on him—forcing him to do the last thing he wanted to.

He swore loudly, braced for the recoil, and put three bullets—close grouping—into her chest. She convulsed, stumbling backwards, landing hard against the corner of the workstation. A mist of blood sprayed from her chest, raining down on Church, coating the visor of his mask in a thin film.

She turned, scrabbling at the top of the workstation as she tried to pull herself towards freedom, making it just two steps before she collapsed, falling to a limp heap on the tiles. Church watched as the blood pool began to spread around her body, rolling sideways to avoid it. He brought his forearm up and raked it across the plastic of his mask, smearing it, acutely aware that it was just an inch from the end of his nose—that he'd hesitated, that he'd almost got himself killed, that his reluctance to pull the trigger had nearly cost him his life.

He felt a heavy hand on his shoulder then, and looked up, seeing Cole dragging him to his feet.

'What the fuck was that, Sol?' he asked, still holding fast, staring down at the woman.

'She surprised me,' Church said. 'I didn't expect—'

'Well, you fucking should have,' Cole cut in, letting go of his jacket roughly. 'We're not here to play nice, and we're not here to rescue civilians. We've got our orders, and we get them done.'

'So what did you want me to do? Leave her in there? Execute her the second I opened the cupboard?'

'Either? Both?' Cole spat. 'Look at her,' he said, gesturing down at her bloodied eyes and rotting fingers. 'Didn't matter what you did. She was dead the second she fucking breathed that shit. And if you're searching for a clear conscience, you're in the wrong line of work, Church. I thought you'd know that by now.'

Church looked down at the woman for a moment longer, hearing Cole's words ring in his ears, and then looked up at his captain.

'Would she be dead?' Church said.

'What's that supposed to mean?' Cole asked.

Church narrowed his eyes at his captain. 'Do you know more about this than you let on? Do you know what this is? What she's got?'

Cole paused for just a second, blinking at his brother, and then glanced down at the woman once more. 'I don't need to,' he said. 'Look at her. Don't take a genius to work out that she's fucked. And if you can't fucking get your shit together,' he muttered, shaking his head and turning away, 'then you're going to be too.'

FOURTEEN

PRESENT DAY

'JULIA? JULIA!' Church repeated, voice hardening, grabbing her attention.

She blinked, peeling her eyes away from the two dead vets in front of her and looking up at Church.

She was no stranger to this kind of thing. But perhaps—realising she was on a direct collision course with the man responsible, this time without any backup, without Interpol or anyone else standing between her and the end of her gun—the gravity of what it was exactly that she was involved in was finally taking hold of her.

Hallberg hadn't heard a word he'd said. Not about the carrier or about the security camera. Was this all too much for her? Did he need to pull the rip cord?

'Julia,' Church said again, focusing her attention.

'We're standing in the middle of a crime scene and the NCA are no doubt homing in on this place as we speak. We need to make a decision here. What are we doing?' Church pressed her, hoping perhaps she might finally say that they were in over their heads, that they were going to hand this over, that they were going to call this in and then take a step away.

It was the smart thing to do, it was the obvious thing.

The moment her brow furrowed, Church knew it wasn't what they were doing though. She seemed to process his words with delayed effect, compiling them in her head before she answered. Like a car sputtering before it came to life.

'The carrier is gone,' she said slowly, looking around, confirming back to Church what he'd already said, but this wasn't him. She nodded to herself, glancing up at the camera in the corner of the room. 'We need to know what happened to him.'

She seemed to gain confidence with each word, turning and heading back down the corridor towards the front. She stepped into the reception area and made a beeline for the computer, tapping the enter button, the screen lighting up.

She stared at a lock screen and hummed unhappily.

It was right about now, Church thought, that she would make a call, get Fred to crack it for her. But Church didn't think that he'd be able to do that over the phone.

Though apparently they didn't need tech support after all.

Hallberg scoffed a little and reached down, pulling a sticky note off the desk next to the keyboard, holding it up for Church. It bore the word *password*, then a colon, followed by a random assortment of letters, numbers and symbols.

She put it down again, shaking her head, muttering under her breath as she typed it in.

'What's the point in hashing your password for security if you're just going to write it on a fucking sticky note?' she grumbled, accessing the computer and searching for the app she wanted in the taskbar. She opened it up—recordings and feeds from the security system—and began spooling back through the footage. There was nothing for 24 hours, and then suddenly the screen burst to life with activity.

The receptionist appearing in frame, her feet first moving on her back, sliding towards her desk and up into the chair. A man coming after her, holding onto her wrists like some strange and warped wheelbarrow race. Of course, Hallberg was playing the receptionist's murder in reverse as she scrubbed back through the footage, scanning straight past the execution and back to when the man knocked on the door, the room empty as though he'd waited for his moment.

He stepped inside and turned, pulling the blinds down. As Hallberg played it at normal speed now, a second man followed, both of them dressed in dark jackets, baseball caps. The men moved to opposite windows and pulled the blinds all the way down. The receptionist behind the desk got up and called out to them. But despite her gesturing and waving, the recording soundless, they carried on. And the moment the final blind covered the window, the first man turned towards the desk and shot her with a suppressed pistol, a long and wide baffle attached to its nose—the kind that really would dim the sound of a gunshot.

The receptionist slumped backwards in her chair and the gunman moved swiftly forward, swept past her and down the corridor without returning, the second stepping towards the receptionist, lifting his own pistol, and putting a second round into her heart to make sure before he dragged her off the chair and out of frame.

And then, the feed might as well have been a still image.

Hallberg, eyes sweeping across the screen, searched for the button to switch the feeds and found it, jumping from room to room until she finally found the one at the back. She wound it back to the right timestamp and let it play.

In frame, Church could see two men conversing, both Chinese. The first, his face visibly slick with sweat, was sitting on the metal procedure table, the sleeve of his sweatshirt rolled up over his elbow, a thin piece of white gauze taped to the crook of his arm, while the vet in the polo shirt at the side of the room was hunched over a microscope, studying something. A blood draw, Church thought, and he guessed Hallberg did the same.

A moment later, the door burst open, the first gunman stepping into view.

The carrier, sitting on the table, lifted his hands, turned his head away, as though begging for his life.

The vet barely managed to turn in his chair before the gunman levelled his pistol at him, fired, killing him where he sat, before returning to the carrier. There was a moment of stillness, and then suddenly the gunman was sprawling, tackled from behind by the second vet.

The carrier wasted no time, diving off the side of the table, scrambling towards the back of the room and the fire exit. The gunman got to a half stance, the vet still holding onto his waist, and fired, chasing the carrier out with bullets.

The holes in the wall, Church recounted.

When the carrier was through the door and gone, the gunman turned, throwing his elbow into the top of the vet's back, kneeing him loose. He stood up, didn't even manage to raise his hands before the gunman executed him. He fell to a knee, clutching at his sternum, and then flopped onto the ground.

Before he'd even fallen still, the gunman was out the back door after the carrier, and not a second later, the second gunman was hurdling over the dead vet, and out the back door as well. And then, once more, apart from the slowly spreading pools of blood beneath the two dead men, the image was still.

Hallberg let out a sigh, and lowered her head.

'This is more than 24 hours ago,' she said.

'But it's something,' Church assured her. 'At least now, we have a better idea of what's going on.'

'Do we?' she asked.

Church nodded. 'Those two men that came in, the only reason they'd be chasing the carrier is if China got wind of the deal and wanted to put a stop to it. Those guys, whether they were flown in, or whether they've just been embedded here, they're trained operatives. MSS. Got to be,' Church said. 'Who knows how big the operation is—but either way, they're looking to reclaim what they think is their property. Hell, maybe the pathogen, whatever it is, was stolen from a Chinese lab. Either way, their job is to apprehend, not kill. Shooter number one had a chance to execute the carrier the second he walked into that room. He didn't, because he wanted to capture him and take him back. And the only reason he'd run, was because he knew what he'd be facing if he did.'

'Fucking hell,' Hallberg said. 'This is going to turn into an international incident if we're not careful.'

'Enough to prick up the ears of the Home Office, and the NCA.'

Hallberg looked up at him, brow creasing.

'This has to be enough to light a fire under them,' Church said. 'It's bigger than we realised and we're out on a limb here. It's time to make a call.'

'Make a call?' Hallberg said, as though the words made no sense to her. 'What are you talking about? By the time they muster any kind of serious action, it'll be too late.'

'It's already too late,' Church replied. 'You saw the video, two armed men chasing down one sick guy who's never stepped foot in London in his life. How far do you think he's going to make it before they catch up to him?'

'It doesn't matter,' Hallberg said. 'We're here now, we've got the trail, and we need to keep pushing on.'

'And what happens,' Church said, 'when the NCA come through here, find what we found? Go through the CCTV footage, and see us kicking the door in. How's that going to play, hmm? When they see that we were here and we didn't call them?'

She bit her lip this time, and stood straight. 'You're right,' she said, pulling her phone from her pocket, and dialling a number. She held it to her ear, and Church could hear Fred's muted reply against her cheek.

'Fred, I need to set you up with remote access to a workstation,' Hallberg said.

'Okay, and what am I doing?' His voice was small, barely audible to Church.

'You're scrubbing any existence of me and my partner from the hard drive. Leave everything before it, make it look like a power outage or a system crash, or something. Whatever you do, I don't want any record of us ever being here.'

'You found something at the vet's clinic,' Fred replied.

'We did,' Hallberg said.

'Right,' Fred muttered slowly, knowing what he was being asked to do—which was destroying evidence in an official NCA investigation.

'Fred, do this for me,' Hallberg said, 'please. And when you're done, wait an hour, then place an anonymous call to the NCA, say that you heard some strange noises coming from the vet's clinic yesterday. You didn't call them in, but you've just walked past now, and see the door has been kicked in, and that you think there's blood inside.

'That should get the NCA scrambling, at least.'

'Will do,' Fred said, pausing as though apprehensive, as though wanting to say something.

'What is it?' Hallberg said, reading the silence.

'Are you sure about this, boss?' Fred said. 'This is all sounding...' He trailed off, not wanting to use any of the words that he should have to describe this situation.

Fucked, was the one that came to Church's mind.

'I'm sure,' Hallberg said. 'You need to trust me. You need to let me work. And look, Fred, I hope it goes without saying, but if any of this blows back—it's on my shoulders, not on you. I'll make sure of that.'

'You're right,' Fred said. 'It does go without saying.'

Hallberg let out a small sigh of relief. 'Good. In that case, how's that sat flyover footage coming?'

Fred tutted a little. 'It's not much, but I've got something.'

'Historic, too?' Hallberg replied.

'Last couple of days,' Fred said.

'Okay, well find the vet's clinic and tell me where the three guys that bolted out the back door at 2.15 yesterday went?'

'Alright, give me a second,' Fred said. 'I'm not a miracle worker.'

Hallberg turned to Church, grinning, despite the fact that he certainly was not grinning back.

'You know what, Fred?' She laughed. 'I don't believe that for a second.'

FIFTEEN

2010, NOBILSK

As MUCH AS he hated hearing it, Church knew that Cole was right.

He usually was.

Church had often been accused of being a bleeding heart, told that he was in the wrong line of work. But there was something inside him that kept him holding on to what he thought might be humanity. Although, these days, he wasn't really sure.

He'd pulled that trigger and there'd been a flare of regret, of remorse, of pain. But as quickly as it had come, it had faded away. And as he stared down at that woman's body, he felt nothing.

It was what he'd always feared—going numb to the darkness. And yet here he was, in the darkest corner of the world imaginable. Knowing what was ahead, not fearing it, just doing it.

He stayed on Cole's shoulder as they moved, flecks of the lab technician's blood still on his visor. He tuned it out, homing in on the objective, and came up on the next door. Cole slowed and turned back to them.

'All right,' he said, looking up at the wall next to the door, a sign there emblazoned with an icon for the lifts and stairs. 'This is it. Through this door, the elevators that lead down to the lower levels. Intel says the lab where the good doctor was working is on full lockdown —that's on level four. Lifts won't go down there, and the stairwells are all sealed magnetically until the lockdown is lifted or overridden.

'When Zorin got his message out, he said he managed to sabotage the pressure seal on the airlock in his lab, which means that seal integrity is broken, which tripped the ventilation system's failsafe too. That's preventing the lockdown from being lifted until circulation's restored. So no one can get in or out of level four until it's manually reset first.

'I'm sure our Russian friends are doing everything they can to lift the lockdown, but with the filtration system shut down, they're at a dead end. This is our chance to get ahead of them, but that means we've got to split up—reset the recirculation system and hit the control room at the same time.'

He looked at the team. 'Divide and conquer. Everyone understand?'

Nods from the men.

'All right.' He motioned them forward, pushing through into the corridor with a pair of elevators on the right. Cole pressed the call buttons for both, and they started to come up from the floors below. 'Zorin's intel says that the mechanical level is on three, so Foster, Mitch—I want you to head there and restore the pressure. He says there's four breakers—one for each floor —that need to be flipped off together, and then back on one at a time. That'll reboot things and get the fans going. Once we hear the air begin to circulate, we'll do the rest. Got it?'

The two men formed up and nodded.

'Church—you're with me,' Cole went on, checking his weapon. 'We're going to hit that control room. Lift the lockdown, then we regroup on four, get the doctor, and we're headed home.'

They looked at each other for just a moment, knowing their roles and their objectives, and divided into two pairs. The doors opened simultaneously and Mitch locked eyes with Church for just a second before he disappeared into his elevator, Foster at his side. Church stepped into his own with Cole.

He pushed the button for level two, and the doors slid closed and sealed with a hiss, the cables and pulleys easing them down into the earth. Church felt the weight of it pressing in on him immediately, and though it was a short ride, he felt like they'd edged a lot closer to hell.

'Radio silence,' Cole whispered to Church.

If the Spetsnaz weren't on the top floor, that meant there was a good chance they'd be on this one. If Cole was right that Zorin's sabotage of the filtration system had kept them from lifting the lockdown, then Church had no doubt they'd still be in the control room trying to get it done.

The doors opened in front of them, revealing another plain white corridor bathed in harsh light. Before exiting, Cole inspected the signs on the wall opposite, his Russian clearly better than Church's, and motioned for them to head right. He took one step forward and Church reached out, putting his hand on Cole's shoulder, guiding himself out of the elevator behind him, the pair of them covering the corridor ahead with their weapons. They started moving as one, Church removing his hand and laying it back on his MP5 to steady it, keeping it glued on the far end of the hallway.

It split in a T, and facing them was a bank of windows. Behind it, what looked like an office replete with screens covering the entirety of a wall, all of them showing different surveillance feeds and other measurement data from around the building—a schematic of what looked like tubes and pipes flashing red, and big warning symbols scattered across it.

Church figured it was the filtration system Cole had mentioned, and that was confirmed by the three people in that room gesticulating at each other—two of them dressed in black with full-face rebreathers, the same Russian standard-issue rifles hanging from their shoulders.

The third man, however, wasn't wearing a mask or military gear at all. He was in a pale blue polo shirt, sitting on a swivel chair, a dark blue jacket hanging behind him, the same star on the shoulder Church had seen on the burned guard upstairs. The man had his hands up, facing the two operators, his mouth bloodied, cheeks bruised.

They'd been beating him.

He was no doubt one of the security team, Church thought, and the Spetsnaz were trying to get him to fix the problem.

But judging by how swollen his face was, it wasn't something he could get done.

Cole slowed and motioned Church down, the two men lowering to a crouch, creeping forward under the line of the windows. The two Russian soldiers were side-on, as was the security guard. They hadn't seen them creep up. Church and Cole reached the wall and pressed themselves against it, just under the lip of the window, Church feeling Cole's eyes on him.

'You good?' Cole mouthed, barely a whisper.

'Yeah,' Church whispered back.

'Sure?' Cole risked confirming.

Church found his eyes behind the mask, meeting him with a hard stare. He didn't like being asked twice —it meant Cole thought there was something wrong. But the conversation was cut short by a loud thud of knuckles colliding with someone's face, echoing through the glass above them. The security guard pleaded with the men in Russian, but they weren't hearing it, and they hit him again. Judging by how they'd handled the rest of the workers in this lab, they'd keep hitting him until he either fixed the problem or was dead.

How long either would take, Church didn't know.

But Foster and Mitch were closing in on their objective, and no doubt would get it done. When they did, all those warning labels would disappear off the screen, the security guard would do what the men asked, and then the entire mission would be in jeopardy.

The thing that struck Church was that the security guard sitting in that room, face bloodied to a pulp, didn't look like the others they'd come across. His fingers weren't blackened, eyes not bleeding. Had he been protected inside the control room, or was he simply not sick?

Church didn't get a chance to think much more about it before a gunshot rang out. He and Cole both lifted their eyes to the sill of the window, peering into the control room—the still-smoking barrel of a pistol hanging a few inches from the security guard's forehead.

He sat still for a second, and then his head fell backwards, blood draining from the gaping hole in the back of his skull.

Negotiations had broken down, it seemed—the soldiers reaching the end of their patience.

Church and Cole looked at each other, weighing what came next—whether the soldiers would stay there, vacate the room, whether they could let them go, or whether they'd have to go in there and take them out. These wouldn't be run-of-the-mill soldiers. The Spetsnaz were some of the most highly trained operators in the world, able to go toe-to-toe with the SAS, Navy

SEALs, or any other special forces unit. Going in there all guns blazing was a last resort, and yet, like most of the decisions they made in the middle of a mission going wrong, the choice was taken out of their hands completely.

The chatter and rattle of automatic gunfire rose up through the floor beneath their feet, and suddenly there was heavy breathing in their ears—Mitch opening his comms from the other end.

'We've got full contact,' he panted, running hard. 'Four tangos, and they are *not* happy to see us.'

Cole knocked his head backwards against the wall under the window.

'Bloody hell,' he muttered, letting out a long, steadying breath.

'We've got to help them,' Church added quickly, but before he could even move, Cole's hand was on his arm.

'No. Mitch and Foster have got their orders. And you've got yours. We take the control room, and we take it now,' he said, reaching down to his weapon and pulling back on the slide, making sure there was a round in the chamber. 'Weapons free, Church. Let's move.'

SIXTEEN

PRESENT DAY

CHURCH HAD to admit that having a friend like Fred was pretty great.

Not only did he seamlessly gain remote access to the workstation with a few simple directions to Hallberg, but he also managed to do exactly what she'd said—scrubbing her and Church from the security record, crashing the system like a pro so it'd simply look like it cut out on its own. Not a moment later, he was walking Hallberg through the route that the three men had taken out the back door—the carrier and his two pursuers—and Church and Hallberg were quickly on the trail again.

He guided them down streets, Hallberg striding out in front, Church trailing behind, noting that she was on rails, not checking her surroundings, not watching her back.

Though Church expected that was the reason he was there, he kept a firm grip on his pistol, ready to draw it at any moment.

About half a mile from the clinic, Fred guided them down a narrow alleyway towards what looked like an old industrial building—red brick with wonky walls, large windows with rotten Georgian-style framing.

Hallberg finally slowed to catch her breath, looking back for the first time to check Church was with her.

'This is it,' Fred said, voice tinny in the narrow alley, playing out of Hallberg's phone on speaker for Church's benefit. 'They cut down this alley and I lose sight of them on account of the angle. But they don't come out the other side, so it's either the building on your right or the one on your left.'

Church glanced at the other option. Flat concrete walls, steel roller shutters. What it was a part of he couldn't say, but the pedestrian exit didn't even have handles, could only be opened from the other side. Fire escape, he surmised. There was no way the carrier went in there, not unless the pathogen he was exposed to gave him the powers of a spider and he climbed up the walls. Church doubted it was anything as novel, which only left one option—the brick building. Windows smashed and roughly boarded over from the inside, old wooden doors half rotted through. Plenty of ways inside.

Hallberg started trying every one, finding on the third try a window with a sheet of plywood that looked like it had been kicked loose. She pressed on it and it flapped inwards, and without hesitation she stuck her head inside. Church was right behind her and reached out, grabbed her by the collar and pulled her back into the alleyway.

She turned on him, trying to elbow his arm free, but he kept a good grip.

'What the hell are you doing?' she said.

'What the hell are you doing?' Church replied. 'You want to get your head blown off or do you just stick it in every hole you find?'

'I don't know if you've forgotten,' she retorted, 'but time isn't something we've got a lot of right now.'

'You'll have none of it if you keep doing shit like that,' Church said. 'I don't know if you've ever been shot but I have, and I'm not trying to get shot again. Especially not because you literally stick your nose into the middle of an MSS manhunt.'

'Right, well what's your big idea then?'

'Caution. Sense,' Church said, finally releasing her collar and tapping his temple with his finger. 'If there's one thing I never thought you were, it was impetuous. You ever heard the term slow is smooth and smooth is fast? No? Well learn it. It's something to live by, something to not die by.'

Hallberg scowled. 'So you want to go first?' she asked, proffering him the hole.

'Yeah,' Church said. 'I do.'

He stepped past her and drew his pistol, reaching out and moving the plywood sheet an inch or two, inspecting the rusted nails that had broken from the corners, the slight depression in the wood where someone had thrown a boot into it, the freshly broken pieces of wood frame where someone had climbed inside.

Hallberg's instinct was correct—this was where they climbed through—but she was lucky that they hadn't been waiting on the other side.

Church levered the plywood a little wider, looked inside into the darkness, listened for any hint that the place was occupied, and after a few seconds, satisfied that it wasn't, he slowly drew his body over the sill, pushing his head and shoulder through the gap, climbing into the building clumsily, his size making it difficult.

He held the wood up to Hallberg and she climbed in after him.

'See,' she said. 'Empty. And how much time did we waste?'

'Seconds,' Church replied flatly. 'Now be quiet, we don't know who's in here, and if anyone is, we don't want them to know that we're coming.'

They crept through what would have been a store-room a long time ago, the smell of damp and dry rot seeping into the air. Church moved through the old building, now abandoned, the floors above rotted, the floors beneath bowed and weakened.

Half the walls were collapsed in, or threatening to at least.

To restore a building like this would cost more than knocking it down and replacing it. But something this old, Church thought, was probably tied up in some kind of history or heritage. Listed, maybe even. So instead of being preserved or renovated, it was just left to rot, mired in red tape and bureaucracy.

It was dark inside except for thin bands of light coming through the upper floor windows and streaming through spaces between the floorboards above, just giving enough of a glow to move by.

Church went ahead, stepping slowly, following the tracks in the dust, stepping over a pile of broken boards, a flood of light coming through a hole above, lighting the way. He saw one man running, two following, their pace quickened but even. Stalking their prey.

The carrier and the two MSS operators.

At his shoulder, Hallberg was breathing hard. Loudly, he thought. Louder than anybody had ever breathed before, it felt like.

As they drew close to another door, Church detected something, froze instinctually. A faint sound from the other side. He held his fist up signalling Hallberg to stop, but either she didn't know the sign or she wasn't paying attention, because she bumped right into his back and stumbled a little.

Church whirled, reaching out, grabbing her by the shoulder of her jacket, keeping her from falling.

He raised his pistol and touched the cold steel against his lips, a gesture she would definitely understand.

He released her jacket and touched his finger to his ear, then pointed through the door.

Hallberg stepped a little closer, leaned in, heard it

too, her eyes widening—the voices dim, distant, speaking in Chinese.

Why they were still here, Church didn't know, but the fact that they were was undeniable.

Hallberg lifted her hands then and sort of shrugged, looking around as though asking which way to go.

Church had no idea what was beyond the door, but he knew that getting them into a firefight—or even putting her at risk—was stupid at best, but more likely suicidal for them both.

He gestured the other way, backtracking a little until he reached the hole in the ceiling he'd passed beneath earlier. Church motioned Hallberg up. She nodded, understanding that they could move in from above, get a better look at who they were listening to, maybe catch a few words.

Church crouched a little, put his hands on his knee and offered her a leg up.

She stepped onto it and he lifted her easily up through the gap.

She was lighter than he expected and more agile, clambering onto the upper floor with ease before she turned around, offering her hand down to him.

He stared up at her. 'Really?' he whispered.

'How else are you going to get up?' she frowned back.

The corridor was narrow though, and this wasn't the first time Church had had to do something like this. He put his foot on one wall, the treads of his boots biting into the rough bricks, then hopped upwards, putting his heel under his hamstring, wedging himself in the hallway with some difficulty—immediately realising this was much easier the last time he'd done it, which was probably fifteen years ago now.

He extended his body upwards, shuffling his feet up the wall, gaining inch by inch until he could reach the floor above.

Hallberg took his arm and pulled at him, though he didn't know if it made any difference at all.

With his knees screaming and sweat beading on his brow, he managed to lift himself onto the floor, pulling himself onto his stomach and then rolling onto his back, breathing harder than he would have liked to admit.

'Graceful,' Hallberg smirked at him, staring down at his rapidly rising and falling chest.

He didn't dignify it with a response, simply lifted his middle finger and gave her full view of it.

She grinned and offered her hand again.

He took it and she pulled him upright, the pair of them resigning themselves to silence as they crept forward, shuffling their feet to not make any noise, lowering themselves down to their hands and knees as they drew over the top of the wall and the door they'd stopped at below.

The space ahead of them was vast and open, the entire second floor only interrupted with brick pillars, the rest of the space totally empty.

The voices grew louder as they crawled, ringing up from the floor beneath.

They moved on their bellies, making sure not to

disrupt the conversation as they manoeuvred into position, able to spy through tiny gaps between the floorboards.

Church signalled to stop, moving his head left to right to see, counting more than the two men who'd chased the carrier. Maybe that's why they were still here. They were waiting for backup to arrive—and probably lying low in case anyone had managed to get into the vets clinic and see their handiwork.

Church could see four in total, one of whom seemed to be injured. The injured man was sitting on a chair in a square room, having his upper trap tended to by another of the men. They were all Chinese, all wearing dark clothes—jeans or cargo trousers, jackets long enough and baggy enough to conceal ballistic vests and holsters, but plain enough to be innocuous. Clothes designed to blend seamlessly into a crowd. To allow operatives to move unseen.

How the man sitting down had got his injury, Church didn't know, and his Chinese comprehension was zero. The third man was standing, arms folded, staring through a thin slat of light in a boarded-up window, looking out into the street beyond, while the fourth man was having a conversation on a phone.

Church guessed whoever was giving them their orders. And though the words were lost on him, the tone was readable. Frustration. From both sides. If they weren't moving, it likely meant they'd lost their target too. Church recognised the injured man as one from the security tapes. It looked like the carrier had got at least one good shot in. Got the drop on him in the building, probably, then disappeared.

And now the MSS had redoubled their effort, drafting in two more guys as they waited for more intel on the carrier's location.

Church's nose tickled with the dust under his chin as he breathed softly, watching them, noticing that Hallberg next to him had her phone raised in front of her face, a voice-notes app running, taking a recording of the conversation below.

And then, at the worst possible moment, the worst possible thing happened.

The words 'incoming call' flashed up a half second before the phone started vibrating, bathing Hallberg's face in blue light.

She gasped a little too loudly and thumbed the lock button on the side, muting the call, pulling the phone tight to her chest, staring down through the gap at the four men below—all four of them now stock still, heads turned, eyes fixed on the ceiling in the corner of the room, right where they were lying.

The ceiling made of half-rotten planks, Church realised coldly.

Planks that would do nothing to stop bullets if the men fired.

And then, without hesitation, they did.

SEVENTEEN

2010, NOBILSK

THEY MOVED AS ONE, Church and Cole sliding from beneath the window and heading around the corridor towards the door.

The Russian operators had their backs to it, discussing their next steps, but the second they turned, Church and Cole would lose any advantage. They needed to strike fast, and they needed to strike now.

Cole came up on the door first, spun across it, stood with his back close to the wall on the other side and waited for Church to get into position. The pair of them pushed their SMGs down under their ribs, drawing their pistols instead. They'd be no more than six feet from the target as soon as they stepped inside the room, and even a weapon as compact as an MP5 wouldn't be as nimble as a pistol in such close quarters.

They'd rehearsed this countless times and done it

live dozens too. They'd open the door—Cole filing in first, Church right on his shoulder—Cole taking the one on the right, Church the one on the left. Almost simultaneously. A single bullet to the back of the head before either could turn around. Quick, clean, deadly.

Cole pulled his pistol in close to his sternum, two hands wrapped around it, and lifted three fingers of his right hand, counting down.

Three.

Two.

One.

Church reached for the handle and pushed inwards, Cole twisting into the room first. He lifted his Beretta, Church right behind him, and fired before Church's pistol was even fully up. Church registered the spray of blood mist—the first operator dead before he hit the ground—but the second was fast.

Though Church's pistol was rising, he was already sighting empty air above the man's head. The trigger pull came an instant too late, the bullet flying an inch high and punching into the far wall.

The Russian dropped to a knee, ripping his weapon from its holster. Church chased him with his sights, squeezing off a second round, catching his shoulder and bedding into the top of his ballistic vest. Cole tried to go after him too, but the man lunged forward, shunting the rolling chair—with the dead security guard still in it—back with his heel. It slammed into Cole's knees and toppled him forward over the man, sending a shot into the wall rather than the target.

Church, unencumbered, kept firing—round after round into the man's centre mass as he scrambled forward, diving beneath one of the desks. Only Kevlar, Church thought, swearing as he jumped forward, hurdling the desk, his left hand on the surface, sliding across his hip, landing on the other side just as the man was trying to get to his feet.

Winded but still mobile, the Russian brought his weapon up. Church's left hand shot out, taking his arm out of the air before he could sight, pinning it to the wall behind him, driving his knee into the man's gut to knock the rest of the wind from him, trying to bring his pistol over the top to execute him there and then.

But if a full-face respirator did one thing well, it was to kill peripheral vision. Both wore the same kind of clear mask, breath amplified in their ears, the inside fogging with each heavy pant—so Church didn't hear or see the blow coming.

The soldier's elbow came out of nowhere, smashing into the side of Church's head. There was a terrifying hiss as the mask seal broke for a split second before it sucked back to his face.

His grip loosened. The blow dazed him, and he stumbled back, bringing his Beretta up and firing blindly into the space where he thought the soldier was —but when his vision cleared, the man was gone.

Instinct took over. The Russian was in his blind spot again, trying to get behind him, trying to wrap an arm around his neck. But Church was bigger, stronger. He drove him back into the desk, feeling the man's body crunch between it and his own weight.

The Russian shouted, voice muffled behind the mask, trying to bring his pistol to Church's temple. But before he could, Church snapped his head backwards, the back of his helmet cracking into the plastic visor of the Russian's respirator.

The man swore, crying out, throwing a hand to his face in panic. His grip loosened.

Church elbowed him hard in the solar plexus, twisted away, and brought his pistol up one final time.

The man froze square in his sights.

Church exhaled softly, squeezed the trigger, and watched as the crack he'd made in the visor was replaced by a bullet hole—the round punching straight between his eyes.

The operator sagged onto the desk, then slumped to the floor. Church doubled forward, panting hard.

At the other end of the room, Cole was getting to his feet. The whole exchange had lasted just a few seconds. He gave Church a single nod.

'You having fun over there?' Church asked, dragging himself upright.

'Just giving you space. Didn't want to get in your way,' Cole said with a little shrug. 'Knew you had it handled.'

'Yeah,' Church replied, huffing. 'Had nothing to do with you falling down, did it? Somebody throw a banana peel or something?'

He lifted his hand to his ear, pressing the comms button. They could stay there and banter all night, but they weren't the only ones locking horns with the Russians.

'Mitch, Foster—still alive down there?'

The airwaves crackled in Church's ear and relief washed over him as he heard Mitch's strained and tired voice.

'Yeah, just about. These Russian fuckers are a handful though. If you come across them, watch your arse.'

'Yeah,' Cole said back, glancing at the two dead men in front of him. 'We will do. You managed to get the ventilation system going?'

'Just about,' Mitch said. 'Everything's in fucking Russian.'

'Yeah, pretty inconsiderate of them not to print the signage in English.'

'Yeah, a little. Damn Russians.'

Cole chuckled. 'Not exactly a conscientious bunch.'

As charming as their exchange was, Church's attention had moved elsewhere—to the bank of screens in front of him, displaying feeds from various security cameras around the lab. He leaned over one of the keyboards and began tapping, cycling through them until he paused on one labelled *Level Four Biolab C*— what he guessed was their prize.

Two feeds covered the same location: one showing an outer room with a few cots and a bookcase, the books strewn across the floor; the second showing the inside of the lab itself. A man sat in the corner in an inflated white hazmat suit. One desk's computer looked like it had been taken apart; an electrical panel had been removed from the wall, wires spewing out and trailing along the tiles until they hooked up to the machine. That must have been how the virologist got the message out, Church thought as he inspected the image, unsure whether it was a still or a live feed. The man wasn't moving—and if he'd been sitting there in that locked lab for 36 hours, Church wondered if he was even still alive.

'Oi,' Cole called out, snapping his fingers. 'You can look at dirty pictures when we get home. We've got a job to do.'

Church scowled inside his mask, turning the screen to face Cole. 'Is that our HVT?'

Cole holstered his pistol and walked over, squinting at the feed.

'Seems like,' he said, sticking out his bottom lip as he studied the man. 'He's not dead, is he?'

'My thoughts exactly,' Church muttered.

Cole let out a long sigh. 'Alright, well, let's try and pick up the pace, eh? I think the whole of fucking Siberia knows we're here by now.'

Church hummed in agreement, but before he could reply they got confirmation that Mitch and Foster had managed to learn enough Russian to complete their objective. Above them, a fan spooled up, the hum echoing down from the aluminium duct overhead, a gentle wash of cool air descending into the control room.

'That's the ventilation system sorted then,' Cole said, glancing up at the wall of screens as the flashing red network of tubes began to turn green section by section. On the Level Four feed, the figure in the hazmat suit looked up, staring at the ceiling, aware the air was moving again—but with no way to know if it had been done by those coming to save him or those coming to kill him.

'Let's get this system rebooted,' Cole said, moving to another workstation and tapping on the keyboard there.

Church kept watching the small figure on the screen. The man stood, leaned back against the wall, put his hands in the small of his back, and stared up at the vents. His eyes slowly turned to the camera, locking directly with Church's.

The dead man behind the wheel. The severed foot. The charred bodies in the hallway. The woman in the cabinet...

The images flashed in Church's mind as he looked at the man whose life was—apparently—worth more than all the others combined. The man responsible for their deaths, and for everyone else's in this city.

Church didn't know how to feel—but didn't have time to think. On a neighbouring screen showing a security feed from the main entrance, a dozen black-clad figures came flooding into view, bursting through the front doors, armed to the teeth in the same gear as the two dead men at his and Cole's feet.

'How we looking?' Church asked stiffly, peering over the top of the screen at Cole.

'I'm working on it,' Cole replied. 'But rebooting this security system—in fucking Russian—isn't exactly trivial.'

'You're going to have to find a way.'

'I'm working as fast as I can!' Cole snapped.

'Well, work faster,' Church urged, tapping the screen with a thickly gloved hand. 'Because we've got company.'

EIGHTEEN

PRESENT DAY

CHURCH SHOVED HIMSELF SIDEWAYS, the muzzle flash blinding him through the cracks in the floorboards.

He rolled, arms tight to his chest, seeing stars, shoulders banging on the rotten wood. Not worried about the sound now—hoping even that it would draw their attention, and their aim. Hallberg didn't have the same instinct, covering her head instead, pressing her face to the dusty floor. A pointless move if a bullet found its way to her. Holding her hands over her face would do nothing except stop her from seeing her own death coming.

Church grunted, shunting himself to his knees. Running sideways, pistol drawn, firing blindly through the floor. He stopped, doubling back, hoping that the thundering noise of footsteps above would confuse the men below. But Hallberg hadn't even made it to her feet yet, face still pressed to the floor.

'Julia!' he snapped. 'Move!'

She looked up at him, terrified, but did as she was told, pushing herself up, trying to get to her feet. But Church had already turned away, knowing what was going to happen next, what had to happen next if he had any hope of getting them out of there alive.

He charged back towards the hole in the floor that they'd climbed through, throwing himself down onto his hip, sliding through the dust and over the jagged edge, plunging eight and a half feet to the floor below. He landed hard, knees giving out, and collapsed to the ground, pain radiating in huge waves through his ankles and up through his legs and into his back.

Dazed, he tried to force himself to a stance, everything hurting, and twisted, dragging himself forward towards the door that they'd first detected the Chinese through, dropping his shoulder and launching it into the wood just as it began to open from the other side.

He knew that the Chinese would give chase, knew that they'd come through that door. And that he had to buy time for Hallberg to make her way down.

He threw the slab of wood back towards the frame, heard a loud crack as it collided with the skull of a man on the other side. Someone called out in pain, stumbled backwards, and Church gave himself space too, bringing his pistol up now, levelling it at chest height and firing cleanly through the old wood, hoping to hit someone on the other side—and at the very least make them think twice about running through blindly, buy them a few seconds.

As he turned back towards the hallway, Hallberg's legs were dangling through the gap. She pushed herself free and dropped to the ground just as Church reached her, scooping her almost out of the air and carrying her forward, pushing her into a sprint as they hammered back through the abandoned building towards their exit.

Behind them the door opened.

More gunfire.

Plumes of plaster and dust puffed from the walls and ceilings around them, little geysers.

They shunted through door after door until they got back into the storeroom, Hallberg darting for the window, pushing the wood out and climbing through.

Church came after her, not waiting around, gripping the plywood in two hands and tearing it right off the frame.

The nails groaned as they came free, the sheet clattering to the ground behind them, bouncing a few times before it came to rest.

And by the time it did, they were already back in the alley and running hard.

Church glanced over his shoulder, but there was no one behind them.

He wondered whether or not the Chinese had simply lost them in the building, or if they'd decided not to give chase at all. As they reached the street, doubling forward, hands on knees, panting, Hallberg's phone still in her hand, it began buzzing again.

She lifted it, seeing Fred's name for a second time, answering angrily.

'What is it?' she said. 'You know you almost just got me killed!'

'What?' Fred stammered back. 'What do you mean?'

Hallberg shook her head, grumbling. 'Talk,' she said, cutting him off. 'Tell him you've got something solid.'

'The carrier's phone,' he said, 'just connected to the London Underground Wi-Fi at Mile End station. I wanted you to know,' Fred said, almost apologetically, launching into what was sure to be a grovelling monologue.

Hallberg didn't even let him start though, turning to Church.

'If we know, they know,' she said, still out of breath.

'That's why they didn't chase us,' Church said. 'Maybe that's what they were talking about on the phone.'

They could conjecture all afternoon, but ultimately they were only headed for one place. And they'd exited to the wrong side of the building, which meant that they were behind the MSS.

And Church figured that they wouldn't be hanging around.

As they took off down the street, ready to make a loop towards the tube station, Church pieced it together in his mind. The MSS must have chased the carrier into the building but they'd lost him. Maybe he'd ducked into a side room, doubled back and exited out the window, gotten the drop on a pursuer, or just climbed up to the second floor and hid like they had.

Either way, the MSS hadn't managed to get hold of him, and he'd slipped through the cracks. And now, he was making a break for it—no doubt trying to organise a way out of the country. Hoping, perhaps, that the Underground would shield his phone from being tracked.

But either way, he couldn't have been more wrong.

And Church figured, if both they and the Chinese were converging on Mile End, that it was likely that the NCA were too.

Finding their way to the vets clinic and picking up the trail had them one step ahead of the official investigation, but tracking the guy's phone was low-hanging fruit, and no doubt they'd already be scrambling to set up officers at every station on the line, waiting for him to get off so they could snatch him up.

But Church and Hallberg were close, a few minutes at a run, and if they were lucky, they might just be able to intercept him before he boarded a train.

The crowds thickened as they neared the station.

No sign of the MSS, but Church didn't know if that was because they were behind or ahead.

They thundered down the stairs into the station, shouldering their way through a throng of people, slowing as they reached the bottom step, and bottomed out onto the platform.

There were two trains, one running east, one west.

And there was no way to tell which the carrier was boarding.

Hallberg was too short to see over the heads of the crowd, Church just tall enough to do it for her. But he stuck out enough as it was. And a great way to get spotted was to stand on your tiptoes, a head above everyone else, and turn your head around like a meerkat.

No, this had to happen quietly. They had to close in on the carrier and take him silently. They couldn't risk an incident here. Not with trains barrelling down the line. Not with hundreds of bystanders around.

A hand on the shoulder, a pistol in the small of the back. Steer him somewhere quiet. Somewhere away from the crowd.

Church and Hallberg exchanged a glance, both knowing what had to happen.

'We split up,' they said in unison.

'I'll take east,' Hallberg said.

Church nodded. 'I'm on west.'

She began backing up, melting into the crowd.

'Call me if you see him.'

Church nodded to her and peeled away, began his comb through the station, keeping himself slouched to blend in, his eyes roving the faces of commuters heading home, denizens of the city running errands. A mess of millions, Church thought, London a melting pot of ethnicities and lifestyles. A living, seething mass. One whole that constantly melded and reshaped itself every second of every day.

The most heavily surveilled city on earth. But still,

one of the easiest to lose yourself in if you wanted to. And somewhere hiding in this crowd was the man that had worked so hard to do that.

Church tried to recall his face from the security feed at the vet's clinic, but the resolution wasn't the best, and all he had was a rough, blurry image of the man in his mind. One that fit a dozen people by the time he'd made it a quarter of the way along the platform.

Someone shouldered past him and he turned, scanning the opposite platform across the way, searching for Hallberg, checking on her, making sure that she was alright.

He didn't find her.

But what he did see was a Chinese national in a dark jacket, slithering through the melee, eyes fixed forward, hand under his jacket, on collision course for something.

Either the target or Hallberg, Church thought, unsure which was worse—or better—already moving, already closing down the angle to intercept him.

He got within ten feet, quickening his pace, but doing everything he could not to shove or bump commuters out of the way, not to raise alarm, not to let the MSS agent know that he was coming up behind him.

When he was just out of arm's reach, Church saw her.

Hallberg.

Her back to the guy, looking left and right, almost at the edge of the platform. Time seemed to slow down as all three came together, the man's hand coming free of his jacket, a knife glinting in the harsh halogens overhead, a hot rush of air flowing over the platform as the train began to approach, the screech of metal rollers on steel rails echoing towards them.

Hallberg straightened, turned, caught Church's eye, glance fleeting, shifting to the agent in front of her.

Her mouth opened, a sharp intake of air.

Church's hand leapt out.

The MSS agent thrust the knife towards her gut, Church seizing it out of the air.

The tip swished across and sliced Hallberg's shirt, exposing the tan flesh to the left of her navel.

The agent, surprised, not expecting the force, couldn't resist as Church moved the blade upwards, the man finally catching sight of the person responsible, turning his attention towards Church.

The agent tried to react but was too slow, tried to resist, but Church was bigger, stronger, the knife already arcing up and back towards him, angling downwards.

The man's eyes widened, knowing it was coming an instant before the blade sank into his chest, his fingers still around the handle.

It met resistance, crunching into his ribs and he bared his teeth, trying to fight back, but Church had two hands on it now and with a mighty shove, buried it to the hilt, straight into the top of his right lung, Church thought, probably severing a major artery on the way through.

He called out, spitting blood as he did, it reddened his teeth, splashed on the side of Church's face.

He turned away, still holding fast, and twisted the

knife roughly, feeling the man's left hand beating and pawing at his side. The agent's knees began to buckle as Church forced him backwards, down onto his knees, a scream ringing out in Church's periphery—a bystander noticing what had happened, not seeing a fight for good and evil, or a fight for the city, just one man stabbing another in the middle of the day, in the middle of a crowded tube station.

Another shrill screech rose in the air, followed by another, and then suddenly everyone was moving like a sea, roiling and pulling, waves of bodies crashing against him, elbows and knees against his arms and hips as people sprinted for the exit, the train grinding into the station, Hallberg doing her best to fight against the sudden river of meat sweeping her along.

'Church!' she called out, hand stretching over the backs of the fleeing commuters.

Church reached out for her, letting go of the agent finally, his body swallowed by the crowd instantly, but she was gone before he could grab her, swept away in the current.

Someone barged him roughly, twisting him round, and he lost sight of her completely. Instead, spying across the platform, the face of the person they'd gone there to hunt.

Grainy image in his mind or not, there was no doubt that this was the person he was searching for. He was wearing a black hoodie, face slick with sweat, dark circles under his eyes—a sick man if Church had ever seen one.

He stood still for a second, at the very edge of the platform, at the back of the ocean of commuters, eyes locked on Church, Church staring back.

He took a step forward and the man plunged beneath the surface, immediately disappearing into the fleeing crowd, moving with it.

And though Church couldn't see him anymore, he knew that if he lost him here...

They might never find him again.

NINETEEN

2010, NOBILSK

COLE HIT the button and then they were running.

He and Church streaked out of the control room, heading for the elevator.

'Mitch, Foster,' he said, touching his hand to his ear again, 'we're heading to you. Take the elevator down, we regroup on level four.'

'Wilco,' came a hasty reply, the two men running as well. Church figured they had about thirty seconds' head start on the Russians—if they were lucky.

The Spetsnaz were sprinting in from the front door one level above, but mercifully the elevator had remained on their level. The moment they pressed the button, Church and Cole stepped inside, Church's toe tapping, Cole's fingers drumming on the barrel of his MP5.

Cole jabbed the button for level four and the doors

rattled shut, a gentle, inoffensive tune playing in the background. The two men paused and glanced at each other before looking up at the ceiling.

'Für Elise?' Cole asked, brow furrowing.

'Blue Danube,' Church replied. 'You can hear the oom-pah-pah.' He nodded his head along with it. 'Three-four time signature. Classic waltz.'

'Didn't know you were a connoisseur of the arts,' Cole smirked.

'Not just a pretty face,' Church replied. 'And I take umbrage at the implication.'

Cole laughed. 'Umbrage, eh? That word-of-the-day calendar's working out well for you.'

Church barely had time to let out the first note of a laugh before the elevator bottomed out, the doors opening to a bloody scene—and they fell silent.

The corridor stretched out ahead, the white walls splattered with blood, littered with bodies.

'Jesus Christ,' Cole muttered, his MP5 snapping to attention, Church's right next to it.

They hadn't known what to expect, but it wasn't this.

Next to them, Mitch and Foster's elevator arrived. The doors opened, their gasps of shock ringing out too, the clack of their weapons punctuating the silence of level four. Cole looked back towards the buttons in the elevator, reached out and punched the emergency stop with his knuckles.

An alarm rang, the light in the elevator turning red, and then he stepped out into the carnage.

Putting the elevator on stop would slow the Russians down even more, and Mitch did the same on his end. The four of them regrouped in the hallway for the final push towards Zorin's lab.

'Jesus Christ…' Mitch muttered, scanning the bodies with the sights of his gun.

The upper floors had been devoid of fresh corpses —the Spetsnaz had already cleared them out or torched them. But down here had been on lockdown. They were the first to set foot on level four since the lockdown had been triggered. This was ground zero, where the virus—or whatever the fuck it was—had first broken out.

This was where it hit first and hit hardest. Where those infected would have had it the longest. Where it would have done the most damage.

It was clear someone had gotten out before the lockdown was triggered—and the second it had, the elevators to level four had been shut down, the stairwells sealed. But it had been too little, too late.

It hadn't worked.

Not for the rest of the facility, and not for the people on this level either.

None of the team seemed keen on moving inwards, all of them scanning the bodies for any hints of life, any signs of movement.

'Let's get it going, lads,' Cole said stiffly. 'And if it's any consolation—if we're going catch it, we would have caught it already. Going another fifty yards isn't going make a bit of fucking difference.'

'That's not really a consolation,' Mitch grumbled, following the captain and stepping over the dead.

They were thickest near the elevator—as though, when they knew the breach was happening, they'd tried to make an escape.

And failed.

A door to a stairwell on their right was secured with a keypad, and Church saw that one unlucky lab technician had collapsed below it. Her ID card was still in her hand. She'd made it this far, tried to let herself out—the door locked magnetically, sealing them in with a pathogen.

What must that have been like, Church thought. Knowing your death was coming. Knowing there was no escape. Screaming, pleading up at the security cameras for help, for a way out... already knowing one wasn't coming.

They moved deeper, past labs, the stench of death strong in their nostrils, the coppery taste of blood pervading even the filters on their masks.

Church wondered how that was possible—how he could smell that and not be infected. He tried to put it out of his mind, but the question kept rearing its ugly head with every new body they came across.

Cole pushed open a set of double doors and stopped, staring down at a man with no trousers.

He was face down, a pool of blood spread around his head, leaked from his mouth and nose, from his eyes.

Church looked at him too—in just a vest, shoes,

socks and underpants. His pasty white legs screamed that he hadn't seen sunlight in a very long time.

'Looks like someone was having a good time,' Cole remarked, though the vain attempt at humour didn't quite cut it that time and he was met with silence.

Nobody felt much like laughing just then.

They entered a large central room, a line of leather sofas across one wall, a bank of vending and coffee machines across the other.

Three dead bodies were sat on the seats—one collapsed sideways, one hunched forward, head between the knees, blood pooled between the man's feet, poured from the mouth—and the third was a woman, her head laying back over the cushions. The smell of urine drifted from an open bathroom door on the right, the stench of vomit underpinning it all.

The double doors whined shut and then clipped against the frame behind them, the four men standing in the middle of the room, taking stock of it before moving. But before they could, the woman on the sofa did—her head lifting off the headrest.

Her eyes were swollen and red, her long brown hair matted, her skin pallid and slick with sweat. She blinked at them as though unsure if they were real, or if she'd just awoken in some terrible nightmare, and then, with some effort, tried to speak.

'Help,' she said in Russian, lifting a weak hand. 'Help me, please.'

The men stared back at her as she tried to heave herself from the sofa, failing the first time, and then rising to a weak and swaying stance on the second attempt.

She was wearing a black blouse, a white lab coat, the left sleeve bloodied at the crook of the arm where she'd been coughing into it. This was the first time they'd all gotten a look at someone who was clearly sick, and the reality seemed to set in for the others just as quickly as it had for Church when he'd come face to face with the woman in the cabinet.

'What the fuck were they making down here?' Mitch asked, bringing his SMG up to his shoulder, hoping he wouldn't have to kill the woman—that seeing his gun aimed at her would encourage her to stay where she was, to stop her slow, ambling advance towards them.

But it didn't.

'Stop,' Church called out. In Russian. But she was deaf to it. The woman just kept coming forward, right arm stretched out, fingers extended, nails blackened, necrotic almost. Whatever this thing was, it was vicious —it seemed to be eating its victims from the inside out.

Mitch stepped forward now, weapon still raised, and tried himself. 'Stop,' he ordered in English. 'Stay where you are.'

But the woman either didn't care or couldn't hear. And it was Cole who made the decision, moving between them and lifting his MP5 mercilessly, putting two rounds into her chest before she could take another step.

In any other situation, Church thought he would have tried to intercede, would have tried to stop the captain—or at least would have voiced his displeasure at that. Allowed his morality to rise up, allowed himself to question the nature of what they were doing, the difference between right or wrong. And yet, as he watched the woman fall, listened to her hit the ground, dead weight, thudding against tile, he had no words and no feelings—nothing except perhaps gratitude that she'd been put out of the pain she was in.

He closed his eyes behind his respirator and risked taking a full, deep breath.

Like Cole said, if they were going to get it, they would have gotten it already. What they did now didn't matter.

Cole slowly turned back to his men. 'Anyone want to get out of this fucking place, or just me?' he practically growled.

Church nodded. Foster grunted. Mitch raised his hand.

'Then it's unanimous,' Cole sighed, turning and heading to the next set of doors, not giving the woman another glance.

They moved with more speed and conviction now down to the next corridor. Pausing at one of the bodies, Cole reached down and pulled a keycard free of the man's belt, coming up on a door with a biohazard symbol on it and, without missing a beat, he held the card against the reader to its right and pushed through, Church instantly recognising where he was.

It was the outer room from the security feed with the cots and the bookcase, the place dark and empty. To the right, a brightly lit lab, visible through huge plexiglass panels like a fish tank.

As everyone filed in and looked inside, the man he'd seen on the security feed—the doctor in the inflated white hazmat suit—was standing in the middle of the room, gaunt behind the oversized helmet.

Cole came forward, lowering his weapon.

'Dr Zorin,' he called. 'I believe you called for a rescue. We're here to humbly oblige.'

He spread his arms to the side and gave the man a full bow.

The virologist didn't seem to appreciate the gesture. Instead, coming forward, placing his heavy rubberised gloves on the glass.

'Just the four of you?' he asked, his voice tinny, echoing through the comm system in his suit and filtering back through the speakers around the room.

Cole stood straight and looked at him. 'Yeah, why?' he asked, stepping closer to the glass. 'Four of us not enough?'

'No,' the doctor said, swallowing audibly and looking around at the men. 'It's not.'

TWENTY

MOVING WITH THE PEOPLE NOW, Church sprinted towards the exit, clocking two more MSS agents on the way towards the stairs.

Everyone was going the same way and the carrier was hiding among the crowd. He was here somewhere, and the stairs would funnel everybody into a bottleneck, give Church the best chance of finding him. He put his foot on the bottom step, a flash of black in his periphery, his left hand shooting out reflexively, grabbing the shoulder of a man wearing a hoodie, tearing him upright, shoving him against the wall.

Not him, just a frightened bystander, eyes screwed closed, face turned away, fearing the worst.

Church released him and kept going.

Another flash of black, same thing, a woman this time, in a coat, screaming and clutching at her handbag.

Before he made it another step, somebody was grabbing him and twisting him round. He turned, an MSS
agent right behind him, gun rising through the air.
Church made a grab for it, the muzzle flashing, the
sound deafening in the narrow tiled staircase. He forced
the muzzle low, the bullet nicking the inside of his left
thigh as it flew past. Church called out, the pain instant
and searing, the round pinging off the metal steps,
sparks dancing, people scattering, a hot trickle of blood
running down inside his jeans. An inch to the right, and
it would have taken a chunk out of his hamstring. But
Church had a full grip on the barrel of the pistol, the
slide unable to rack and put another bullet into the
chamber, the trigger held firm by Church's grip. He
could feel it trying to rebound under his hand and knew
that the man's finger was in the trigger guard.

He twisted it sharply, listening to the snap of bone as
he folded the agent's index finger in two, and in one
swift movement, he launched his knee into the guy's
chest, the man two steps below him, the blow throwing
him clean off his feet. His heels came free of the stairs,
his weapon still in Church's hand, and he rolled over the
flattened backs of the crowd, everyone bent double,
cowering away from the gunshot.

He tumbled over them, grunting and cursing, and
disappeared into the darkness below.

Church turned, looking back up towards the light
then, everybody frozen in place except for one man in a
black hoodie, trying to claw his way to the surface.
Church knew ordering him to stop would be useless.

He could shoot him now, raise his gun, and put him down, dousing a dozen people in his blood. But who knew what kind of downstream effect that could have? No, he needed to subdue him without hurting him, without risking anyone else's lives.

Church took off once more, pulling himself upwards, using people's shoulders and backpacks as handholds as he fought his way over the crowd, screaming at them to stay down, not to move.

He made it to ground level a second after the carrier, seeing the man in full sprint ahead. But before he could get onto level ground, he was overtaken by a third MSS agent who must have been stationed on the street.

Whether he heard Church's steps or just sensed him there, Church didn't know. But he turned, drawing his pistol and raising it, firing practically blindly behind him, barely glancing back as he did.

Church ducked and strafed sideways, the bullets zipping overhead, before he charged after him once more, the three of them truncating as they reached the kerb of the busy road, the carrier slowing for just an instant, trying to dive between traffic.

But it was all the time the agent needed and he grabbed for his hoodie, pulling him back, trying to get him into a headlock. Church was there then, a fist coming over the agent's shoulder, trying to knock him out cleanly. But he was fast, expecting it, and in the second it took for Church to find his stance and wind up, he released the carrier and threw up a block, sending Church's punch over his head. Before he could recover, the agent's fist collided with Church's ribs, knocking the wind out of him.

He staggered backwards, looking low, waiting for the pistol to come back up, anticipating it, moving to the right, and reaching out for the agent's arm instead, pulling it under his elbow, taking it out of play. The man kicked out for Church's knee, sent his leg shooting backwards, almost downing him.

But Church held firm, taking the agent with him, the man hunching forward, bearing Church's weight. They were locked head to head then, both on their knees, and Church just caught a flash of the carrier, recovering himself behind the agent, turning and beginning his escape once more.

Church had to finish this, and he had to finish it now.

His left hand shot out over the top of the agent, finding the bottom hem of his jacket, ripping it up over his head, blinding him.

He sent a knee into the man's gut, and risking releasing the agent's shooting hand, he threw a devastating uppercut into his jaw. He flipped backwards, jacket flapping in the city air, and landed square on his shoulders, feet in the air, head still tied in his own coat, pistol spilling from his grip and skittering across the kerb.

Church stood quickly, looking around for the target. But most of the crowd had escaped from the tube station now and were spilling out across the street in thick waves, swallowing the carrier once more.

Sirens rose around him, dangerously close. And he knew that there was no more chasing.

That the worst possible scenario had just played out.

And that there was only one thing left to do.

Run.

TWENTY-ONE

2010, NOBILSK

COLE TURNED his head to look at the others, realising that Zorin knew something he didn't—perhaps the scope and scale of the disaster and the kind of response it would elicit from the Russians.

He'd said four wasn't enough, and Church couldn't help but feel he was probably dead on the money.

Though they were ahead of the Spetsnaz, they'd only succeeded in accomplishing what the Russians had intended to do anyway. The lockdown had prevented anybody from getting in or out of level four, but now that it was lifted they weren't the only ones headed straight for Zorin.

'All right then,' Cole said, forcing a smile behind his mask. 'Let's show this prick how wrong he is.'

Cole seemed to harden with each word and, with a

short inhale to strengthen his resolve, he began barking orders.

'Mitch, Foster—you start planting charges. I want this place fucking incinerated, all right?' He pointed around the room. 'In and outside of this fish tank. Church—hard drives, pull them all and make sure you don't miss a thing. And you and me, Doc,' Cole said, turning back to the glass, 'we're going to get a bit better acquainted and you're going to walk me through exactly how we're going to get you the fuck out of there.'

The doctor blinked at Cole and then nodded.

These were the cards he'd been dealt and he didn't really have another choice.

Cole clapped his hands. 'Hop to it, lads—double time.'

Mitch and Foster swung their packs off their shoulders and immediately started fishing out explosive charges, Church moving forward automatically towards a bank of workstations at the back of the room, pausing halfway there and looking back at Cole.

'Why do you want me to pull the hard drives?' Church asked, thinking on his order. 'We're destroying everything, aren't we?'

Cole hesitated for just a second—just long enough for Church to guess he was lying. Or about to, at least.

'Yeah, of course,' he said. 'But I'm not leaving that to chance. You know those things are protected inside fucking computers and we're not going get a chance to come back here. So we pull them out and we make sure there's nothing that can be salvaged.

'Once I get the doctor out of this thing, you're inside and you're going to sort out the computers in there too. Scoop them all in a bag, we take them with us. And when we get the chance, we'll cook them properly.'

Church's brow crumpled, but he didn't have the time nor the inclination to stand there and argue. This was the exact kind of thing the SIS would do—standing for the greater good on the surface, playing both sides under the table. They wanted Dr Zorin on British soil to question him about the Russians' bioweapons programme. And what better way to get a jump on that than with all of his data in hand? They might want this place destroyed, and they definitely wanted the Russians to think all Zorin's hard work had gone up in flames. But even as Church began pulling the hard drives as requested, he realised it was all an act.

With gritted teeth, he began breaking open the cases of the desktop computers and levering out the hard drives with little care, digging the end of his combat knife underneath to pry them free, breaking screws and bending metal as he did. The less of what Zorin was doing in this place that saw the light of day, the better.

Mitch and Foster worked in silence, moving around the room, wiring up charges as they went, stringing blast wire between them to ensure a simulta-neous detonation, while Cole went round to the airlock and, under Zorin's instructions, began typing in the necessary security codes to get him out of there. By the time Church had finished with a trio of computers on his end, Zorin was already inside the airlock, turning slowly in his overinflated hazmat suit as jets of compressed gas washed over him and UV lights blasted away any remnants of virus and bacteria.

The outer door hissed open and everybody froze, watching as the doctor stepped out. The difference between the protection he was afforded inside his suit and what they were afforded behind their masks was instantly apparent.

'Church,' Cole called, snapping his fingers and pointing through the doorway. 'We'll keep it open for you, don't worry.'

Church moved forward almost hesitantly, slowing as he reached Cole, the man's hand outstretched now, requesting the hard drives Church was holding.

He stared at him for a moment and then handed them over.

Anything else would have been too suspect.

Right now, they couldn't argue. This was the mission and Church had an order.

He drew and tried to hold his breath before he stepped into the lab, the white light blinding, his breath seeming to echo inside the space. There were two more computers in here and he sorted them quickly, working quietly, trying to hear what Cole and Zorin were saying to each other.

'You in one piece, Doc?'

'Yes,' Zorin replied, nodding. He spoke perfect English, albeit accented. 'But I'd rather like to get out of this suit,' he said. 'I've been wearing it for almost two days—you don't want to know what it smells like in here.'

Cole couldn't help but laugh at that. 'Yeah, you're right. I don't. The question is, how the fuck do we get out of here? Because last time we checked, there was a dozen Russians armed to the back fucking teeth headed right for us. I don't think we're going to have a good time if we try and punch through the middle of them. So please tell me there's a back door out of this place.'

Church worked methodically, keeping his eyes on his task but his ears on Cole's words, hating that distrust was creeping into him.

Cole was a good man and a good captain.

Church had been under his command for over a year and, during that time, had seen him as nothing but a beacon of honour, a man of real fortitude. And yet, Church thought, just as he was under orders doing something he didn't want, Cole was probably the same. If he'd been pulled aside by the DSF and by Ros Kerr, given this order to recover the data instead of destroy it —and to keep that need-to-know—then Church suspected he didn't really have much of a choice.

The second hard drive came free in his hand and Church was walking quickly back towards the airlock before he could finish his thought, Cole's foot on the threshold, keeping the doors open as promised.

He beckoned Church forward.

'Anytime today, mate,' he said, taking the other two hard drives from Church's grasp before he could ask for them, and slotting them into his waiting rucksack.

Mitch and Foster joined them a moment later, their work done, and Mitch handed over the detonator—a small black device with a thumbswitch to arm the RFID receiver and a pistol trigger to set the explosives off.

Cole nodded to Mitch and Foster and scanned the room, checking their work.

'We've got our plan, lads. Rear fire escape back here leads up to level three and level two. Once the Spetsnaz come down, we'll go up a few levels, across to the main staircase, and up to ground level before they even know we're there.'

Mitch and Foster nodded, about to move out, but Church caught Zorin's eye, seeing the fear there, his gaze fixed on Cole's backpack, knowing it was full of hard drives—full of his work. Work that he too, seemingly, didn't want to see out there in the world.

And though he resisted, he couldn't help himself. 'Captain,' he said, before the men could move.

Cole looked back at him.

'What is this all?'

'Those hard drives,' Church said. 'You're not going to destroy them, are you?'

Cole froze, eyeing him. 'No,' he said. 'I'm not. Because I've been ordered not to. I've been ordered to bring them home. And that's what I'm going to do.'

'They need to be destroyed,' Church said. 'You know they do.'

'That's not the mission.'

'It should be,' Church said. 'You saw what it was like out there.' He pointed back through the main door.

'That fucking corridor... Up on the streets, piles of bodies. That's one city. You want that to be the whole world?'

Cole's jaw flexed behind his mask.

'It's not my decision, Church. I've got my orders, and so have you. And our orders are to get Zorin and this data out of here in one piece.'

'But—' Church began.

Cole didn't wait for him to finish, surging forward instead and grabbing him by the lapels of his jacket, pulling him forward so that their masks clacked together, their faces a few inches apart.

'You're a soldier, Church, and soldiers follow orders. I don't like pulling rank, but you seem to be needing a reminder: this is not a fucking democracy. So if you don't want to move, then be my guest and fucking stay here. But I've had enough—I've had a fucking tits full of this place, and I'm leaving.'

He let go of Church and turned towards the fire escape.

'And if you've got any sense in that fucking head, then I suggest you lot do the same.'

TWENTY-TWO

PRESENT DAY

CHURCH TOOK a gamble that he and Hallberg would be thinking the same thing.

Firstly, that they needed to regroup and the best place to do that was out of the area, back where they'd first started, near the train station where Hallberg's car was parked. And once he'd gotten a few streets away, dodging police cars as he did, trying not to limp, his leg throbbing where he'd been grazed, he felt his new phone buzzing and pulled it out, jabbing at the screen with bloodied fingers to answer it.

He pulled the thing to his ear, hearing Hallberg's breathless voice.

'Solomon,' she said, the relief audible in her tone. 'Tell me you're okay.'

'I'm okay,' Church said, slowing to a walk, his pace

now more casual not to arouse suspicion as he put further distance between him and the crime scene—the scene where he'd just killed at least one man and perhaps one more depending on whether he could take a punch or not.

'I'm headed to the car,' Hallberg said.

'Me too,' Church replied.

'I know,' Hallberg said. 'I'm tracking you.'

Church pulled the phone from his ear and looked at it, wondering whether or not it was really just a digital dog collar.

'I'm one street over,' Hallberg said. 'Keep going and I'll meet you.'

'Wilco,' Church replied, cutting off the call and keeping his heading, tucking his bloodied knuckles into his pockets, head on a swivel.

He clocked Hallberg before she saw him, coming down the street to his right, the two of them falling into lockstep on the final stretch towards the car.

Church could practically hear her grinding her teeth as they walked, and though he knew she didn't want to hear it, he felt like he needed to say it at least once more.

'It's getting to that time,' he told her.

She slowed for a second as though almost bowled over by the remark, and then regained herself, closing her eyes.

She didn't argue, knew that she couldn't.

'Julia, you've got to make the call,' he said. 'Otherwise they're going to pull CCTV, they're going to see your face, know that you're involved in it. This shit's coming to your door. You've got to deal with it before it does.'

'I know,' she muttered. 'Fuck, fuck!' She raised her voice, almost shouted the word, and Church glanced around to make sure that no one had heard.

They crossed back towards the vets clinic now, and were only a few minutes from the car, but Church didn't know if there was any time to waste. And Hallberg was smart enough to know the same thing. She opened her phone, and started searching for a specific number, dialling it and pulling it to her ear, clicking her teeth as though thinking about what to say.

Church wondered how she was going to spin this, whether or not there was any way she could, whether she could worm her way out of it.

'Paul,' she said the second the phone was answered, 'don't talk, just listen. The dead Chinese and Albanians —I know you told me to leave it alone, but I didn't. The Home Office were wrong to try and quash this, to try to keep it quiet, and I brought in an outside investigator to track down our missing man.'

Hallberg glanced up at Church then, as though checking to see how annoyed he'd be that she was hanging him out to dry. But Church knew that there was no escaping this, that if she was going to be on who knew how many cameras, then so would he too.

He could hear Paul's voice rising on the other end of the phone already, could see Hallberg pulling it away from her ear an inch or two to spare her eardrums. Who he was, Church didn't know, but he suspected that he was pretty high up at Interpol if Hallberg was going straight to him.

'Paul—stop,' she said then, screwing up her face against the onslaught, 'please just listen to me. I brought in an investigator because I thought the Home Office were making the wrong call—and I was right. It's not just us looking for this guy, the MSS are in on it too— yeah, the Ministry of State Security—the Chinese are here, Paul, in London. Boots on the ground—'

His voice exploded on the other end of the line again, Church catching the words this time.

'You're in London? Please tell me you're not involved in whatever the fuck just happened at Mile's End station. It's all over the news, Julia! That better not be your doing.'

'It's Chinese intelligence,' Hallberg insisted. 'They're running an op on British soil, trying to extract the missing Chinese national, and by the time the NCA are able to mobilise any kind of response and investigation, it's going to be too late. They'll snatch him and they'll be out of the country before the NCA even pick up their trail.'

'That's not your problem,' he said. 'Interpol—we're not an operational agency, we provide support, intelligence, not whatever the fuck you think it is you're doing now. And if this outside investigator is the same one that you've been using the last few months—'

'That *we've* been using, Paul,' Hallberg cut back in.

'Don't forget you're complicit in all of this. From day one, I never did anything without running it by you first, so don't you dare think about throwing me under the bus on this one.'

Church could hear the tension simmering through the line, could hear Paul reining himself in.

'Look, Julia, I don't know what I can do, but I'll try and shield you from this as best I can. But if you're in security footage, if you're in the middle of this… just please, please walk away,' he insisted. 'Step away from the investigation now and give me some time to do damage control. I'll say that you were in the wrong place at the wrong time. That two overlapping investigations resulted in the coincidence of the fucking millennium. I'll try and sell that to the NCA and to the Home Office for you, but you have to cooperate with me now, Julia. You have to get out of the city and you have to go home. That's non-negotiable.'

Church could see Hallberg seething, could see her knuckles whitening around the phone as her car came into view.

'Are you listening to me, Julia?' he repeated. 'You're good at what you do, but this isn't it. You know what your job entails and you know how far off the reservation you are right now. I don't need to tell you that, do I?'

Hallberg cleared her throat, teeth gritted, the silence stretching on, but Paul wasn't going to say another word until he had confirmation.

And when Hallberg finally seemed to realise that, she let out a small forced breath and replied.

'No,' she said, 'you don't have to tell me, Paul. I know what my job is.'

'Good,' Paul said. 'Then I suggest you start doing it. If the Home Office fuck this up, if the NCA fumble the investigation, that's on them. This is their country and this is their investigation. If they need Interpol's help, we'll be there. But it's out of our hands and you have to realise that. Now, do what I ask and let me make some phone calls. See if I can't snuff out this fire you started before it burns down the whole fucking agency—and our relationship with the Home Office and the NCA while it's at it.'

The line went dead and Hallberg pulled her phone away from her ear, wound up as though she was going to hurl it clear across the road, stopping just before she did, bringing it down and staring at it angrily instead. She hummed a low note of displeasure and shoved it roughly into her pocket, pulling out her keys instead and unlocking her SUV. She climbed into the driver's seat and Church circled round, climbed into the passenger seat, staring out at the city, the faint cry of sirens still echoing in the distance. He allowed himself to breathe a little sigh of relief then, though he didn't show it.

'So then, we're going home… aren't we?' he found himself asking the question, eyes turning to Hallberg, realising that she wasn't starting the car, wasn't putting it in gear, wasn't turning round and heading away from the scene.

'You're following orders, aren't you?' Church risked asking again, knowing the answer before she even looked at him.

'No.'

'No?' Church replied back, his eyebrows lifting.

'No,' Hallberg said, cocking her head a little. 'You heard him.'

'I did,' Church said, 'and what I heard wasn't phrased in uncertain terms. Paul—whoever he is—'

'Director of Operations for the UK,' Hallberg added.

'—Right, well, Paul—the Director of Operations for the UK—told you pretty explicitly that this is now out of your hands, that we're out of our depth, and that whatever is going on is not our jurisdiction or our job. If anything, it sounds like I'll be lucky if the NCA don't show up at Mitch's door before the night is out.'

'You'll be fine,' Hallberg muttered, as though it wasn't even a question. 'Nothing will happen to you. Paul knows that if the NCA get you into a room, that it'll just cause a never-ending shitstorm for him, me, and about a dozen others at the agency. He'll never let it get that far. You're a bit of a nuclear deterrent.'

'But I don't know anything that could ruin them,' Church said.

'Yeah,' Hallberg said coolly, 'but I do. Plenty. And I've got the evidence to back it up, so trust me, you're safe,' she assured him.

And he couldn't help but believe her.

But it didn't alleviate his feelings about the situation at hand. 'That still doesn't change the fact that we're not just treading on toes now, we're stamping on them, and with what just happened at Mile End—if the NCA weren't mobilising before, they are now. Every camera in the city is going to be looking for the carrier.'

'But it won't be enough,' Hallberg said, already defeated.

Church was surprised, her pragmatism seeming to have left her.

'It's what they do,' Church insisted.

'It doesn't matter,' she shook her head, 'we've come this far, we need to finish it. I disobeyed orders, coming here, doing this. Someone was killed on a tube platform, shots were fired, it's going to be a PR nightmare, and I'm right at the centre of it. Paul wants to shield me, because if he doesn't, he knows I can take him down with me. But if there's no other option, he'll sell me down the river regardless, step down from his own position to avoid any heat from what we've been doing. He's five years from retirement, got a bloated investment account, a villa in the south of France. He'll be fine. Hell, once he comes to terms with it, he'll probably be happy about the whole thing. And once he realises that, he'll shove my head on the chopping block and hold back my hair.' She tutted and shook her head, convincing herself of something. 'Right now, the only thing that we've accomplished is fucking up an NCA investigation, but if we get to this guy first, if we capture him, and we bring him in, and we hand him over to the NCA, wrapped in a neat little bow... then that could be enough, that could be enough, to placate the

NCA, the Home Office, Paul too, everyone. Keep the train on the tracks, you know?'

She looked over at Church expectantly, but he gave her nothing.

'If we get there first, if we catch him, the carrier—he's our leverage, he's what gets me, and you, out of this.'

Church couldn't help but shake his head.

'That's a lot of ifs, Julia. A *lot* of ifs. And I don't think it'll be enough, even if you do find him.'

'Maybe you're just getting cold feet,' she said lightly. 'There's been something off all day, you haven't wanted to be here. I know it, you know it… and this is your chance. Walk away now, I won't blame you,' she said, 'just get out of the car, disappear, run back to the farm, and hide from the world, forever.' The bite was growing with every word. 'But I'm staying, I'm going to finish this.'

'You're not thinking this through—'

'And when do you ever think?' she snapped, almost scornfully. 'You just go charging into fights, into shootouts, into goddamn *explosions*, like it's nothing, like you're fucking invincible, and the second that I want to do something that could save an entire city, you're telling me no—'

'I'm telling you no,' Church bit back, 'because *I've* got nothing to lose. If I charge into a fight, or a shootout, or a burning building, it doesn't matter if I don't come back. The world goes on like I was never even here. But you? You've got so much to lose. You've worked for so much. You don't want to throw it all away—trust me, not for this.'

'Not for nine million lives?' she said evenly, tempered now like quenched steel. 'Every minute we sit here, that carrier is running through the city, breathing on people, coughing on them... who knows how many could be infected already and how many will be infected if we just let this go. Another hour, another twelve before the NCA catch up? It could be beyond containment already. And if it's not, it will be soon. We're here, we know the stakes, and by the time the Met get a handle on that scene, analyse the CCTV, figure out what the fuck is happening, link it to the NCA case, get them in on it... hell, if the MSS haven't already grabbed him by then and gone, then the other option is even worse. Either way, China will deny any involvement and we'll be back in the midst of another pandemic before we even know which way is up. So politely, Solomon, this is the end of this discussion. You either get out of the car, or you help me, but either way, I'm not wasting another second talking about it.'

Church just shook his head to himself, wondering how he could convince her.

But no matter what he said, he didn't think there was anything that could.

She, like he had done so many times in the past, had made a decision, had weighed her life against the lives of others, and saw clearly which way the scales tipped.

And she was right. He had charged into the jaws of his own death a hundred times before without a second thought. But now that she was here, alongside him, he was scared. He did want to pull back. And as Hallberg cranked the engine and pulled away from the kerb, taking his silence as agreement, he came to a stark realisation.

That he was scared because her life meant so much more to him than his own.

TWENTY-THREE

2010, NOBILSK

THEY HIT the fire escape in single file—Cole at the head of the train, Zorin right behind him, Mitch and Foster in the middle, and Church bringing up the rear. When they reached the next floor up, Cole paused, looking down the length of the corridor as though deciding whether or not to get out here.

He turned back to look at Zorin and then Mitch.

'How much explosive did you plant down there, Mitchy?'

'All of it,' Mitch said back diligently.

Cole stuck out his bottom lip, looking around the stairwell as though trying to measure the structural integrity of the building.

'All right... maybe one more floor, is it?' He chuckled, doubling back and heading up the next set of stairs.

'Sol,' he called, foot on the bottom step, looking

back down at Church on the landing. 'You head back down to four, keep an eye on that corridor. When our Russian friends arrive, you shout up and I'm going to blow it. Bring the whole fucking floor down on them.'

Church stayed exactly where he was. 'You want me to go back down to level four and then you're going to blow it?'

'Well, I'll give you five fucking seconds to get up the stairs, won't I?' Cole said back, sighing as though it was obvious he wasn't going to murder Church where he stood.

'Five seconds?' Church asked.

'Fucking hell, ten seconds then,' Cole said. 'Look, it wasn't a polite request—get moving.'

Mitch and Foster both glanced back at Church, a lingering stare as though they were bidding him goodbye forever. But Church knew Cole wasn't trying to kill him, rather trying to teach him a lesson. A lesson about trust, about hierarchy, about following orders, about being a team player.

Church gave a solid nod.

'Wilco,' he said, turning his back and scuttling back down to the fourth floor, camping out at the fire escape and cracking the door just an inch so he could see into the lab. Above him, the footsteps echoed as the men climbed up and out on two, the door squeaking open but not shutting—Cole waiting there in the frame for his go.

Church breathed easy, trying to calm himself, but from here he could see all of the explosives—at least eight separate charges that would engulf the room and most of the lab—hell, most of the floor—in a fireball. The moment he saw the Russians, he needed to shove the door closed, call out, and then run. Climb as quickly as he could and get out through Cole's door before he pulled the trigger and condemned the Spetsnaz to death.

Distant steps began to echo down the length of the corridor ahead, filtering slowly to him as the Russians made their way towards his position. Church kept one hand on the frame, one on the door, ready to slam it closed, the heavy steel slab thick enough to stop bullets, he guessed, but not the explosion.

The footsteps grew in intensity, the men closing in.

Church's heart pounded.

They'd be here in seconds, their shapes already swimming beyond the frosted glass panels in the door to Zorin's lab. He anticipated they'd press in and instantly realise that Zorin was gone and they were surrounded by explosives.

Church knew then he couldn't wait until they were inside. It had to be now—he had to pre-empt it. He let out a breath and shoved the door closed, clanging it against the frame, turning and taking a bounding leap up the first four steps.

'Contact!' he called, hauling himself up the stairs as quickly as he could, his heavy breaths fogging the inside of his mask as he pounded on the concrete steps, his thick clothing sealing in his body heat and sweat. His skin was on fire, his blood pressure fiercely high as he made his way up, passing the door to level two and carrying on. Below, the squeak of steel rang out, the bar on the fire door clanging against the metal. The Russians now not only in Zorin's lab but at the fire door as well.

They must have heard him.

Which meant they were right on his tail—

—and that Cole couldn't wait any longer.

A few seconds more and they'd be up the stairs behind him.

Which only left one option.

'Blow it!' Church yelled. 'Blow it now!'

He heard Cole swear harshly above him. Church wouldn't have yelled it if he didn't mean it, and Cole knew he didn't have another choice. He pulled the trigger, the click of the mechanism sounding above. Church was on the middle landing, could see Cole in the doorway, the door open just wide enough for a body to slip through—and then suddenly he was gone.

The shockwave of the blast rippled through the entire building, the fire door above slamming shut as Cole shielded himself from it.

The only thing Church could do was dive forward, pin himself against the wall.

The explosion rocked the facility, a column of fire blasting into the stairwell through the open door below and shooting up through the middle in a column of flame. Church felt the heat on his back, felt his eardrums threaten to burst with the sudden increase in pressure. It still felt like he'd been hit by a train.

But the majority of the blast had been directed into the lab and through the double doors and deeper into level four—but that didn't mean it wasn't large or fierce enough to damage the structure on that level and the ones above.

As Church peeled himself off the ground and looked around, eyes aching in the dust and heat, he could see cracks in the walls and beneath his feet too. He crawled forwards, looking down into the blackened abyss below, thick plumes of black smoke billowing into the stairwell, the entire first flight of stairs missing.

The fire door creaked open above and Church looked up, seeing Cole there once more.

'You still alive down there?' he yelled, a loud and shrill fire alarm now blaring all around them.

Church nodded and gave a tired thumbs-up, pushing himself to his hands and knees and then to his feet, climbing shakily upwards the final stretch of stairs.

Out of the fire, though—but into what?

TWENTY-FOUR

PRESENT DAY

THE MOMENT that Hallberg's phone connected to the car's Bluetooth system, she was calling Fred.

It rang for longer than it had before, and when he answered, he seemed almost a little reluctant.

'Boss?' he said.

'It's me,' she confirmed.

He let out a slow breath on the other end. 'Tell me you weren't in the middle of that mess at Mile End?' he muttered.

'Of course not,' she replied.

He paused for a second, as though reading the lie for what it was. Something designed to give him something resembling deniability if he was asked about her involvement there.

'Okay…' he said after a second. 'But you're alright?'

'I'm fine,' she insisted.

'They're saying two dead,' Fred went on, 'gunshots fired, somebody got stabbed?'

Hallberg instinctively put her hand over the slash on the belly of her T-shirt, feeling the jagged edges of the material where the knife had sliced through it, millimetres from her skin.

'I wouldn't know,' she said easily. 'But, look, I need you again, Fred. We're close. We had eyes on him, but the MSS were in play too. He slipped through our fingers—'

'I don't know, boss,' he replied. 'This is all getting—'

She cut him off before he could say another word.

'Just do what I ask you. My promise still stands, you're safe in every conceivable way. But I need you to pull the CCTV footage from the station and the surrounding streets. The carrier—wearing a black hoodie—gets chased by two men, they get into an exchange, and he slips into the crowd. I need you to find him, and I need you to tell me where he's going. This could be the only chance we have to get out in front of the Chinese. Fred, we can end this now, and you can save nine million lives.'

'Of course,' he replied, as though she didn't need to remind him of the stakes.

Church thought, if he was asked, he would have tied himself to a stake, stepped up onto the pyre, and willingly, if it came from Hallberg.

'Jacking in now,' he muttered.

And Church had to smirk. He wasn't a big movie guy, but he'd seen *The Matrix*, could picture the techs tapping away on their computers, the endless green digits scrolling in front of their eyes. That's how it all seemed to him, anyway.

'Okay, here we go,' Fred said, the seconds ticking by. 'Just scrubbing through the footage now, and there they are—'

He sucked in, a sharp intake of breath between his teeth.

'What is it?' Hallberg asked.

'Those two guys that got into it,' he said. 'The big one ripped the small one's jumper over his head, and then it looks like he knocked his head clean off his shoulders. Jesus, wouldn't want to be that guy.'

Church sort of grimaced. To hear his exploits reeled back to him—what was done in the heat of the moment, what was compartmentalised almost instantly by his years of training—he didn't like to be reminded of it, either soon after or a long time later.

Hallberg seemed to read it in him and hurried Fred along. 'We need to know where the guy in the black hoodie goes.'

'Yeah, yeah, I'm on it,' Fred said, going as fast as he could. 'Okay, I've got him, moving through the streets, here we go. Got him on another camera. Following...'

He clicked his teeth as he tracked the carrier through the city.

'Here we go...'

Church heard furious tapping on the keyboard on the

other end of the line, and as Hallberg pulled up to a set of traffic lights, Fred came back to them with their final destination.

'Okay, I've got him. Heading into an apartment block about a mile from the station. But after that, I don't know where he goes.'

'Alright,' Hallberg said. 'Keep digging, check out the block, see what you can find. Let me know if you can narrow it down for us.'

'Give me a few,' he said. 'I'll get back to you.'

And as he hung up, Church was sure that he would.

Hallberg drummed her fingers on the wheel, the address coming through over text.

With a couple of swipes and taps on the screen, she synced it to the car's navigation system, and their route suddenly laid out in front of them. Not long, just ten minutes of driving, crawling through the city streets, red light after red light.

Hallberg was growing anxious. More anxious by the moment. And at what seemed like an overly long stop at a pedestrian crossing, she turned around and reached into the back seat, awkwardly unzipping her black duffel bag there, and reaching inside, pulled out a clear full-face respirator, dropping it into Church's lap.

'What's this for?' he said, looking down at it.

'That's an N99,' she replied, 'rated for bacterial, fungal, and viral particulate. Should protect us if we get into close quarters with this guy.'

Church arched an eyebrow. 'It's a bit late for that,

isn't it? Why didn't you give me this earlier?' He couldn't help but keep the bite out of his voice.

Hallberg's brow crumpled as she looked over. 'We were keeping a low profile in public,' she retorted. 'What, you wanted to run around London in a fucking respirator?' She bit back just as hard.

Church bristled, adjusting himself in his seat, grip tight around the mask.

Hallberg let out a sigh. 'Look, we're going into the same room as this guy. I just want to be safe. At the station... he looked sick. It's the smart move.'

Smart move, Church thought. Smart move would have been cuffing her to a radiator in Mitch's rather than letting her run off on this crusade. At least they'd be safe there, even if the whole world went to shit.

But no. They were in the middle of the most densely populated city in the country, edging closer to the carrier of an unknown pathogen by the second.

Suddenly, Church had no words. All he could do was wonder how he'd got himself into this mess.

He stared down at the mask in his lap and it seemed to stare back up, featureless, shining and new, and yet for him, carrying an entire history he'd done all he could to forget.

He scratched reflexively at his arm again and swallowed, turning the mask over so it wasn't looking at him.

'So what's the plan when we get there?' he asked, voice thin.

'We find out what apartment this guy's holed up in,

we bust in there, we subdue him, call the NCA and the UKHSA, and we quarantine him there.'

'And after that?'

'And after that,' Hallberg said, 'we wait. When the men in the big white suits arrive, we pray that we made the right call, that what we did was enough, and that we weren't too late.'

The words hung soberly in the air as the light turned green and they pulled off, gaining speed, charging through the city towards patient zero.

And the end, Church hoped, of what was proving to be an extremely long day.

TWENTY-FIVE

2010, NOBILSK

WHEN COLE PULLED Church onto sub-level two, the sprinklers were already raining down around them, soaking the floor and the walls, the fire alarm blaring its mournful tune, the emergency lighting painting the floor a bloody red.

There was no sign of Mitch and Foster—just Cole and the virologist standing behind him, the water pattering loudly on his plastic suit.

'Where are the others?' Church asked as he shunted the door closed behind him and leaned back against it, panting hard, his body ringing like a bell.

'Cole and Mitch pushed on, securing our exit,' Cole replied. 'But I wasn't letting Zorin out of my sight.'

Church could see now that he had his hand firmly locked around Zorin's wrist.

'And now that the band's back together, we can get the fuck out of here. So, shall we?'

He turned, pushing the doctor along, forcing him into a run.

He loped forwards, the huge baggy legs of the hazmat suit clapping together and tripping him. They caught between his feet and he stumbled, twisted, and then fell to the ground, sliding through the water, sending ripples and waves down the length of the tile corridor ahead. Cole reached down and grabbed the back of his suit, trying to haul him to his feet, but the rubber gloves and boots only slipped and sloshed in the liquid, the man unable to get to a stance.

'You've got to move, Doc!' Cole yelled at him.

'I can't—it's this suit,' he said breathlessly. 'I need... I need to change. I haven't eaten, I haven't drunk anything, please, please, I can't go, I can't go on like this.'

Cole looked back at Church, as though sizing him up to see whether or not the two men could carry him out, but Church didn't think it was doable.

Zorin was going to be ungainly, cumbersome, moving slow, wearing that—and a much larger target to boot. The time it would take to get him changed would make them much slower to exit, but they had 200 miles to cover before the exfil, and there was no way he was going to wear that the entire time.

'Where?' Church asked him. 'Where can you change? The whole place is fucking contaminated.'

'Here,' Zorin said, pointing to a lab to their right.

'It's level two, but they have a clean room like downstairs. There are respirators, like yours—the pathogen, it's... it's airborne, but... but your masks, they'll work. I can get inside, I can get out of these clothes, and—'

But Cole didn't let him finish, the bumbling explanation seemingly good enough for him.

'Fine,' he said, hauling Zorin to his feet with both hands and shoving him through the doorway. 'Get moving, now,' he told the doctor, ordering him forward into the lab.

Zorin slowed and looked around, squinting about the large room before making his way towards the far end, walking around workstations and computer desks towards a bank of lockers set before the same style of airlock that was on level four.

Church watched him for a moment before Cole filled his vision.

'Those charges may have slowed them down,' he said, 'but I doubt the Russians sent the full platoon down to get Zorin. The rest'll be on us before we know it, so watch the fucking door while I hurry this fucker up.' Cole growled, pointing back out towards the corridor.

He turned, advancing quickly on Zorin, who seemed to be sifting through the lockers for spare clothing and appropriate protective equipment.

Church made his way back to the door, soaked through by the sprinklers, and hung in the corridor, resting the knuckles of his left hand against the frame, steadying his weapon against it, sights locked on the door. The first flight of steps was destroyed below, but that didn't mean the Russians wouldn't make their way up regardless. If any survived, they'd be doing all they could to give chase—roping, climbing, boosting each other, whatever it took.

And they seemed to be doing just that.

It was only a few seconds before the door opened, forcing Church to duck back into the lab and ease his own closed. He let out a low whistle, darting towards Cole, who was shoving Zorin into the airlock with an armful of clothing.

'Contact,' Church called out as loud as he dared.

Cole twisted towards him, reaching up and slapping the flat of his hand against the red button next to the door.

The airlock began hissing closed and he turned back to Zorin. 'You get down, you stay out of sight until you hear my voice, all right?'

The man nodded behind his hazmat suit and laid down on the floor, disappearing from view as the door closed in front of him, locking him inside the airlock, the decontamination process already starting.

'Church,' Cole said, moving towards him now, 'lights.'

Church nodded, doubling back towards the door and flicking all of the switches down, bathing them in darkness—just the red security lighting next to the sprinklers staying lit, drowning the room in a bloody glow.

Reflexively, Church reached up to his helmet and levered down the night vision goggles, still fixed there, pulling them tight against his mask and flicking them on.

The room lit up in a white so bright it stung his eyes.

He squinted against it, waiting for them to adjust, homing in on Cole, who was beckoning him towards the back of the room, motioning him down behind the workstations there—just in time, as the door opened behind them, swinging wide, two Russian operators stepping in, streaked with concrete dust, more sliding through the corridor behind them.

The door swung shut, sealing Church and Cole in with the two hunters.

'Quick and clean,' Cole told Church. 'You take the one on the right, I'll take the one on the left.'

Church nodded, watching as Cole lifted three fingers, counting them down to two and then one, making a fist briefly—the go sign.

They popped up from behind the desk, lined up their targets and fired.

The two operators, shoulder to shoulder, were difficult to hit. Church, just in front, managed to get the angle and clip the first target in the chest and shoulder. Cole, aiming higher for the head, had his bullet zing off the Russian's helmet. The one Church shot stumbled sideways, tried to wrestle his gun free and took two more shots—this time to the upper chest and throat. He scrabbled at his neck, falling backwards, the sound of choking and coughing punctuating the moments of silence between the sirens.

The one Cole had shot was still on his feet though,

now ducking, charging forward. They chased him with gunfire, lighting up the room. The man scrambled behind a workstation. Cole swore, motioning Church to flank, and he did so—the two of them sweeping around in a pincer move. They locked eyes across the room. Cole nodded and they stepped into the corridor between the workstations, finding their target. He lifted his rifle and fired towards Cole, just as Church pulled the trigger.

Two shots, two bullets—Church's finding the space between the bottom of the Russian's helmet and his vest, punching into the top of his spine. He crumpled forward, sprawling on the floor, and Church was on him in a moment, left boot on the man's right wrist, ensuring that he couldn't pick up his gun. But when Church saw the wound, he knew that he'd shot through—that the man was dead. He wouldn't be reaching for anything.

Church looked up quickly, searching for Cole, but didn't see him. Not at first, anyway. He wasn't on his feet—he was on his back, his heels just visible beyond one of the desks.

Church ran forward, expecting to find the worst, sliding around the corner in the water, spraying the wall as he laid eyes on his captain, flat there on his back, clutching at his arm.

'Cole,' Church called out, kneeling at his side, patting the rest of his body, searching for any other wounds.

'Piss off,' Cole said, batting him away. 'You want to do that shit, you got to buy me dinner first.'

He forced himself onto his side and looked down at his right arm, the Russian's shot having taken a chunk out of it.

'Oh, that's a fucking bleeder.' Cole grimaced from behind his mask.

'You're a better shot with your left anyway,' Church assured him, offering his hand. 'No great loss.'

Cole frowned and then smirked in turn, taking his arm—the two of them getting up together. Ahead, the airlock opened, Zorin stepping back out into the lab without invitation, the hazmat suit gone. He was now dressed in a pair of dark chinos, a fleece top, and a respirator mask—not unlike the one that Church and Cole were wearing. He stared at the both of them, his eyes falling to Cole's arm, widening as they did. The thought seemed to strike Church and Cole simultaneously.

'That shit you've been working on...' Cole practically spat now, coming forward towards the doctor. 'I better not be fucking infected.'

He opened his hand, showing the deep, fresh wound there.

Zorin stared at it for a moment.

'No,' he stammered, 'you shouldn't be. It's an airborne pathogen... You'd need direct contact or exposure via the nose, the mouth, the eyes, something like that. Here, in this lab, the risk should be minimal. But we do need to cover that up. Make sure it's bound and sealed.'

'Then cover it up,' Cole snapped at him. 'Make sure it's bound and sealed.'

Zorin swallowed and raised his hands. 'I'm not that kind of doctor.'

'Tough shit,' Cole snarled back at him. 'I just took a fucking bullet for you, so tonight, you're that kind of doctor. All right? And if not, then I think we're running out of fucking uses for you.'

TWENTY-SIX

PRESENT DAY

BY THE TIME they reached the apartment block, Fred had narrowed down their options to four possibilities.

The first two were owned by a property management company registered to a Chinese national who lived out of the country and had former ties to the Chinese government. The third was a property owned by a woman from North London who had spent 20 years living in Beijing—and who, Fred said, had been investigated for espionage. Twice. And the final apartment was owned by an LLC that was part of a holdings company registered out of Luxembourg. That company was looked after by an Andorran management fund whose CEO was a resident in the Cayman Islands, and whose shareholders were a random assortment of companies with names like Executive Incorporated and Business Partners Ltd.

It was the exact kind of setup that Church had suggested to Hallberg when they first came up on the house where the initial bioweapon deal had gone wrong. She'd scoffed and told him it was Airbnb at that time, but now his suggestion could very well be right on the money.

They exited the car, Hallberg's duffel slung over his shoulder, the respirators tucked safely inside. There was no need to raise suspicions until they found their way to the right apartment.

Church was determined to go down the list from most likely to least likely—his holdings company first on the block, followed by the Chinese national, and then finally the businesswoman who had been investigated for espionage.

They headed to the twelfth floor by lift, neither of them speaking as they ascended, Church making sure his Glock was loaded and ready before they stepped out, Hallberg doing the same, looking a little more apprehensive than him, casting sideways glances as he carefully pulled back the slide and checked that there was a round in the chamber.

'The mission is to subdue him,' Hallberg reminded Church. 'We quarantine and keep him there until backup arrives.'

Church just grunted in reply, nodding.

'Solomon,' she said firmly, pulling his attention to her. 'Tell me you know that's what we're doing.'

He just looked over at her. 'I can follow orders,' he replied, 'even if I disagree with them.'

'So what would be your plan? Execute him instead?'

Church didn't want to voice his opinion on that one. And he would give Hallberg the benefit of the doubt, would try his best to end this without firing a shot. If he could put him between the sights across the room, get him to lie face down, hands behind his back, if they could cuff him with the cable ties in Hallberg's bag, then maybe, maybe he would spare him. But if he tried anything, Church wasn't going to hesitate.

They exited onto the right floor and walked along to the door in question, Hallberg slowing as she got there, glancing at Church, checking if he was ready before she raised her knuckles to knock.

Church reached out and took her by the wrist, pushing her hand down, shaking his head.

They didn't need to alert this guy that they were there and give him any kind of chance to escape. And this time, Church had come prepared. His go-bag contained spare clothes and a ballistic vest, petty cash, his passport, along with the Glock 19 and extra magazines. But, among other things, it also contained a flip phone with a prepaid SIM card, a handwritten list of vital numbers, a baseball cap to obscure his features from facial rec—and a lockpicking set too.

It was a skill that he'd learned over the course of his career and one that had come in handy more times than he could count. Quiet entries were part and parcel of special ops. Sure, there was a need sometimes to stick C4 to a door and blow it off its hinges, go in all guns blazing. But often enough, quiet was best.

And this was one of those times.

He slipped the kit from his pocket and opened it, showing Hallberg the picks and torsion tools.

She raised her eyebrows, looking down at them and then up at Church, the fine instruments dwarfed by his heavy, calloused hands.

She was dubious, as though he wouldn't be able to work the delicate tools with his indelicate fists. But he was happy to prove her wrong, slipping a rake and a torsion tool from the case and slotting them into his pocket. He knelt, feeling her eyes on him, as he slipped the pieces of metal into the keyhole—a standard five-pin barrel lock. The apartment building was old and dated, likely not up to modern fire code, which meant this would probably be a standard latch lock that automatically closed after you entered. And he was banking on that being all there was.

It took him a few seconds to find the right tension before he started raking at the pins, finding the first two easily, the third with some difficulty, and then the fourth and fifth in quick succession. The barrel turned, Hallberg letting out a low whistle and sticking out her bottom lip, impressed but not willing to tell him that.

Church carefully removed the picks, holding the toe of his boot against the door, just keeping it off the frame to stop it closing. If it clacked against the frame, it would make noise. Alert whoever was inside. He leaned in and cracked the door an inch, slotting his fingers through the gap and running upwards, looking for a chain or bar. When he didn't find one, he eased the door open another few inches, lowering his head to the gap to listen, not daring to draw a breath.

He could hear the sound of running water inside, could feel warmth drifting out from the room beyond, and turned back to Hallberg, giving her a nod. This was the right place, a random safe house kept by whoever the financiers of the initial sale were.

Church wasn't surprised. He himself had spent many nights in apartments just like this in cities all over the world.

He motioned to Hallberg to take off the bag—that it was time for masks on. She did as instructed, handing one to Church and, with his pistol still in his hand, he slipped it over his head, shivering as he felt the familiar rattle of his breath through a filter, the experience hurling him backwards in time 15 years. When it was secure, he reached out, checking the seal around Hallberg's face, cinching the strap at the nape of her neck a little tighter. There was no point taking risks, and she stared up at him through the clear plastic as he did, a heel still against the door, neither of them saying a word before they stepped inside.

Church led with his pistol, stepping slowly, reaching backwards with his left hand to ensure that Hallberg stayed on his six. Whether or not the carrier was expecting them, he'd be prepared for when his pursuers caught up with him next. He hadn't seemed to have been armed in the station, but that didn't mean he wouldn't be now, that this safe house wouldn't be stocked with weapons of some kind. And if he did manage to get a shot off, there was no way Church was letting Hallberg take a bullet.

As the thought crossed his mind, he was glad that he'd taken an extra minute to slip on the ballistic vest from his bag when he'd pocketed the lockpicks. He hoped it wouldn't come to it—getting shot was never fun. The opposite, in fact. But he'd still do it without a second's hesitation if it came to it. He'd take a bullet for her. But he'd also shoot first if he thought it was going that way.

He told her neither of those things as they filed into the darkened living room in a vertical stack. Church took stock of it: small kitchenette on the right, door at the back into a bedroom, one on the left leading into a bathroom.

Water was clattering on the other side.

Someone taking a shower.

Church continued to catalogue the room—soiled clothes in the middle of the carpet, the same black hoodie the carrier had been wearing when he'd made his escape. And on the small dining room table, a black zipped first aid case lay open, bloodied gauze wadded next to it, a syringe used and empty on the surface beside a clear bottle of liquid.

He glanced up towards the bathroom door once more, the water still running, and stepped cautiously towards the table, reaching out for the bottle. He paused halfway, his eyes homing in on a clear bag of nitrile gloves sitting on top of the first aid case. He licked his lips, knowing he didn't have time, but unable to help himself. He stretched out for them, opened the bag and withdrew a pair, pulling them on as quickly as he dared before reaching for the bottle once more.

As he touched it, the sound of running water stopped, the squeak of a metal valve echoing through the door.

Church froze, feeling the bottle in his hand, and looked up towards the bathroom. Hallberg swam close to him now, hurried, looking down at the thing in his hand.

'What's that?' she risked, whispering, Church's eyes still fixed on the door.

'Interferon,' he muttered back, turning his body towards the bathroom and lifting his pistol. 'Broad spectrum antiviral,' he added.

'How do you know that?' she asked.

But Church didn't give her an answer.

More sounds rose from the bathroom now—retching, someone vomiting.

Interferon was tough on the system, the list of side effects longer than the purported benefits.

He grimaced behind the mask, glad that it was obscuring his face, that Hallberg couldn't see him, and advanced a step on the bathroom, putting Hallberg behind him once more.

Instinctively he slotted the interferon into his pocket and brought his left hand to the grip of the pistol, training the sights on the bathroom at chest height—the exact place he knew the carrier's heart would be when he opened the door.

And then he did.

Light cracked through the frame, filling the darkened apartment, and the man stepped out, an open wound on his left shoulder weeping blood, stitched up but angry and purple.

Church noted no steam was drifting from the bathroom.

A cold shower, he immediately thought.

But despite that, the carrier was still slick with sweat, his skin pale, the virus taking hold. He was running a fever, the shower a vague attempt to cool himself off, perhaps clean himself off. But it was in vain. Too late for him, Church thought, levelling the pistol at centre mass.

He realised he wasn't alone then and froze, towel over his shoulder, a pair of grey sweatpants already cinched around his waist. The shock passed quickly, his eyes narrowing, staring at Church and Hallberg.

He glanced around the room, calculating, his expression sharp, an intelligence clear in the way he was holding himself. Not just anyone would be recruited for a bioweapon sale. Was he ex-military? A PMC? Not that it mattered. Church knew the type. Not to be underestimated.

'Who are you?' he asked, maybe buying time, maybe a genuine question.

Hallberg stepped from behind Church despite him holding his hand out to keep her out of the firing line.

'We're here to take you in,' Hallberg replied evenly, her voice tinny from inside the mask.

'You're infected with something,' she said. 'That much is clear. We need to know what it is, and we need to know now. Cooperate, tell us everything, and we'll make sure that you're cared for. That you get the treatment you need.'

The carrier curled a little smile, standing across the room from them, pulling the towel slowly from his shoulder now, as though in full knowledge that Church wasn't going to pull that trigger.

His finger flexed on it anyway, not liking the challenge to his convictions, but he stayed himself for Hallberg.

'You can't help me,' he replied in near-perfect English, the towel dropping to his side, obscuring his right hand.

Church moved forward a step, making sure the carrier knew that if he made a move, Church would shoot, no questions asked.

'I'm fucked,' he said then—the word finite, decisive almost. 'We're all fucked,' he added, his grin widening.

Church stiffened at that. What did he mean? That he was contagious, that they were all infected? That the masks wouldn't do enough, wouldn't do anything to stave it off? Before he could make up his mind, the towel dropped, something glinting in the light coming out of the bathroom behind the carrier.

A knife in his hand.

Church inhaled, steadied his aim, ready to shoot, but Hallberg stepped sideways in front of him, pushing his weapon away with her shoulder, preventing the shot.

He let her, but decided: if the guy gained an inch, Church would shove Hallberg to the ground if he needed to, kill this man where he stood.

But he didn't come forward, didn't threaten them with the knife.

Instead, he brought it across his body, held it to the palm of his left hand, and drew the blade across the skin.

A cut deep enough to bleed immediately.

'This,' he said, holding the wound up to them, the blood running over his palm and down his wrist. 'This is what you want, is it?'

Church stood there, watching the blood drip from his skin onto the carpet.

The carrier began to laugh, brandishing his hand at them, and Church could feel his heart thundering in his chest. This disease, whatever it was—was it blood-borne, was it airborne? Had the carrier just sealed all of their fates?

Hallberg, as though sensing that Church was about to shoot, held up her hands, her own gun aloft. A show of peace.

'We're not going to hurt you,' she assured him. 'But you need to come with us, now. You need to put down the knife, and you need to start talking. Otherwise, I can't help you.'

She was hell-bent on not killing him, Church thought. Perhaps knowing that if she did, her career would be well and truly over. Or perhaps it was simply the fact that murdering this guy here in the middle of

London might infect everyone in the building. Either way, Church knew if he did what he wanted—if he killed the man—that it might mean the end for them, and certainly for Hallberg. Even if she managed to get out of this alive. Killing him was killing her career too. One bullet for both. And Church knew her well enough to know that it was the only thing she had.

The carrier took another step forward, his eyes flitting to the table behind Church, to the case there, to the syringe, as though looking for the interferon, the bottle that was in Church's pocket.

His mind churned, looking for the optimal outcome to the situation.

In a swift movement, he holstered his own gun, showing his empty hands before reaching into his pocket and holding up the vial of interferon.

'This is what you want,' he said to the carrier, gently pushing Hallberg out of the way so that she wouldn't be between them.

The carrier didn't reply, but couldn't hold his poker face.

'It is, isn't it?' Church asked. 'You know what you've got, and you know that this is your only chance. That's why you're here. They stocked this place special for you in case the deal went sideways and you needed to hole up somewhere, right? Gave you a contact who connected you with the vet you got killed, gave you this address. An intermediary to save your skin and protect their own. I'm guessing that the people whose interests you represent want to make sure they erase any trace of their product's existence. Especially here on foreign soil. They want to make sure that you're not scooped up by the UK government, or worse, your own.'

The blood continued to drip from the carrier's palm, but he said nothing.

'They've organised an extraction for you, haven't they?' Church went on. 'Arranged to get you out of the city, out of the country. It's the only way they can be sure that you're not going to talk. But they need you to make it that far.'

The man swallowed visibly.

'Good,' Church said. 'That suits me. The quicker you're out of the UK, the better. You want to start an epidemic, you do it somewhere far from here.'

He held the interferon between his forefinger and thumb then, showing it to the carrier as he turned his back and stepped towards the table, lowering it into the medical case.

Slowly he flapped the lid over and zipped it up, turning and offering it at arm's length to the carrier. 'This is what you want, isn't it?'

The carrier's eyes settled on the case, then flitted to a backpack next to the door. A go-bag of his own, Church thought.

'Take it,' Church told him, risking a step closer. 'Take your medicine and get out of here. Leave London. Now. And don't come back.'

He could hear the anger in Hallberg's breathing to his right, but this was the right call. He was sure of it.

All that blood—there was no way they'd be able to

subdue him, get him on the floor without getting covered in it. Without risking infection. That's what he was ensuring when he'd cut himself. Mutually assured destruction. And Church wasn't about to risk that, whether it meant the carrier slipping through their fingers or not.

Slowly, the man came forward and reached out with his bloodied hand, grabbing the top handle. Church removed his grasp from it instantly to avoid the blood.

The carrier smirked at that, the knife still in his right hand, blood trickling now over the bag and spotting the dirty carpet with crimson.

He held the knife up threateningly and backed towards the door, putting the case over his shoulder and then picking up the rucksack, fumbling blindly for the door behind him, eyes still fixed on the two of them. He opened it, lingering for a second longer and then, still bare-chested and slick with sweat, disappeared into the hallway, leaving Hallberg and Church alone.

The moment the door latched, she surged forwards, heading for it. But Church reached out and caught her by the waist, scooping her cleanly off the ground, holding her back as she struggled against him.

'What the fuck are you doing?' she said.

'We can't just let him go! We had him. We fucking had him!' Hallberg said, her voice strained, almost on the verge of tears.

Church held fast, looking at the door for a second longer before he met her eyes, their masks knocking together as he turned her towards him.

'We don't know what he had,' Church said, 'and he was willing to get shot. He never would have come quietly. It was escape or death for him. He'd accepted that. You wanted him alive. He's alive. If I had it my way, I would have killed him the second he stepped out of that bathroom. Hell, I probably would have gone in there and shot him in the shower. Would have been cleaner. But you didn't want that. And I did what you asked. I didn't kill him.'

'But you let him go! And now we have no idea where he is, or where he's going!' she snapped, tearing herself free of his grip and throwing her hands in the air.

'And killing him here,' Church said calmly, 'we would have risked infecting this entire building. Hundreds of people, all ready to stream into the Underground, into the streets, to spread this everywhere. Right now, he's contained. The virus is contained inside his body. And he's trying to get out. And if he's trying to get out, he knows that he has some time left before it's too late. If you know you're going to die, you don't shoot yourself up with interferon. Trust me. It's adding a layer of pain on top of pain. This is better. For everyone.'

'How exactly is it better this way?' Hallberg shook her head furiously.

'Because this way,' Church said, 'you're not only going to get him, you're going to get whoever picks him up. And then, you're going to track them back to whoever financed this whole thing. You thought bringing in this one guy was going to be enough to save your job? What about bringing down the entire network? The lab that made this shit? The people that helped this guy get into the country?'

Hallberg stared up at him, blinking, doing a double take. 'What are you talking about? What are you saying?' she asked.

In that moment, when Church had been staring down the barrel of his gun at the carrier, he'd been struck not just by a thought, but by an idea. One that might not just save the city, but also Hallberg too.

'Admit it—you were just afraid,' she spat then, before he could say anything else.

Caught off guard, he looked down at her.

'There's something you haven't told me. Something big. You've been hiding it from me ever since I came to you with this. Something that's got you terrified. And I don't appreciate being lied to, Church. I came to you because I thought I could rely on you. And all day, I've been telling myself that I could. But this? Just now? This proved it. You're not who I thought you were. You're not the man I thought you were.'

Church, skewered through, looked down at her, wondering if she was right. If he wasn't the man she thought he was. The man he thought he was.

'Maybe not,' he muttered, after what seemed like an interminable silence. 'Maybe I'm not the man you think I am. But that doesn't mean I'm not going to try to do what I think is right.'

'And you thought that was right?' Hallberg said.

'Letting him walk out the door? Condemning this city to death?'

Church gritted his teeth, looked down at her, sure of his answer.

'Yes,' he said. 'If it means saving your life I'd do it again. Without a second's hesitation.'

TWENTY-SEVEN

2010, NOBILSK

CHURCH WATCHED the door while the doctor set about patching up Cole's arm, his captain keeping a firm grip on his weapon through the whole process, as though to remind the doctor what would happen if he failed to take care of him.

Down the corridor, gunfire rang out—sporadic and grouped.

Three small bursts and then silence settled after, the dull drone of the alarm and the rattle of falling water an ever-present din in the background.

Cole reached to his ear and toggled his comm.

'Mitch, Foster, report,' he said, the strain in his voice now evident.

'We're here,' Mitch replied back. 'Caught them with their pants down. Ruskis never stood a chance.'

'Copy, we'll be with you momentarily.' Cole

glanced down at his arm and, satisfied, pushed Zorin off, came forward, moving his arm in a circular motion as though to test the quality of the doctor's work. Satisfied, he motioned the doctor to keep up and, as a trio—this time with Church in the vanguard—they eased into the hallway once more and set off towards the far end, stepping over two more dead Russians.

Mitch and Foster waved them over as they closed in on the other fire escape, the one nestled next to the elevators—the one the woman on level four had died trying to access.

'Lifts are dead,' Mitch said. 'Probably on account of the alarm.'

'Or the giant explosion,' Church offered.

'Either way, we're taking the stairs,' Mitch replied with a shrug.

'Roger that,' Cole said. 'Lead us home, Mitch.'

Mitch and Foster filed into the stairwell together and, shoulder to shoulder, took the steps.

When they were a flight ahead, Church—with Zorin right on his shoulder—followed them up.

He could hear the doctor breathing hard in his ear and, when he looked over, he caught him pulling the sleeves of the fleece down to the backs of his hands, noticing now that he was wearing a pair of latex gloves. He fussed with the cuffs continually, as though trying to eliminate any exposed skin. Church realised then that Zorin was staring right at him, and he wasn't sure he'd get another chance to ask.

'So what exactly is this shit, Doc?' Church couldn't

help himself as they climbed the stairs towards the ground floor.

The doctor let out a shaking breath. 'Simply put,' he muttered, looking around nervously, 'a variant of the Marburg virus. Weaponised to increase its lethality. We combined it with—'

'Hush,' Cole cut them off. 'Stay on mission, Church. You two can braid each other's hair when we're safe and sound and on a fucking plane out of this place. For now, stay quiet and keep your eyes open.'

He reached out and pushed Zorin up the stairs, hand between his shoulder blades.

The doctor climbed up immediately, the conversation done, but Church had heard enough. He thought he'd heard of the Marburg virus before—a cousin of Ebola, from what he understood. One of the haemorrhagic diseases, which basically meant that, with enough time, it liquefied your insides, and everywhere there shouldn't be blood coming out of, there'd be blood coming out of.

Which explained the symptoms they'd seen on the people downstairs.

They formed up with Mitch and Foster on ground level and waited for Cole's go.

He signalled that Mitch and Foster split out the door —one covering left, one covering right—that Church stay tight with their HVT, and that they'd exit left, back towards their initial point of entry.

They broke through the door, the hallway clear, and

started to move, heading towards the back of the building, pausing only when Mitch drew up to a set of double
doors, peeking through them before they went any
further.

He backed up immediately and turned around,
raking his fingers across his throat.

'No go.'

He motioned back the other way, and Church and
Cole both took Zorin by the arms and guided him
quickly in the other direction, reading the immediacy in
Mitch's movements.

Foster was ahead, the train reversed, and Cole came
up behind him, put his hand on his shoulder, and pushed
him onwards.

'New plan,' he muttered. 'Looks like we're going
right out the front fucking door.'

Foster gave a stalwart nod and picked up the pace,
the MP5 in his grip looking like a toy gun against his
immense bulk.

Church remembered during their selection that one
of their senior officers had made the comment that he
wasn't sure whether Foster could even be in the SAS.
And when one of the other captains had asked why not,
he'd said, 'Well, we're supposed to be a covert unit,
aren't we? There's no fucking hiding him, is there?'

They'd got a good laugh out of that at the time.

But now, no one was laughing—because they were
heading in the direction they'd seen that horde of
Russian special operators come from.

They picked up the pace, blasting through double doors after double doors until they reached a final set. Beyond it, there was an atrium of sorts with a small glass entryway and a rounded desk that would once have been to receive visitors.

And beyond the glass lay the streets of Nobilsk, snow piled up against the sides of buildings, the streets covered now that the ploughs weren't moving.

Fires were burning, jets of ignited kerosene streaming through the darkness, lighting up everything around them with a sinister yellow brilliance.

Church could see men clad in full hazmat gear, wearing heavy gas masks, huge canisters strapped to their backs, flamethrowers in their hands, sweeping around the area, setting light to piles of the same yellow body bags they'd seen at the back of the building. Whether they were the same ones, or in the time they'd been inside the Russians had piled up more, Church couldn't say. But either way, they were incinerating any trace of the virus—and they were doing it with prejudice.

'My God,' Zorin muttered from his place in the middle of the back, peeking over Cole's shoulder.

Their captain surveyed the area in front of them, and Church did the same.

It looked like two men were roving with the flamethrowers, and Church picked out at least three or four more operators dragging and carrying bodies down the street in the yellow bags. How many were out there in total, he couldn't say—but too many for them in open ground, he suspected.

Cole had come to the same conclusion.

'We keep this quiet,' Cole said. 'They've got their backs to us and they aren't expecting it, so we slip out of here, bolt left, squeeze up tight to the buildings there, and the first alleyway we see, we take it. Put as much distance between us and this fucking lab as we can. Everyone copy?'

He glanced around, not waiting for compliance before he put his hand on Foster's shoulder once more.

'Lead the way, big man.'

Foster just hummed his acceptance and pressed forward, opening the door and slithering through the darkened entryway with surprising fluidity for a man of his bulk.

Ahead, there was a revolving glass door, and to its left a single hinged door. They angled themselves towards it, Foster easing it open and stepping out, covering them as they all filed through, sprinting for the wall of the nearest building, heels crunching on the gritted pavement.

They kept their heads down, moving fast, Cole pointing towards an alleyway fifty feet ahead. To their right, the two men with flamethrowers arced their liquid fire through the gently falling snow, splashing it over the ever-growing mountain of bodies.

The air was filled with the acrid smell of burning plastic and sizzling flesh, the flames struggling to catch as they crawled over the funeral pyre.

'Double time,' Cole urged them, and they picked up as much pace as they dared—their enemies' backs turned to them, but perhaps only momentarily. As they neared the entrance to the alley, Cole slowed, shoving Zorin through in front of him, and then waiting for Church and Mitch.

They both stepped into the darkness, and Cole swept after them, urging them on.

But another noise, above the crackle of flames, had now pierced the night, sending a shiver up Church's spine.

The cries of a child.

He stopped and twisted back towards the light, feeling Cole pushing him, trying to turn him.

But he wouldn't budge.

He watched across the street, hidden by the darkness of the alley, as two Russian soldiers marched a line of civilians out of an apartment block at gunpoint and ordered them to line up against the wall.

Church felt his hands tighten on his weapon, watching—knowing it was a firing squad before it even took shape.

Cole was looking back too now, his hand firmly on Church's chest, stopping him from moving but unable to move him.

'Don't even think about it,' he muttered. 'That's not our mission, and this is not our fight.'

Church cast his eyes along the line of men, women, and children.

Sixteen, he counted in total.

All of them in various states of undress, pulled from their beds and from their homes, none of them wearing masks. A few had wrapped cloth or scarves around their faces in a vain attempt to ward off whatever was infecting their neighbours, but Church couldn't tell whether any of them were sick from where he was.

Instinctively, he tried to take a step forward to get a better look.

Cole pressed harder, putting two hands on Church's chest now, trying to force him backwards—but Church was bigger. Stronger.

'That's not our fight, Church,' he grunted, the strain in his voice evident.

But Church didn't care.

The Russians were about to execute women and children.

'Look at them, Church,' Cole urged him. 'Not a mask between them! And you heard the doctor—this shit's fucking airborne. Fucking Marburg, Church. You know what that means? It means in a few fucking hours, they're going to be spitting, crying, and shitting blood. You go out there, you maybe save them from a bullet, but you'll condemn them to a much worse fucking fate. There's three men here that need you—that need you to get out of here alive. You can't save them, Church, even if you go out there. But what you can do is get us all killed.'

Church set his jaw, looking down into the face of his captain, carved in stone behind his mask.

'He's right, Church.' Mitch's voice rang from behind them.

Slowly, Church turned back, the pleading cries of the civilians rising in the frigid air behind him.

Mitch and Foster stood there in the alleyway, the doctor standing between them.

'We've got to get out of here now, Sol,' Mitch said to him. 'It's not pretty, but it's the truth.'

The doctor came forward then, wringing his hands.

'The pathogen,' he said almost robotically, 'has an incubation time of six to twelve hours before symptoms first begin to display. Within twenty-four hours, subjects begin to experience massive multiple organ failure and internal bleeding. Those people... they may not look sick now, but there's nothing you can do for them. The virus has a ninety per cent mortality rate—even with treatment. Your captain is right. If you intervene now—if you manage to save them... by the time the sun comes up, they'll know that a much worse fate is in store for them than a bullet.' He swallowed audibly, his hands trembling. 'I know what horrors I've done. But please—you must let them continue. This virus... it cannot get out of Nobilsk. It cannot.'

Church stayed there for what seemed like a long time, listening to the cries.

And then, with difficulty, he nodded and felt Cole's grip loosen on his chest, his captain breathing a sigh of relief.

'All right,' he said, 'then let's move.'

'Wait.' Church muttered, turning back to the firing squad once more.

'Wait for what, Church?' Cole asked him.

'Just wait,' he said.

'What, you want to watch them die?' Cole's brow creased behind his mask.

'I don't,' Church said back, his voice strangled in his throat. 'But I have to.'

TWENTY-EIGHT

PRESENT DAY

HALLBERG GLOWERED AT CHURCH. 'How could you do this?' she muttered. 'How could you just let him go like that? We had him, Church. We had him. And you just had to play the hero, didn't you? Saving me?' She shook her head. 'Don't you understand? What happens to me doesn't matter. All that matters is containing this.'

Church blinked in astonishment and then laughed a little.

'That's rich,' he said. 'If I said something like that, you'd come down on me like a tonne of bricks. In fact, you have. Every time I take a risk, you tell me it's not worth it. You chastise me for it. But now that it's you, what, it's suddenly okay?'

Hallberg scowled, realising she wasn't just toeing the line of hypocrisy. She was way over it. And yet her anger still stood.

'It doesn't matter,' she said. 'I risked everything coming here. Not just my life, but my job too. This was our last chance to get him. And you, you stopped that from happening. We had him, Church,' she repeated again, as though it might hit him harder the tenth time.

'And if you hadn't stood in my way,' he replied coolly, 'then he'd be lying dead here on the carpet. But you did. And that gave me time to think.'

'Oh, great,' she said, rolling her eyes. 'A great philosophical revelation, I'm sure.'

Church ignored the comment, surprised it came from her with such vitriol, but he gave her some leeway anyway.

'No,' he said grouchily, 'I just thought that doing this in the middle of an apartment block was probably the wrong choice, regardless of whether he was alive or dead. Shot, he'd be bleeding out all over this floor. Contaminating this room. The one below it. And hell, maybe the entire building if this thing is airborne. And if we took him down and held him here, then he was only going to get sicker. More contagious. He was bleeding already and that meant unnecessary risk to you and to me—'

'So you let him just go gallivanting off into the city?' she interjected.

'Yeah,' Church said. 'And we know that he's going to try and get out of the country. We know that he's going to link up with whoever his contact here is. And wherever that happens, taking him there is going to be better than doing it here. Out in the open, away from people. Somewhere that if everything goes sideways, no one else gets hurt.'

'Oh yeah, and how exactly do you propose to find him this time? Chasing this guy all over London has been like trying to pin the tail on the fucking donkey. There's only so much that Fred can do—'

'This time we don't need Fred,' Church cut in, reaching down and turning out his pockets—two white flaps of fabric. Empty.

Hallberg looked at them and then shrugged. 'What am I supposed to be looking at?' she said. 'You want me to buy you lunch or something?'

'No,' Church replied, stepping forward. 'The present you gave me this morning.'

Hallberg screwed up her face. 'The phone?'

'The phone,' he said. 'Why did you give it to me?'

'So I could keep track of you,' she said.

Church nodded, waiting for her to clock on.

Her eyes flitted to the table then. To where the medical bag had been. 'Did you...' she started.

Church nodded. 'I did,' he said. 'Right before I handed it to the carrier. Along with the life-saving drug that he's going to want to keep on his person. At all times.'

She scoffed then and looked up at him, stepped forward, grabbed him by the ears. 'You genius,' she said. 'I could kiss you.'

Church smiled down at her. 'Maybe later. And maybe once we've both got a clean bill of health, eh? Now come on. Let's stay tight on his tail. And if this comes off and we nail him and his contact, get a line on whoever put this together? Well, you might just get out of it in one piece.'

'One piece?' She laughed. 'If we do this right and we nail the whole network... they'll probably give me a fucking promotion.'

TWENTY-NINE

2010, NOBILSK

THE COLD WAS UNRELENTING, the night taking its toll on them.

They were all running hard, moving through the streets in their heavy gear, their masks arresting their breath.

Church still had a lump in his throat, unmovable since the firing squad. He ran numbly, but he wasn't sure if it was because of the weather or something else. They needed to find a way out of the city, and that meant they needed a vehicle—something capable of battling through the tundra and the soft snow outside. Which eliminated every civilian vehicle they passed, four-by-four or otherwise. Snowmobiles made the most sense and there would be no shortage of them here, but two hundred miles on a sled through these conditions would be suicidal.

They were geared for the winter, but not for a journey like that. Which left only one option.

Something big. Something militarised. Not quite a tank, but something close. Something with enough ground clearance and enough power to churn through the loose snow and get them to their exfil.

But that didn't leave them many options, and the ones they did have would be under armed guard—the military kind.

When they were a safe distance from the lab, they paused for breath, Cole taking out a tablet from his pack and pulling up the satellite images of the city, annotated by the SIS, giving them all of their potential infill routes, points of interest as well as potential escape options.

Near to the wall on the north side was the military garrison.

And as Cole pinched and zoomed in on the car park outside the main building, it became clear there was a line of what looked like armoured four-by-fours—perhaps the only thing capable of getting the job done.

But it was clear as day that getting them wouldn't be easy.

They crossed over a kilometre of open city, dodging roving teams of soldiers and Spetsnaz clearing buildings, throwing yellow biohazard body bags onto piles, more men with flamethrowers, more firing squads, an endless wash of them.

Church kept reminding himself what the doctor had said—ninety per cent mortality, even with treatment.

It didn't matter whether they were showing signs of having it. Because they were already dead, one way or another.

They made their way through the final alley, Cole signalling for them to slow down at the mouth, pausing to look out across the open stretch of ground at the outer perimeter fence of the military garrison.

'The gate's open. Building's dark—looks abandoned,' Mitch said, casting his eyes along the outer wall.

Cole pulled his monocular to his eye and scanned it more thoroughly.

'It does,' he said.

'So where are the fucking soldiers?' Mitch replied.

Church grimaced. 'Would you hang around? If they're not out there lining up civilians and executing them, then they've already made a break for it. And I doubt that the Russians go easy on deserters.'

'So dead or killing their own,' Mitch muttered back. 'Well, at least they won't be around to bother us.' He tried for something like humour and fell miserably short.

'Either way,' Cole joined in. 'Keep your heads on a swivel. We do this quick and clean, all right? We get inside there, we find the right vehicle, we hold there with the doctor. Foster, you're with me. Mitch, recce the area, make sure we're alone. And Church—you find us some keys. Can you handle that?'

Church nodded, their group splitting up without further instruction, Church peeling off towards the entrance to the building, Mitch down the road along the outer fence while Cole and Foster pressed on towards the row of armoured vehicles parked inside the gates. They were hulking four-by-fours, armoured-plated with huge wide tyres designed to carry speed over all terrains, snow included. The front was littered with huge spotlights, the massive flat bonnet no doubt concealing a monumental power plant to keep the thing moving.

Church made his approach towards the front doors, the brutalist design of the complex on full display. A big slab of concrete with small windows. Gold lettering inscribed above the front door. A pair of flags fluttering next to it, waving gently in the wind coming over the walls, displaying the Russian red, white and blue.

He headed towards the entryway, weapon against his shoulder, night vision goggles still against his eyes, looking for any movement. But there wasn't any. The smell of death already invaded his senses. He reached out with his left hand and pulled the door open, leaning to scope the inside. A large vaulted entryway, the walls covered in photographs and plaques. Lists of names inscribed into the concrete. Men who'd accomplished unknown feats. Who'd given their lives for their country. Maybe names that would never be learned again. That would be forgotten after this night, wiped from existence, he thought.

He shook that feeling off and moved deeper, the cold in there omnipresent. There was no wind, but it seemed like any semblance of heat had abandoned this place.

Along with its inhabitants.

Doors and windows left open, no care for the place once the decision had been made.

It only stood now as a monument to everything these men had betrayed.

The welcome desk stood empty, the chair on its side, a thin layer of frost settled over it, a veil of tiny ice crystals drifting through the darkness.

Church continued moving, keen to get this done, to be away from this place. To bury this mission, along with the others, in the recesses of his mind. Dying for a drink. Dying for fifty of them. Enough to turn this whole thing into a blur.

It wasn't a good way of dealing with it, but it was the only one he had.

He made his way down a long corridor, unsure what he was looking for. Probably something resembling an armoury. Some kind of equipment room.

That was where they kept the keys at Stirling Lines, and he figured that the Russians would be no different.

He followed the hallway around to the right, turning a corner and realising suddenly why it was so cold in here. At the far end, a set of double doors led out into the darkness, and they were wide open, snow already beginning to build up on the tiles inside.

He could make out the silhouette of a pair of bodies. One lying face down, the other propped against a wall. As he crept closer, he wondered whether they'd been infected and already succumbed to the virus.

As he made up the ground, he realised that wasn't the case at all.

These men had tried to make a run for it and had been killed for their actions.

The one face down bore three bullet holes in his back.

The one against the wall was gut-shot and then double-tapped in the head. No doubt he'd caught a round slumped there to die and had been finished off by his comrades.

Church grimaced, stepping through the open door and into the night once more to get his bearings.

He could see the snow-covered remains of several more men, just undulations in the snow.

He walked towards the nearest one and rolled him over, shedding his white husk, his skin paled by the cold, but his eyes red and bloodied, nose bleeding too.

The virus moved fast.

How long these men had been out here, he couldn't say, but the illness had already begun to set in.

This one too had been shot, and as Church stared down at him, he had to wonder whether or not a bullet really had spared him from a worse death. If the doctor had been right. That thought was one that he would no doubt ponder across many sleepless nights—this one included—but he had an objective to accomplish, and the faster he did so, the faster they could put Nobilsk in the rear view.

He swept back inside the building and began

checking doors, looking for that armoury, each one revealing a fresh horror.

Bodies everywhere he looked.

Men shot in their bunks, shot in the back of the head while they sat at a table to eat their dinner.

It seemed that, infected or not, those with the orders had been indiscriminate, killing anything and everything that had dared to breathe the air.

Church couldn't imagine that all of these men had managed to catch it, but it didn't matter. The priority was containment at all costs.

The only thing Church could promise himself was that he wouldn't let this happen anywhere ever again.

That before the night was out, orders be damned, he wasn't letting those hard drives and this data make it out of the country.

He opened another door, glancing around inside, closing it before he'd even realised that it was the room he was looking for, so desperate to be out of there.

He did a double take and pushed the door wide once more.

The room he'd found was small, segmented by a partition wall with a steel door leading into the next compartment, a meshed window with a slot large enough to pass weapons through sitting next to it.

This was the armoury, and it seemed to be somewhere that had been fought over.

Even in the small room where Church was standing, three men lay dead, hammered by bullets, mowed down where they stood.

Soldiers who'd tried to arm themselves, to fight off their own kin, and who'd suffered for it.

Church grimaced and looked them over. They wouldn't have come here if they didn't think they could get through the locked door. Reluctantly, he leaned down and padded their pockets, finding what he wanted on the second body, pulling out a set of keys.

The man had several chevrons on his shoulder, a ranking officer, but Church could see the rank meant nothing in all this mess. He lifted the keys and spooled through them until he found the one he wanted, trying it in the laser-cut lock. He twisted hard, the heavy frozen mechanism sliding out of the frame with a heavy clunk, the door creaking as he pulled it wide and swept his weapon around the room beyond.

The left and right-hand walls were entirely lined with racks of weaponry—rifles and pistols, long guns, carbines, light machine guns, everything you'd need to defend from an invading army. But it seemed like the enemy that had claimed Nobilsk, that had overrun the city, wasn't one they were ever prepared for.

There was only one man inside—the man who'd cut down his brothers-in-arms. The quartermaster, Church figured. He wasn't in military garb; he was wearing a grey polo shirt with army fatigues, blood splattered all down his chest, his mouth and lips and chin scarlet, the liquid crystallised in the cold. His fingers were blackened, nails half rotted, a Russian AK-12 lying spent on the floor next to him—the weapon he'd used to gun down his own men before they could get inside the armoury.

What he'd been trying to accomplish, Church didn't know. Protecting the weapons? Protecting himself? Either way, he'd made his stand, done his job, held out as long as he could, and then slumped down and succumbed to either the disease or the cold.

Church didn't know which, and he wasn't hanging around to check.

He surged forward towards the man, propped against the wall right beneath a wooden case—the exact kind they had back in Hereford, where they kept all the keys to their vehicles.

Church breathed a sigh of relief, moving towards it, pushing his MP5 down under his arm so that it hung at his ribs, pinned there by his elbow, giving him both hands free.

He put one foot between the quartermaster's knees and leaned over him, pulling the keybox wide, exposing rows of hooks, all filled with exactly what he was looking for. But which did he need? He stared in at the options, solely focused on choosing the right one, on making the right choice. And in doing so, made the worst mistake he possibly could.

Eyes fixed on the keys, he didn't notice as the man below him tilted his head slowly back and opened his eyes, staring up at Church.

He moved quicker than Church thought possible for a dead man, reaching up, grabbing Church by the arm, a deathly rattle escaping his throat as he raked in a frozen breath.

Church leapt backwards, his night vision glasses narrowing his field of vision, reacting to the touch alone, ripping his arm back as hard as he could and drawing his knife from his belt reflexively, driving it sideways with deadly precision straight into the skull of the frozen quartermaster.

The man's eyes lolled for a moment and then fluttered closed, the blade lodged in his brain up to the hilt.

Church, heart pounding, focused on his hand, willing his fingers to uncurl, and when they did, the man slid sideways and fell into a heap on the ground. Church was breathing hard, staring down at the quartermaster, cursing himself for being so hasty, for not checking before getting so close.

He shook his head and breathed a little sigh of relief.

That could have been a lot worse.

He let his eyes fall to his knife, still in the man's head, and reached down—freezing halfway there, noticing something else. Not on the quartermaster this time, but on himself.

On his arm.

His left sleeve was pushed up halfway to his elbow, a five-inch stretch of skin exposed.

And there—three deep red scratches in his skin.

Church's mouth ran dry, his brain finally identifying what he was looking at.

He could taste vomit then, nausea twisting through his guts.

At the end of the darkest, deepest scratch, embedded in his arm, was a single jagged, rotting fingernail.

THIRTY

CHURCH AND HALLBERG stepped from the apartment with spirits renewed.

And before they'd even made it out the door, Hallberg was already tracking the carrier through a sophisticated GPS app that showed a detailed map of London along with a flashing red dot that she assured Church was accurate to a metre and updated in real time.

Which meant they could hang back and follow from afar, watch and wait, and when the time came, make the interception or simply hand it over to Hallberg's superiors—in exchange for immunity for her transgressions, of course.

But sadly, their hope was short-lived. They didn't make it five steps out of the apartment before Church slowed, looking to his right out of the long bank of windows and down into the streets below.

'What is it?' Hallberg asked, a few feet ahead, turning back.

Church narrowed his eyes, following a navy blue BMW 5 Series that swung quickly around the corner and screamed to a stop at the kerb behind Hallberg's SUV.

Before the two men in baseball caps and grey jackets stepped out, another BMW—same make, model and colour—followed the first and parked right behind it.

Church knew plainclothes police cars when he saw them, and he knew the walk and posture of armed police. These men were trained and they were carrying. The NCA, likely zeroing in on the apartment block in the same way Fred had. A tick behind, but close on Church and Hallberg's tail.

He surveyed the four men forming up in the street to exchange information, to solidify their plan before they made their ingress, and he let out a little sigh of relief. Four was easily avoidable. They'd likely all come up the lift together.

But before he even formed that thought, two more cars appeared—these ones marked—and four more officers climbed out. Eight in total now.

Difficult, but still doable.

And then, a long sleek Volvo estate closed out the group and four more plainclothes, armed officers climbed from the vehicle, making twelve in total.

He looked over his shoulder down the length of the corridor, towards the fire escape and the stairwell on the far side, then the other way towards the two elevators and the main staircase leading down.

Twelve was enough bodies, Church thought, to cover every conceivable exit. Four in each lift and one in each stairwell to sweep and make sure they weren't flanked, leaving two on the ground to cover any escape. That's how he'd do it, and he thought they'd probably come to the same conclusion.

'We need to move,' he told Hallberg, taking off towards the lifts. She too had now seen the officers below, craning her neck to look down through the window.

She jogged to catch up with Church, swearing under her breath, heading for the lift.

'No,' he said, 'stairs. If we get in the lift, we don't know what's going to be there when the door opens.'

Hallberg paused, finger hovering a few inches from the button, and pulled it back, nodding to Church as he opened the stairwell door and swept through it, keeping his pistol firmly in its holster, wondering whether or not they could just walk casually down the stairs and past any officers coming up. Whether they'd have pictures of them, courtesy of Hallberg's boss. Whether they'd know to stop them, or know to be on the lookout for them.

Church figured that they'd be able to track her car if they needed to. Hell, they probably recognised it the second they pulled up. And though he was sure the carrier was their first priority, there was a good chance that both he and Hallberg were secondary targets.

They started down, not running, but keeping a

steady pace, reeling off the floors. Eleven, ten, nine... and they were practically on eight by the time the ground-level door squealed open and footsteps echoed dimly up to them.

Church lifted his hand, motioning Hallberg to slow down, holding his finger to his lips to hush her.

'What's the plan?' she risked whispering.

'We head down,' Church told her, gesturing to the stairs. 'Another floor or two and then we get off, cross slowly to the fire escape on the other side and then keep descending, hopefully missing the officers coming up the other side. If we time it right, we'll pop out behind them.'

Hallberg gave a firm nod and Church offered a brief smile, trying to reassure her as they carried on, meandering down to the seventh floor, the quickened steps of the officers below growing in volume as they took the stairs two at a time.

Church put his hand on the handle of six and eased it down, the squeak of the sprung mechanism echoing gently in the bare concrete shaft. He bared his teeth as the hinges groaned too and they let themselves out, knowing that the officers coming up from below would have heard it. But they had no choice now. They had to follow through with this plan. Church just hoped that they wouldn't be made on sight.

He ushered Hallberg onto six and told her to walk slow. Church filed out behind her, easing the door closed as quietly as he could and then caught up, shielding her totally from behind, hedging his bets: if the police were looking for a man and a woman together, perhaps just seeing a man alone might throw them off. They might discard him, he hoped, as a random resident. But even as he strode he became aware there were a lot of ifs and hopes in that plan.

He moved casually, stepping as though he didn't have a care in the world, but only made it twenty feet before the door opened behind him and he had to make a snap decision as to what was more suspicious: looking back or staying the course.

'Keep going,' he told Hallberg, continuing to shield her, keeping his hands softly at his sides.

The door didn't close behind him but he heard no footsteps in the corridor.

He knew without looking that the police officer was standing there making a judgement, watching him walk away.

'Hey.'

A voice rang out from behind him.

Church kept walking.

'Hey,' the call came again, 'stop.'

But Church didn't.

'Police.'

The word rang through the hallway and Church could hear Hallberg's quickened breathing in front of him, the steps hurrying a little.

'Walk slow,' Church murmured to her, staying at a constant speed.

'Sir,' the police officer called out, 'police. Stop where you are.'

Footsteps now, coming after him. A few slow, then faster, then running to catch up. But that wasn't the noise he was listening for. The slither of metal against plastic—a pistol being pulled from a holster—was what he was waiting for.

And almost instantly, the officer obliged.

'Armed police,' he called out, sharp and authoritative now. 'Don't move.'

Church did as he was instructed, stopping dead. Hallberg risked looking back, and Church nodded for her to take a few more steps, trying to give her a little bit of distance. A head start, if nothing else.

But this time, she didn't listen, looking back at him, wide-eyed.

'Don't move,' the officer said as he advanced. 'Keep your hands where I can see them.'

Hallberg mouthed something to Church then.

'I can fix this,' she said.

And Church knew what she meant—that she could come clean about who she was, about why she was there.

And it might do just that. Or it might do nothing at all. They'd still end up in cuffs, in custody for interfering with an investigation. Hallberg would still lose her job, and this whole thing would come crashing down.

Which left Church with only one option. And it was one he didn't like.

He was going to have to take care of this.

But he hoped not in the way he was fearing.

The officer was on him now, six feet behind and holding steadily out of arm's reach, out of lunging distance.

'Turn around. Slowly,' he ordered. 'Keep your hands at your sides.'

Church turned, palms forward, fingers spread, and spun slowly in place until he was facing the officer.

The man was a few inches shorter than him, wearing a black, unbranded baseball cap, a grey bomber jacket, a Glock 19 in his hands levelled straight at Church's heart.

There wasn't a hint of a waver in his grip, the finger steady on the trigger as the man appraised him, tightening his grip on the weapon as he seemed to recognise in Church the same thing that Church recognised in the officer—that this man wasn't just a civilian.

'Identify yourself. Now,' the officer demanded.

'Show me your badge first,' Church replied coolly.

He thought that was going to go one of two ways. Either the officer would oblige, dig for his warrant card, give him his name, badge number, or he was going to react badly. Either way, Church would learn something.

'On your knees. Now. Do it.'

With a sigh, Church slowly got down onto his knees, Hallberg standing silently behind him. And it was only at that moment that the officer seemed to notice her.

'Back up,' he said, pointing at Hallberg. 'Turn around, put your hands on the wall above your head.'

Hallberg did as she was told.

Church could feel her eyes fixed on him, but she said nothing. Trusting him.

Just a little longer, he thought.

'You,' the officer went on, looking back at Church, 'interlock your fingers behind your head. Slowly.'

Church did as he was told in silence, lifting his hands to his shoulder and then to the back of his head, careful not to make a sudden enough movement that his jacket would flap open and expose the pistol tucked into the waistband at his hip, in the concealed holster there.

'Who are you?' the officer asked once more, risking coming forward.

But Church just looked up at him. 'I'm not answering any questions,' he replied. 'Not until you give me your name and badge number and I've talked to my solicitor.'

The officer's jaw flexed and he took his off-hand from the pistol, coming forward, reaching out to give Church a pat-down, but thinking twice about it, staying his hand.

Church had shown no sign of aggression—nothing except calmness, quietness—hoping it would be enough to persuade the officer that his first instinct was wrong, that perhaps this man, big as he was, might just be a normal guy.

Cautiously, the officer came within striking distance, reaching to his belt, dragging a pair of cable ties from a pouch affixed to it, circling around Church, giving him some space as he did, half-expecting something to happen.

But reluctant or not, Church knew that eventually he'd have to get close. Eventually he'd have to loop the straps over Church's hands. And in that split second, he'd have his one and only chance.

Church had done nothing wrong so far, other than failing to identify himself, and though the officer had refused to give his name and number, he didn't think he'd go so far as to put the gun against the back of his head while restraining him.

'Am I under arrest?' Church asked slowly.

'You're being detained,' the officer replied. 'Under Section 24.'

'What does that mean?' Church asked him then.

'It means—' he said, not getting to finish.

The moment Church felt the plastic touch his fingers, he launched himself backwards, throwing the back of his head into the gut of the officer, reaching up sharply and grabbing him by the lapels of his jacket, wrenching him forward over his head and flat onto his back.

The officer landed hard, a puff of air escaping his lips, the impact winding him.

He was dazed for a moment, but a moment was all Church needed. He sprawled down on top of him, grabbed for his wrist and twisted hard, the weapon coming free, spilling onto the floor.

The officer tried to fight back, but Church was too heavy, too fast, twisting on top of him and taking him by the arm, rolling him over so he was face down, Church's hands lacing around his neck like a boa constrictor, closing his windpipe, making it impossible for him to call out for help—for him to breathe.

But it wasn't his throat that Church was aiming for, it was the carotid arteries on the side of his neck, and with his forearm and his bicep he closed them entirely, pressing down with his full weight on top of the officer, who struggled for just a few seconds before he began to slip into unconsciousness, Church's sleeper hold taking effect.

And only once he was sure that the officer had fallen still, that he was out cold, did Church release and roll off him, reaching down and unplugging the radio from his ear, tugging the receiver from the back of his belt and hurling it into the wall hard enough that it smashed into a dozen pieces.

Church took his pistol next and ejected the magazine, popped out the round in the chamber and dropped the carcass on the ground, taking the extra ammunition for himself.

And only once he'd gone through those instinctive, mechanical steps did he look over at Hallberg, who still had her hands pressed to the wall.

'What did you just do?' she asked him, staring down at the officer.

'I just saved us from being arrested,' he replied.

'You assaulted a police officer,' Hallberg muttered back.

'I'm glad that's all I had to do,' Church said, stepping towards her, reaching up and taking her wrist from the wall, pushing her hand into his and lacing his fingers between hers so she couldn't pull them free.

'Now come on,' he said, 'we've got to finish this.'

Hallberg stood there for a moment, shaking her head, still looking at the officer.

'Stay if you want,' Church told her, 'but when he wakes up he's not going to be happy. Right now, he doesn't know who we are or anything about us.

'In about 90 seconds, if we're lucky, he's going to start screaming. And if we're not out of the building by then, we're going to be in big fucking trouble. So tell me, what do you want to do?' He pulled on her arm, grabbing her attention. 'Julia, are you with me?'

She dragged her eyes slowly from the officer and fixed them on Church, swallowing audibly.

She didn't nod, didn't say anything, but he felt her fingers tighten in his, and he knew.

And then, without wasting another second, they were running.

THIRTY-ONE

2010, NOBILSK

CHURCH STARED down at his forearm, the nail sticking straight up out of his flesh, greyed like stone.

Like a headstone, he thought morbidly.

A small bead of blood began to bubble up around the edge of it, and he reached with shaking fingers, plucking the piece of nail from his skin with a little twinge of pain.

The red jewel of blood continued to grow, congealing and freezing by the moment in the sub-zero air inside the building. He knew that squeezing at it, trying to expel the poison, would be pointless.

If it was in his system, it was already coursing through him. Infecting him.

Dr Zorin's numbers flashed in his mind.

Ninety percent mortality rate.

Even with treatment.

First signs of symptoms in six to twelve hours.

Death within twenty-four after that.

Fatal, he thought.

There was no way of getting around it.

He closed his eyes then, lowering his head and letting out a slow, solemn breath. When he opened them again, he found himself staring at the man below him, his knife still buried in his skull to the hilt.

He pulled it free, not wanting to leave any evidence behind that they were ever there.

That was the mission, he thought, smirking to himself.

The fucking mission.

Like it mattered now. Not to him at least, but to everyone else. His eyes found the dead man once more, infected. And he too was the same: a ticking time bomb. He was never leaving this place. Not Russia, at least. But they weren't out of the woods yet, and he wasn't in the ground yet either. They still had a mission to complete. And Cole had been right about one thing— that it wasn't just the lives of the people here, or the lives of the people back home, he was saving.

It was Mitch, Foster, Cole himself.

While he could still pull the trigger, he could still fight. And he knew there was probably one last stand ahead before they were in the clear. The Spetsnaz would be out for blood. They'd been trying to get hold of Dr Zorin, and to know foreign forces had got there first? They'd be taking no prisoners.

Church rolled his sleeve down grimly and tried to

ignore the growing throb in his forearm. He could already feel the poison in his system. No, he was just projecting that. Though it wouldn't be in his imagination soon enough. This was going to get real all too fast, which meant he didn't have a lot of time to wait around. His heart was throbbing in his ears and he did his best to steady it, breathing deeply as he scanned the keys in front of him, looking for the right ones.

Unsure which he should take, he grumbled to himself in frustration and hunted around for some kind of receptacle, finding an ammunition box and dumping out the tray of 7.62 in it, unhooking and throwing in every key in the box instead. It jangled and rattled as he walked back into the corridor, his MP5 still hanging loosely from his shoulder, the keys in his hands. He should have had it at the ready, but what did that matter now? He strode straight out of the back exit and into the freezing cold air, making a loop of the building, stepping over the bodies like they weren't even there, until he came around the corner and saw Cole, Foster and Zorin standing waiting for him.

He approached from behind, not announcing himself, and when he got close enough for them to hear his footsteps, they turned, aiming their weapons right at him. Usually, he would have quipped something like, 'Don't shoot, I come in peace'… but he just didn't have it in him just then.

He dumped the keybox on the bonnet of one of the armoured SUVs, avoiding Cole's gaze.

Cole was watching him carefully, perhaps the rounded shoulders or the lack of communication alerting him that something was wrong.

He nodded towards Church's gun. 'Just for decoration, that?'

Hands now free, Church reached down for it and pulled up to a lazy ready position. 'There's no one here,' he grunted back. 'No one alive at least.'

Cole appraised him but didn't seem to know exactly what was going on.

He narrowed his eyes behind his respirator, taking a stab at it. 'You're not still crying about that firing squad shit, are you?'

Church drew a breath.

Cole was wide of the mark, but he didn't need to know that.

'You got me,' Church said back, shrugging.

'Listen,' Cole said, 'I know it's not right, I know it's the furthest fucking thing from right, but we've got a mission—'

'And that's all that matters,' Church finished for him.

'Yeah,' Cole replied slowly. 'Took the words right out of my mouth.'

His words were extended, detached almost, as though his mouth was forming them automatically while his brain did its best to work out what was really going on. But luckily, Mitch's voice over the airwaves interrupted them.

'I got movement out here,' he said. 'Beyond the fence, five hundred metres and closing. Looks like an armed patrol. How's it going over there?'

'Church is back,' Cole replied, touching his ear, his eyes fixed on the man in front of him. 'He's got the keys, we're just sorting them out now, and then we're out of here. Regroup.'

'Music to my ears,' Mitch replied, huffing and panting over the radio as he turned around and began running back.

Cole licked his lips behind the mask, reaching out to the box that Church had brought, tipping it on its side and spilling the keys across the bonnet of the vehicle.

He spread them out with his hand and then looked in the box to make sure, turning it over as though it was going to give him some clue to what was really going on. When he came up with nothing, he let out a long sigh and stepped forward instead, taking Church by the shoulder, squeezing firmly but not painfully, and for what seemed like a long time.

'It's all right, Church. We'll be home soon enough. I promise you, we're all getting out of here.'

'Yeah,' Church said. 'It will be over soon enough.' He forced a smile and then turned away from his captain, beginning to separate the keys into grouped piles. 'Now, let's figure out which one of these is the right one and get on the road. I think I'm ready to leave Nobilsk. And we've got a long road ahead.'

'Yeah,' Cole said. 'And not a lot of time.'

Church smiled sardonically, wanting to say it out loud but knowing he couldn't. *You don't know how right you are, Captain.*

You don't know how right you are.

THIRTY-TWO

PRESENT DAY

OTHER THAN ASSAULTING the police officer, Church's plan came off without a hitch.

They stepped into the opposite stairwell and descended smoothly, footsteps ringing out above as the other officers climbed up to twelve, unaware that one of their own was still lying unconscious several floors below.

Church and Hallberg exited onto the ground floor and made a beeline for the exit, stepping onto the street, skirting the wall away from the last two police officers who were camped out at the front, chatting to each other in full knowledge that their team hadn't reached the right apartment yet and, keen to keep their operation quiet, were allowing the denizens to go about their days as normal.

Church was banking on them not getting intercepted

twice and he was right. By the time either of the officers even looked up, Hallberg and Church were around the corner and out of sight, heading after the carrier. Hallberg brought her phone up when she was sure they were safe and homed in on the red dot once more.

'Where's he going?' Church asked.

Hallberg bit her lip, zooming out, triangulating their position relative to his, watching as he continued to make turns. The destination was seemingly only one place.

'Canary Wharf,' she said, brow creasing. 'The water?'

She quickened her pace and Church kept up with her, his strides long and easy.

'You think his contact has got a boat? Definitely be an easy way out of the city.'

'I don't know,' Hallberg replied. 'But either way, we need to catch up.'

She broke into a light jog and Church did the same, the pair of them reeling the carrier in by the moment. They backtracked practically on the route they'd taken to get there, unable to use Hallberg's car—the police vehicles were parked too close to it. It would arouse too much suspicion going for it, which meant they were on foot. But if anything, it was quicker than driving. The afternoon was wearing on, the traffic increasing by the moment as rush hour bore down on them.

They traced a path back towards Pennyfields, passing the opening to Saltwell Street. Fred's call had done as Hallberg had hoped: a sea of marked police cars and police cordons surrounded the veterinary clinic.

They carried on, pushing back towards the overland rail and past the station, hanging a left towards the entrance to the Wharf, the buildings suddenly leaping into the sky around them, the smell of the Thames growing in Church's nostrils, the gentle breeze picking its way along the water, rolling over him uncomfortably.

He stopped as Hallberg stepped onto the kerb and announced that they were within striking distance of the target.

'Up ahead there,' she said, looking up from the screen and pointing across an open stretch of concrete and water towards a bridge spanning one of the slips.

On both sides, high-rises shadowed the area, the sun hanging low in the sky, night approaching quickly. There was a bite in the air now, and Hallberg shivered, zipping up her jacket. Church narrowed his eyes, immune to the cold when he was working like this, when he was focused.

The carrier was alone for now, leaning on a rail, looking left and right, directly in the middle of the bridge, waiting for someone.

They weren't too late.

Church wasn't surprised at the meeting point.

Londoners and tourists alike slowly crossed the bridge behind him, filing up and down the busy promenades, taking pictures, heading in and out of restaurants or in and out of the expensive apartment blocks that perched above them. The area was open around the meeting point. It would be easy to see anyone coming and going, easy to spot any kind of unwanted approach, easy to tell whether or not someone had been followed. No doubt the contact who had set the meet point knew this and had chosen it for that reason, wanting to make sure that the carrier and those dogging him hadn't formed some kind of alliance. As bad as things would be for the carrier if the MSS scooped him up, for the contact it would be just as bad. Crossing the Chinese government was a fool's game, the punishments severe. So it was no surprise that they were being overly cautious.

Hallberg was tentative, unsure what to do, or perhaps just unhappy at their only option: waiting.

They could take him then and there, draw weapons in the middle of Canary Wharf and hold him at gunpoint once more. But he'd already expressed a willingness to die over being captured by either side. So doing that was a zero-sum game. All they could do was hold fast until his contact arrived, keep tailing them in some fashion, wait for the next move, and then when the time was right either swoop in and make the arrest or hand it off to the NCA.

'I don't like this,' Hallberg said, shifting from foot to foot.

They were camped out at the corner of the Docklands Museum, watching from a little under a hundred yards away. Church was used to it, had spent countless hours, countless days and weeks, holed up in far worse places, waiting for far more mundane things to happen.

It was the nature of the job. But, just like throughout his career, when you were waiting for something, it meant you had nothing but time. And very often people wanted to fill that with conversation. Church could feel Hallberg watching him, her eyes boring into him once more.

'Are you finally ready to tell me what's going on?' she asked.

Church looked down at her.

'Why you've been so cagey all day, so tentative, why you've been zoned out? And snappy.'

'I haven't been snappy,' Church said back, snappily.

Hallberg arched an eyebrow, her gaze heavy, weighing on Church.

He let out a long sigh. Perhaps it was finally time, the end in sight now. Perhaps he could tell her. Perhaps he should. Perhaps he had to. Not just for her, but for himself.

'You're always ready to lay your life down on the line,' Hallberg told him, 'to jump in with both feet, but this time you've hesitated every single step. Why?'

Church swallowed, a hot lump forming in his throat.

He cleared it, clenched his fists a few times, willing the pins and needles there to abate.

'Because I've lived this before,' he said, lifting his eyes to the carrier, his voice quiet. 'I've experienced this before—this exact thing, it feels like—and I've seen the worst possible outcome of what can happen if you're not careful enough, if you let your guard down.'

He reached out for his left forearm then, rubbing it harshly, the old, knotted scar tissue there itching ferociously all of a sudden—the site where that rotten nail had bedded in. A constant reminder that hesitation, that being cavalier, reckless, does kill.

Before he could stop himself, Hallberg's hand reached out, laid itself over his, stopping the scratching.

He flinched, but she didn't take her fingers away, lacing them under his palm, squeezing instead. He looked down at her and could see she was seeing right through him, reading him like a book.

'I don't know what you went through,' she said softly. 'But you can't live in fear, Solomon.'

'I don't,' Church said back. 'But I live with the knowledge and experience of what happens if things go wrong.'

She nodded slowly, thinking on that.

'So let's make sure they don't,' she replied, smiling.

And despite himself, he smiled back.

'Let's finish this,' she said, letting out a long exhale, turning her eyes back to the carrier across the border, 'before it even starts.'

THIRTY-THREE

2010, NOBILSK

BY THE TIME they found the right key, Mitch was already back with them.

They opened the doors to the SUV and bundled in, Foster taking the front passenger seat with Cole behind the wheel, Mitch and Zorin packed into the back with Church. He took the left side, making sure his bloodied arm was against the door and not touching the doctor. He thought he had a good chance of pulling the wool over Cole's eyes. But Zorin had created this fucking thing and Church doubted he'd be able to slide even the faintest hint of infection past him. So he kept his left hand on the underbarrel of his MP5, his right hand on the grip, the gun across his lap so that his arm was tucked down next to his leg, his eyes fixed out the window, staring through the tinted, bulletproof glass.

He felt high up as he settled into the seat. The

vehicle was hulking, its wheels coming up halfway on his thigh, the ground clearance practically to his knee, a steel step to climb into the cabin hanging from the underside of the armoured hull. The interior was sparse. Two seats in the front were separated by a massive central console equipped with GPS, radio and a few other instruments that Church couldn't quite work out. Or perhaps he just didn't have the inclination to. Across the back was a bench seat that could have squeezed four and comfortably accommodated three. Behind them was a spacious rear storage compartment, filled with military hard cases adorned with Cyrillic notation that Church guessed was housing heavy weaponry, possibly even artillery.

He wasn't sure what the Russians had been preparing for out here, but it was nothing short of a war by all the kit.

And it seemed like that was exactly what had taken over the city—even if it wasn't the kind they were expecting.

Cole slotted the key into the engine and ran his hands over the wheel.

'Strap in,' he said. 'I think this might get bumpy. We're going to have to carry some speed out of here.'

Zorin and Mitch buckled up next to Church, but he didn't bother.

Instead, he shuffled back into the seat, keeping his breathing slow, trying to control his heart, eking out what time he had left, trying to slow the flow of blood around his body—the spread of the virus.

He could feel Cole watching him in the rear-view mirror, but didn't look up to meet his eyes.

'At least,' Mitch said, almost cheerfully, 'once we're out of the fucking city, we can get these masks off.'

'I wouldn't recommend it,' Zorin replied.

Church stiffened a little at his words, waiting for the accusation to come.

'The pathogen can survive outside the body for more than eight hours. I wouldn't risk removing your masks until at least that time has passed since the last potential exposure.'

Church let out a little sigh of relief—inaudible, he hoped, in the cabin.

'Great,' Mitch grumbled back, looking down at his watch. 'At least it'll be in time for lunch.'

Foster and Cole chuckled a little as Cole finally cranked the ignition, the roar of the engine drumming up, drowning out the idle conversation.

He shunted the heavyweight gearbox into drive and pressed on the accelerator. The engine whined, the supercharger spooling up as it forced air into the huge block.

The wheels began to turn and they shuddered forward, settling into a slow, idling crawl as Cole guided them out towards the gates, headlights off, leaning forward and tapping on the screen in the centre console so he could see their position on a map.

He zoomed out, orienting it, until he knew which way they were headed. When he was satisfied, he dropped a pin in what seemed like the middle of fucking nowhere and hit the green button.

It took a minute to calculate and then gave them their route. Cole's grip tightened on the wheel and he glanced back at them.

'Here we go, lads.'

He didn't wait for a response before he stomped on the accelerator, all four wheels of the vehicle spinning on the icy roads. They slingshotted forwards, the deeply treaded tyres digging into the asphalt and propelling them onwards, short gears bringing them up to speed quickly.

Church was pressed backwards in his seat as Cole charged into the city proper, straight through the open steel gates of the garrison and out into Nobilsk.

Church didn't get a chance to even think about the approaching patrol Mitch had warned of before they were suddenly there in front of them. Cole's hand moved towards the console, and when the men—dark shapes in the distance, their flashlight beams affixed to the ends of their weapons swinging around on the floor —stopped and looked up, pointing their torches towards them, Cole flicked a row of switches. A huge array of lights and lamps on the front of the truck burst to life.

Church's mind catalogued them instantly.

Half a dozen men.

Four in Spec Ops gear.

Two wielding flamethrowers.

All threw their hands up to their eyes to shield them-selves and then reflexively lifted their weapons.

Muzzle flash. A barrage of it.

Bullets danced off the armour plating of the vehicle, sparks spraying upwards over the windscreen. The thick glass didn't even crack as the rounds pinged off it, leaving white flecks behind.

Zorin tucked forward, putting his hands over his head as though out of the firing line, but everyone else remained seated. Church just squinted a little at the brightness of the gunfire, pushing his night vision goggles up onto the top of his helmet once more, allowing his eyes to acclimatise to the last throes of the Russian night.

The four men with the rifles jumped out of the way as the truck rallied past. The flamethrowers let loose, dousing the side of the vehicle in flammable liquid, the whole exterior engulfed in flames suddenly.

But Cole was laser focused.

He kept the wheels straight, kept ploughing forward. And though the flames persisted, rippling and flapping over the bonnet and roof, he didn't slow down.

The soldiers behind them ran back into the street once more, took a knee and squeezed off tight, focused bursts of fire towards their back. Church closed his eyes, numb to the sound as the bullets pinged off the metal sheeting. Mitch twisted to watch them dwindle behind, glancing over at Church as though wondering why he hadn't done the same.

'Well,' he said, turning back to the rest of the team, 'I guess they know we stole one of their trucks now.'

'Ngghh,' Foster replied—not quite a word, not quite a grunt.

'They've still got to catch us,' Cole said, keeping his foot planted as they squealed around a corner, the tyres losing grip, the back stepping out. The supercharger screamed under the bonnet, the rubber churning against the snow and tarmac.

They slid into a row of parked cars, shunting them up onto the pavements, and then peeled away, regaining pace once more as they headed down a long main street, the outer wall visible in the distance.

Church looked to the right now, orienting himself, seeing the great grey slab of the bio-research lab flashing by down the length of a street. He could see the piled-up yellow bags out the front, could see the flames licking upwards, the glow illuminating the swirl of snow drifting above the city.

'Looks like they're rolling out the welcome waggon for us,' Cole half-yelled then, hunching forward in the seat a little more, his foot mashed against the floor.

The engine howled its battle-cry, the SUV accelerating continually, moving so fast now that it was barely finding traction on the icy road, beginning to snake under its own sheer speed and bulk.

Ahead, a line of soldiers had funnelled into the street, all taking a knee, all firing. But it was useless. It didn't matter if there were ten or a hundred men. They were firing 7.62s at best, and the windows—supposedly the weakest part of any armoured transport—were at least two inches of solid plexiglass.

You'd need an anti-tank round to have any hope of piercing it.

Because that's what this thing was.

A tank.

Church just sat back and closed his eyes.

If they did have something big enough to derail them, then it didn't matter whether he was awake or not.

Either their bullets would be shrugged off and they'd be through the gate in thirty seconds, or they'd have something that could take them out and they'd die in a fiery wreck before they made it.

Church wasn't sure which he preferred.

Zorin had told him those people executed by the firing squad were granted a much better death than what the virus would have had in store for them.

So Church couldn't quite make up his mind.

Did he prefer the wreck? Being incinerated by an explosive tank round to the chest?

Or did he want to keep living, waiting for a much worse end?

The gunfire stopped momentarily, distant, dimmed shouts of Russians drifting through the glass and finding their way inside the vehicle. They'd blown through the line without any trouble, were headed into the open tundra at speed.

Slow death then, Church thought, the decision made for him.

'We're in the clear,' Cole said, the relief audible in his voice. 'But everyone hold on. We're hitting the snow at a hell of a lick here!'

Church opened his eyes, staring through the wind-screen at the quickly approaching gate. A different one to the one they'd used to enter Nobilsk. Its barrier was still intact, but no match for the four tonnes of steel hammering towards it. Church reached out, putting his hand against the back of Foster's headrest, waiting for the bump. But it was barely detectable—the wooden beam exploded as the front bull bars collided with it, dousing the vehicle in splinters.

The nose dived as it hit the heavy snow, the wheels biting into the loose powder, Cole fighting to keep them straight. The vehicle slowed and he wrestled with the wheel, keeping his foot planted, until they settled to a solid churn, huge sprays of snow flying up past Church's window.

He watched it go as they drove into the night, Cole killing the lights, plunging them into darkness, following what seemed to be a buried roadway on the GPS.

He was grinning, but Church was aware he seemed to be the only one.

He looked to his right, seeing Mitch staring back through the rear windscreen.

'They're not following us,' he said, and this time Church couldn't help but look.

He twisted to stare back through the gates of Nobilsk, seeing Mitch was right.

The Spetsnaz were just standing there in the road, watching them go, making no attempt to run, to find their own vehicles or give chase.

'They couldn't fucking catch us if they tried,' Cole said defiantly.

But he didn't sound confident.

And after a moment, they got their answer as to why no one was giving chase.

Even above the endless, deafening roar of the engine they could hear it—distant at first, difficult to pick out over the rumble of the snow under the tyres, but growing with every second.

At first, Church mistook it for the throb of his heart, but then he realised how wrong he was.

There was no mistaking the sound of rotors.

And as he continued to look backwards, watching a distant black phantom rise into the air over Nobilsk, illuminated by the glow of the fires burning in the streets for just a second before it was swallowed by the night, he realised the reason the Spetsnaz weren't giving chase was because they didn't need to.

Cole might have been right that they could outrun another vehicle, or anyone on foot, but what they couldn't outrun was a helicopter.

And Church had no doubt in his mind that it was coming for them.

And when it caught up with them…

There'd be nothing they could do to stop it.

THIRTY-FOUR

PRESENT DAY

TIME TICKED ON, people oozing past the carrier.

He was wearing a hooded jacket, leaning on the rail, head over the water, keeping himself facing away from anyone that might be passing. It was clear in his posture, his position, that despite the public nature of the meeting point—something outside his control—he didn't want to infect anyone. Didn't want to start an epidemic. Didn't want that moral weight. He cared, perhaps even just a little, about the fate of those around him. But whether it would be enough, Church didn't know. He could only take comfort in the fact that it was something, at least. An attempt, if nothing else.

And after what seemed like an age, Church picked out a man from the crowd, wearing a black coat, the hood up despite there being not a drop of rain in the air.

He moved slowly, cautiously, checking over his shoulder and to his sides as he walked, making his way up onto the bridge. Six feet short of the carrier, he stopped, hands remaining in his pockets, and said something. The carrier looked up, stood straight from the rail, backpack on his back, black medical case slung at his hip. Tourists continued to move past, unseeing, unknowing, as the two men exchanged a few words—the carrier and his contact.

Hallberg licked her lips, watching in anticipation, picking at her already chewed fingernails.

Church sensed it before he saw it.

A strange phenomenon that had sometimes happened to him over the years. Whether it was a change in the air, something glimpsed out of the corner of his eye, or something even extra-sensory, rooted deep in the lizard brain—the same thing that makes a deer turn and flee in the woods when a hunter sights it through a scope from a few hundred metres away. A flutter of danger deep in the primitive mind. He homed in on the source instantly. The three remaining MSS operatives—minus the one Church had killed in the underground—all converging from both sides onto the carrier and his contact.

They moved up onto the bridge. Hallberg began to step forward as well, but Church took her by the arm and held her, and she didn't struggle. The Chinese, like Church and Hallberg, had no doubt managed to track their target down. And they'd been waiting for the same thing: for the carrier to meet his contact, wanting to scoop them both up at the same time. As they converged, pistols drawn and held inside their jackets—hidden from the public, but clear as day to both the carrier and his contact—the two men froze, realising the situation.

Church heard the first shout then: the contact pointing at the carrier, raising his voice, yelling at him, probably accusing him of a double-cross. The carrier shouted back, turning, looking for some way out, but there was none. The MSS were at the bridge now, boxing them in from either end and closing in one step at a time. The public began to see that something was wrong, sensing it too, herd awareness flashing through the crowd. They began to shove and move as one, dispersing from the bridge, leaving it empty almost instantly. Just the carrier and the contact remained, marooned in the middle.

One of the Chinese agents called out, no doubt ordering them to come quietly, making it clear that they were armed and willing to use their weapons if necessary.

'Fuck,' Hallberg muttered. 'Fuck!'

She swore again, looking up at Church expectantly.

'What do we do?'

Church ground his teeth, thinking. What *could* they do? Except go in there. Except intercede. They couldn't risk letting the MSS scoop the carrier up. It was clear they were well connected here in London, would have vehicles waiting in the wings, an escape route planned. And on foot, Church and Hallberg would never catch them. No. This had to happen, and it had to happen now —and damn the consequences.

Church reached to his hip.

He managed to get his hand around the grip of his pistol, but didn't manage to get it free of the holster before the sudden flaring of an engine to his right jolted him out of his tunnel vision. A police van, mounting the kerb from the street behind at speed, jostled over the pavement and skidded to a halt twenty feet in front of them, blue lights flashing silently.

Church shoved the pistol back into place, turning his back to it, shielding Hallberg from a half dozen armed officers as the doors were thrown open and they launched themselves from the vehicle, charging into the middle of Canary Wharf. Rifles pulled against their shoulders, clad in tactical gear and bulletproof vests, they yelled for the few remaining people on the promenade to get down and move out of the way.

Chaos erupted almost instantly. The three MSS agents—foreign operatives on British soil without permission, carrying unlicensed weapons and committing all manner of crimes—knew they only had one option: fire first.

They turned, bracing themselves against the rails of the bridge, and opened fire, shooting straight into the ranks of the police officers.

The officers dove to the ground, dropping to their knees, moving to the sides to get their angles before they fired back. The rattles of tightly grouped automatic gunfire echoed through Canary Wharf.

People screamed, ran for their lives. Church and Hallberg, watching from the corner of the building, stayed low. Hallberg peeked over his arm, while Church glanced over his shoulder as the armed police scrambled backwards for cover. The highly trained Chinese operatives shot true, chasing them away with well-placed bursts despite being outnumbered and outgunned.

But Church wasn't watching them. He was watching the carrier.

The man reacted fast, turning and sprinting towards the far end of the bridge with the lone MSS operative still closing on him. The operative raised his pistol to fire, but the carrier was too quick, streaking towards the opposite rail and vaulting over it, throwing himself down towards the water.

Church craned his neck, trying to pick out the splash between the shouting and the rattle of rifles. But he didn't hear one. Instead, he saw that the carrier had landed on a small wooden jetty some twenty feet below.

Church stepped from behind the building and began moving forward, running behind the police van to circle the slip. He pushed past Londoners fleeing in the opposite direction, wrestling his way against the current of terrified civilians. Limping as he managed his footing, he finally caught sight of the target: the carrier scrambling up a sloped walkway and back towards the promenade on the far side of the bridge.

The man reached the flat ground and burst into a

painful run, fleeing the gunfire, trying to disappear once more into the frightened ranks of Londoners—the very people who, if Church didn't catch him here and now, he would no doubt come to infect and kill.

One and all.

THIRTY-FIVE

2010, NOBILSK

THE MADE FOR THE HORIZON, Cole's heel jammed against the floor, the vehicle snaked violently as it fought for grip, searching for the hardened roadway beneath a foot of soft snow.

The ground clearance meant that the bottom of the armoured truck raked across the top of the powder, planing where the snow had deepened, and the steering went light, causing the truck to turn side-on before Cole pulled it straight once more, ducking forward towards the wheel to look into the wing mirrors, searching for the gunship coming up on their six.

They were headed directly east and light was beginning to crack the horizon in front of them, turning the sky a dark shade of bruised violet. And Church had seen enough sunrises to know the daylight would be on them faster than they could imagine.

Cole had killed their running lights, which meant that they were flying blind except for the GPS, Nobilsk just a fading collection of dim pinpricks in the far distance behind. But it didn't matter worth a damn whether they were hidden from soldiers on the ground; the gunship chasing them was likely equipped with all manner of night flight capabilities: infrared, night vision, an array of different cameras and sensors, giving the pilots the ability to fly in pitch darkness, cloud, smoke, rain, and of course snow too.

No weather condition was too much for it.

And Church thought it was pointless that they kept running at all.

The ammunition dished out by the ground troops may have been piffling compared to the armoured-plated SUV, but what the helicopter would be doling out would be more than enough to crack its hull like an egg.

'Anyone got eyes on it?' Cole asked frantically, searching all the mirrors.

Foster was glued against his passenger window, Mitch against his, Church too now, ignoring his breathing and his heart rate, instead wanting to deal with the issue at hand—considering the size of that fucking issue.

'Coming up fast,' Mitch said then, glancing back at them. 'At our four o'clock. It's coming out wide to make an attack run.'

Cole swore, turned his head, lowering it to squint up into the ever-brightening sky, picking out not just the shape now, but everything else that he needed to.

'Fucking hell,' he muttered. 'It's a bloody Hind!'

Church leaned across the doctor's lap to look past Mitch's head, confirming indeed that Cole was right, as he usually was.

The Hind was a legendary multi-platform attack helicopter that had been in Russian service since the Soviet era. It had gone through iterations and upgrades, but the base design had stayed the same. An Apache attack helicopter on steroids, it was equipped with S-8 80mm unguided rockets, a 12.7x108mm four-barrel chin-mounted Gatling gun, and a host of other weaponry including guided anti-tank missiles, up to 500kg of ordnance, and was able to carry a team of armed soldiers too, who'd be happy to operate its 30mm twin-barrel cannon mounted on the starboard side.

It was Russia's one-size-fits-all model: a single heli-copter for all engagements. And it had been through them all and come out the other side too.

There were few other choppers on earth that could measure up to it in sheer versatility and deadliness, and certainly fewer land vehicles.

And it didn't take long for the helicopter to pull, to put its prowess on full display.

The second Church saw the nose light up, the cycling minigun there, hammering the tundra with bullets, he threw himself back in the seat and braced for the hit. The rounds punched into the snowy ground, sending up fountains of ice and snow as the helicopter, nose-dipped towards the earth, swept low, carving a path of death diagonally across them.

Cole slammed on the brakes as the fire was about to take their front wing off, and fought to keep it straight, the bumper diving into the snow like a plough, sending a huge spray of it up over the bonnet.

They decelerated almost to a stop immediately, and Church was launched forward into the back of Foster's seat, just catching himself on his forearm before he broke his nose against the aluminium headrest.

He slumped backwards, just as Cole stomped on the accelerator once more and pulled them forward, the line of gunfire slashing just a few feet ahead of them.

A clever manoeuvre, Church thought, but one they wouldn't fall for twice.

'I reckon we're only going to get one of those!' Cole called out, pulling them back up to speed. 'We've got to think of something here fast.'

Church, along with the others, looked around for any kind of cover.

In urban warfare, they could look for narrow streets, bridges, anything that would give them protection from above, that would break line of sight. But out here it was flat and open. For a hundred miles in every direction. There was nowhere to hide, and the gunship would only need to get one good hit off with its front gun to punch through to their engine and disable them, take out a wheel, or hell, just blow straight through the glass and roof and poke them full of holes where they sat.

And that wasn't even considering the fact that they might be willing to waste a rocket to get the job done.

Church let out a rattling breath, staring at his teammates, at his brothers, and then let his eyes fall to the back of his arm.

He could see a little red spot of blood where it had soaked through his sleeve, could feel the wound pulsing, throbbing underneath, constantly driving that infection around his body.

He knew he was infected. He could feel it now, even, coursing through him, weakening him.

And before he even decided, he knew the decision was made the second that he failed to check that Russian soldier for life.

He'd already given his life for this mission. The only thing that was within his power now was how he went out.

He barely finished that thought before he twisted in the seat and leaned over the back into the boot space, fumbling with the latches of the hard cases there. He flipped the first open and saw a rack of small weaponry: half a dozen handguns, modular assault rifles, and plenty of ammunition. But it wasn't different to what they were already carrying, and that wasn't enough to deal with a gunship.

With a grunt, he hefted the case out of the way, shoving it and rolling it awkwardly over to the side, spilling its contents into the back.

'What the fuck are you doing back there?' Cole yelled.

But Church ignored him, dragging the second hard case forward, unlatching this one, and discovering exactly what he'd hoped for.

A light machine gun. A PKP Pecheneg to be exact. The replacement for the legendary RPK-74, the Pecheneg was a heavy-hitting machine gun firing a 7.62 rifle cartridge fed by a belt-fed ammunition system coming out of a 200-round box. The one Church was staring at was equipped with a top rail scope too. And though he wondered if it would be enough to get the job done completely, he knew it would be enough to slow them down, and if he was lucky, wound the ship in some fashion.

Nobilsk was a long way from where the gunship would have flown in from, and Church could only hope that they hadn't refuelled the second they'd landed in the city and that the pilot would have to be aware of its range—that they'd know that if they went down out here, there'd likely be no one coming to rescue them.

Even if Church couldn't take them out, maybe he could hold them off long enough that they'd have to turn tail and head home to refuel, give Cole and the others enough time to stretch out their lead and make it to the exfil.

Church hefted the mighty weapon into the back seat with him and stood it upright, clutching it between his knees.

'Jesus Christ,' Cole called out, looking over his shoulder. 'What the fuck are you doing?'

'Whatever I can,' Church said back, nodding at his captain and reaching for the door handle. 'Keep the speed steady, and if you can, bring the truck around and give me some kind of shot at this thing.'

'It's minus 20 degrees out there,' Cole protested. 'You'll freeze your fucking tits off before you fire a single bullet!'

'And what's the alternative? We sit in here nice and cosy until that thing blows us apart?' Church reached out and threw the mighty bolt on the Pecheneg towards the stock, chambering a round and making it ready to fire.

'This is our only hope, Cole. You know that as well as me.'

Cole was silent for a few seconds, looking to the others for some kind of backup, for Mitch and Foster to tell Church what a stupid idea this was.

But Church was dead right that they were just waiting to be killed unless they took the fight to the gunship somehow.

'Bloody hell,' Mitch spoke up then, reaching out towards the machine gun. 'If we're going through with this stupid fucking plan, at least let me be the one. I'm a better shot than you anyway, Sol.'

He grabbed for the rifle, but Church pulled it out of reach.

Foster twisted round in his chair to look at him too.

Church sighed. 'I suppose you want to be the one to sacrifice yourself as well, do you?'

Foster stayed stoic, just stared at Church.

That was his intention, and Church knew that he and Mitch and Cole would have gladly gone to their deaths for any of them. But they didn't know what Church did.

'No,' Church said, shaking his head. 'It's my stupid

fucking idea, and I'm going to be the one that does it. If you lot want to off yourselves, next time come to that conclusion on your own.'

Mitch, despite himself, smirked a little.

Church leant forward then, reached out, squeezed Cole on the shoulder.

'You bring that fucker right to me,' he said.

Cole's jaw flexed. He took a second to answer, as though finding it difficult to speak.

'I'll fly it right down your fucking throat, don't worry.'

Church smiled at him, and he returned it, weakly, momentarily.

And then, Church was gone.

He pulled back and reached for the door before he could second guess himself, clutching the machine gun tightly and diving out into the snow, knowing that it would be a soft landing.

He crossed his arms over his chest, kept his ankles tight together, landing and rolling, the ground punching all the air out of him, his respirator pulling free of his face, finally, and twisting around his head.

He raked in a frozen, aching breath and came to rest, facing up into the bloody sky. It was an endless, open canvas, the storm having passed in the night, leaving only a wild and untamed nakedness behind. Stars twinkled above, another blotted out of existence with each second as the day continued to slit the throat of the night.

Church lay there, half-buried in the snow, still

clutching the machine gun and stared up into it, drawing a quiet breath—perhaps his last quiet breath—waiting for the ringing in his ears to subside and for the hellish beating of the helicopter's rotors to return.

And they certainly did.

Church sat up out of the snow and pulled his mask clean off his head, tossing it away, completely unnecessary now.

His face ached against the cold wind, his eyes acclimatising to the dawn, picking out first the shape of the shrinking truck as it jostled forwards, and then, above it, the gunship, coming up directly from behind this time so Cole couldn't pull any more stunts. It raked across the SUV's roof with a stream of fire, the distant rattle of the guns echoing across the tundra.

Sparks danced in the distance, and Church drew a sharp breath, watching as Cole slammed on the brakes, the red lights on the back of the vehicle flaring, and sent them into a full sideways slide, sparing them from an extended battering. The gunship swept forward overhead, pulled upwards into a sharp climb, and turned to the left at its zenith before it dove back down, far behind its target.

Church could see Cole ploughing back towards him now, having spun the truck a full 180. It was exactly what Church had asked him to do, and he was delivering.

Without wasting another second, Church swung his backpack off his shoulders and put it sideways in front of him, heaving and dropping the Pecheneg onto it, easing himself into a prone position with the stock against his shoulder, resting his cheek against the freezing cold steel, sighting through the scope up at the approaching Hind.

Its nose was tilted forward once more, the helicopter accelerating feverishly as it hunted its prey.

Cole was a few hundred metres away and accelerating, the Hind doing the same, closing the gap.

Church thought that at this rate they'd both be on top of him at the same moment.

But he had to wait, choose the right second to fire.

Too soon and the bullets wouldn't do enough damage, wouldn't be accurate enough. The Hind would simply peel off, launch a missile at him from a safe distance, and blow him straight out of the snow.

His only advantage at that moment was that he was small enough not to be noticed—not until it was too late.

He hoped.

Two-hundred metres.

One-fifty.

One-hundred.

The Hind was almost on top of the team, the front gun spooling up once more, its hiss and howl ringing through the emptiness.

Church sighted, braced, exhaled, and squeezed the trigger, pinning it against the back of the trigger guard, the reticle settled right over the cockpit.

The pilot reacted fast, but the bullets were faster, covering the hundred metres to the helicopter and punching right through the cockpit windows, shattering them and sending a spiderweb of cracks across the glass.

The pilot—Church unsure if he hit or not—wrestled the yoke left then right, pulling them into a fast turn. Church's bullets now slammed into the underbelly. He lifted the scope, aiming for the rotors on the tail, hoping to clip them, to do some damage, but the gunship was too fast and wheeled away before he could.

The SUV zoomed past, spraying snow, and Church caught Cole's eye for just a split second before they were behind him.

He didn't turn to look, eyes still fixed on the gunship as it came around for a second pass, flying right at Church once more, readying itself for the kill shot.

'Fuck,' he muttered, shoving himself to a stance, realising that the Hind wasn't after the truck anymore.

It was coming for him.

Church was on his feet, pulling the heavy LMG against his shoulder as he began backing up, the weight of the gun making his arms ache instantly. He squeezed the trigger once more, the bullets seeming to do no damage as they pinged off the armoured hull of the Hind as it zoomed forward, a few hundred metres out. Too far to hurt.

It began to rise up then, and Church's blood ran cold, knowing it was gaining altitude to line up a target.

An instant later, a plume of fire exploded from behind one of its wing-mounted missiles, the rocket dropping a few feet and then sling-shotting forward, covering the distance in the blink of an eye.

The only thing Church could do was turn, take a single step and leap.

The missile slammed into the ground behind him and he felt the force blow him clean off the floor, flinging him upwards into the air. He saw sky, then snow, then sky, then snow before he smashed down with enough force that he was surprised he didn't snap clean in two.

At first there was no pain.

He was seeing stars, could taste blood.

He tried to sit up, draw breath. The pain came suddenly, all at once, lancing through his back and into his head, down through his legs and into his toes. Broken back, he thought instantly, grimly, rolling onto his side, clenching and unclenching his toes and fingers reflexively to test whether he was paralysed.

Movement. Painful. But movement.

He grinned through the blood, tasting it in his mouth, and tried for his hands and knees and failed, the pain localising, radiating across his ribcage. He touched at it, could feel at least one, if not more, of his ribs cracked—broken probably, smashed into a thousand pieces.

His head was ringing like a bell, his exposed skin on fire, burnt from the blast or just shocked from the sheer concussive force. The only thing he could do was roll over, press his face into the cold, soothing snow, managing to get onto his side, barely, realising then that his hands were empty.

He groped blindly, looking for the Pecheneg, but it was gone, buried somewhere and he didn't know where.

A dark shadow loomed above him and he tilted his head back, looking up, seeing the underbelly of the Hind no more than 50 feet overhead, cruising slowly, the side door open, soldiers in black leaning out, looking for him, making sure that he was dead.

And though his heart was still beating, he knew he already was.

He could see them in close enough detail, almost smiling behind their masks as they looked down at him, bringing their rifles slowly to their shoulders, ready to finish him off.

Church closed his eyes, hoping that he'd done enough, that he'd accomplished what he'd hoped, that he'd saved the others.

But the only thing that he could rely on, truly, with Foster, Cole and Mitch, was that they were as stubborn as he was.

He heard the engine of the truck before he saw it, heard the wheels lock, the tyres judder in the snow, heard the rattle of gunfire.

Three suppressed MP5s, all letting loose at the same moment, a call of shock and pain, a scream growing in intensity until a body hit the ground somewhere behind Church.

He squinted through the swirl of snow coming off the wash of the rotors, a blizzard whipping up as the helicopter once more tried to give itself some lift, tried to turn and escape.

Church could hear crunching footsteps around him now as the men advanced towards him. He could hear the ruffling of snow somewhere in the whiteout, Foster grunting as he hefted something heavy, a chuckle emanating from the big man.

'That's more like it!' he laughed, his words followed by the chugging report of the Pecheneg he'd rescued from an icy grave.

Church lifted a hand to his eyes, squinting through his fingers, making out just the faintest outline of the helicopter above, the others still wearing their rebreathers, able to see a lot better than he was.

The helicopter's turbine engines spooled furiously, the revs climbing as it tried to peel out of there. Another dull thud of a body hitting the ground rang through the din—and then suddenly the wind was dropping, the rotor noise beginning to fade, the blizzard beginning to subside.

Church sagged back into the snow, taking a full breath, wiping crystals of ice from his eyes with the knuckles of his gloves, just able to pick out the shape of the Hind, now trailing smoke as it limped back towards Nobilsk. Whether it was out of fuel or it was damaged enough that the pilot knew it was more likely to go down out here than win the exchange, Church couldn't say.

But the fight was over as quickly as it had begun.

Cole, Mitch and Foster hauled him out of the snow

and onto his knees, standing him up groggily. He could feel one on each arm, but wasn't sure which was which, his eyes still stinging.

He heard Cole's voice somewhere around him. 'Well, if you were trying to kill yourself, you failed miserably, Church, and if you're trying to be a hero, you did a shit job of that too,' he laughed, 'considering we had to ride in and save—'

He didn't get to finish his quip, cutting himself off a word too soon, the panic clear in his voice.

And Church knew why.

Foster was at his left, holding under his arm, but had his other hand just above Church's wrist, pulling his sleeve up.

Church blinked himself clear, Cole coming into view, staring down at his unmasked forearm.

Church looked there too now, the scratches having turned from red to nearly black, the spot where the nail had gone in darkened too, gnarled, bulging blue veins popping around it.

'What the fuck is that?' Cole snarled, looking at Church, the rage clear in his face.

He reached out, gripping Church by the straps of his vest, shaking him, bawling his fists in the fabric of his jacket behind.

'I asked you a fucking question—what the fuck is that, Church? Answer me, now!'

But Church didn't need to, and Cole didn't need him to either. Not really.

He knew exactly what it was. They all did.

Foster released him, Mitch too, and Church swayed wearily on his feet.

'You know what that is,' he said back. 'I'm sorry.'

'That's the fucking reason you wanted to jump out of the car, take on the fucking Hind?' Cole shook his head at him. 'You fucking idiot, Church, you stupid, pissing, bloody, fucking twat!'

Church smiled at his captain, and then at the others, the three of them standing silently in the vast open tundra. But despite that, Church felt warm, filled somehow. He was surrounded by family, and he knew that he'd done all he could to make sure they lived to see another day. And just then, it didn't matter to Church whether he would or not.

This was the job, and he knew, one way or another...

This was always how it was going to end.

THIRTY-SIX

PRESENT DAY

THE FIREFIGHT RAGED to their left but Church didn't even look over.

Looking made no difference at all.

All he could do was sprint.

The carrier was out ahead, Hallberg right on his tail. They skirted around the slip towards the high-rise buildings, the water on their left, and streaked onto the promenade, dodging fleeing pedestrians and hurdling over the ones who were just pressing themselves against the wall or the floor, hoping not to catch a stray bullet coming across the slip, the nearest MSS agent moving up and across the bridge to signal his partners that their target was getting away.

The muzzles flashed out of the corner of Church's eye, and the sound of bullets hitting the concrete above his head forced him to duck, reach back, grab Hallberg, and push her along in front of him.

The MSS agent closest must have recognised him from the train station, he thought.

The third agent had turned his gun on the pair of them, but the police were too much for them to contend with, and they couldn't cover both. He stopped shooting, ducking behind the rail once more, and in seconds, Church and Hallberg were past and sprinting freely again, the carrier up ahead, looking left and right, unsure which way to turn.

Shouts echoed behind Church, Chinese, his ears detected. Orders to give chase, but he didn't risk turning back, taking his eyes off their target for a second.

They were reeling them in, Hallberg at full tilt, Church right behind her, making sure she was shielded.

The carrier's run was laboured, and he knew he wasn't getting away. Changing tack, he slowed, veering off towards the buildings, towards a woman at one of the doors to the apartment blocks above the shops and restaurants along the promenade. She was fumbling desperately with her keys to get the door open, to get inside, to safety. She managed it just as he reached her, his hand closing above the collar of her coat, ripping her backwards, clean off her feet.

She hit the ground and called out, and he was already inside, the door closing slowly behind him. Church kicked up a gear, bolted past Hallberg to make it, shoving his arm through the gap just as it reached the frame, keeping it open, the metal corner of the door biting into his elbow. He growled with the pain, his leg throbbing horribly from the gunshot he'd sustained earlier, the blood coming again, bursting through the delicate, freshly congealed scab there.

The denim of his jeans had staunched the bleeding, but now it was open and he could feel the blood running down his shin, as he ducked into the corridor inside, reaching back to take Hallberg's outstretched hand, pulling her into safety.

'Go, go!' she ordered him, knowing he'd be faster on the stairs than her despite the injury.

Church hammered straight past the elevator and into the stairwell, the closing door telling him he was still hot on the carrier's heels.

Church shouldered it open, his pistol flying from its holster, covering the stairs in front in case the carrier was waiting to ambush him. He cleared it, slotted his pistol back in its pouch, footsteps echoing down from above. He hurdled upwards, climbing furiously, arms pumping, legs screaming, chest burning as he tried to close the gap. If he got too far ahead and stepped out on a floor—or hell, reached the roof—Church had no idea whether he'd be able to catch him at all. No, this ended here and now, and this empty stairwell was the best place to get this done.

The footsteps above grew louder as he gained ground, step by step, single-minded in his pursuit, his focus broken only when he heard his name echoing from below.

'Church!' Hallberg's voice, called out, the fear in her tone palpable.

He froze, skidding to a stop on one of the landings. Glancing up, seeing a streak of black above as the carrier stretched out the lead once more. He turned and looked down over the rail, Hallberg two floors below. And below that, at least two men, running hard, boots clattering on the concrete, the MSS giving chase, closing on Hallberg. Church glanced up again, the carrier slipping through his fingers... but he couldn't leave Hallberg to the wolves.

Heaving himself along the rail, he galloped back down the stairs, meeting Hallberg on the next landing, scooping her up in his arms, pointing her upwards, urging her on, the two MSS agents bearing down on them both.

'Go after him,' Church ordered, knowing that it would be the safest thing for her to get out of there, out of the firing line, as quickly as possible. The MSS would be taking no prisoners. Their objective now switched, no doubt, from capture to kill, to destroy as much evidence as possible that the Chinese were involved in this in any way, shape or form, and escape the area. They'd want to put down the carrier for good, and Church and Hallberg with him. Which meant that Church had to finish them first.

Hallberg's fingers clenched tightly around his fore-arms and she shook her head. 'I'm not leaving—'

'There's no time. Go!' Church ordered her again. 'Catch him, finish this, I'm right behind you. I promise.'

He nodded at her, peeled her hands from his arms and turned her by the shoulders, pushing her up the stairs just in time. She looked back and then disappeared round the corner above as Church turned, two MSS agents coming into view on the landing below him.

He spotted them just in time, their guns already raised and levelled at him.

He ducked backwards, covering his ears with his hands, diving against the wall as bullets pelted it right where his head would have been. Dust rained down and he screwed his eyes closed, shook the dust from his eyes as he stood, charged, leapt from the top of the landing into the midst of the two men coming up from below, catching them by surprise.

He slammed into the first, sending him flying back into the wall with a loud thud, and reached out, seizing the arm of the second, the pistol aimed at his skull, and drove it sideways, forcing his bullets into the concrete instead.

Church took a step forwards and dropped his shoulder under the man's arm, judo-throwing him up and over the railing into the chasm of space at the centre of the stairwell.

He screamed out, grabbing for the metal bar, just catching hold by one hand, his feet dangling.

Church reached for his gun, looking to end him there and then. But before he could get it from the holster, the second was on him once more, jumping onto his back, trying to wrestle him to the ground.

Church's fingers leapt to his throat instinctively, his

windpipe almost closed as the man clamped down, fixing him in a chokehold. Church saw stars almost instantly, his breathing ragged, blood poorly oxygenated by the fray, and all he could do was launch himself backwards into the wall once more, crushing the agent against it.

He called out but the man held fast, and Church did it again, harder this time, the grip loosening, air clawing its way down into Church's lungs, the light returning to his eyes. The first guy was now trying to clamber back up over the rail in front of him.

Church stretched his fingers out, reaching for his gun again, but the agent on his back threw his knee upwards into his ribs, leg hanging across his hip, preventing him from grabbing it.

And then the first was up, vaulting over the rail and moving towards the stairs, heading for the carrier, for Halberg.

Church gritted his teeth, and with everything he had, tilted forward, throwing himself blindly, breathlessly, reaching out for his coat and missing, his fingers scraping down his back, latching onto the man's belt instead, and clamping down in a vice grip. The man twisted, pistol coming up once more, putting Church right in his sights, forcing him to do the only thing that he could—spinning in place, putting the MSS agent on his back between them.

The shooter stayed his trigger finger, but Church knew that it wouldn't be enough, that it would buy him a second, and no more.

He swung a closed fist over his shoulder, connecting with something hard, the skull of the agent on his back, and the grip loosened once more. His fingers dug into the man's wrists now, and twisted them free, the weight finally leaving his neck.

Church raked in a breath, turned, the two men side by side in front of him, and launched a vicious kick into the gut of the closest, still seeing stars, unable to make out anything except blurry shapes in his oxygen-deprived state.

He was operating purely on instinct, and he hoped that would be enough.

The hitman flew backwards into the stairs, his back thudding against the sharp concrete edges, and the second didn't stick around, turning and climbing furiously once more. Church went after him, reaching for his ankle, the downed agent grabbing on his leg. As he did, the three of them connected suddenly in a chain.

Church yanked at the man ahead of him, launching a heavy punch upwards into his cheek, dragging him back down onto the landing before he could get his legs under him once more. But by the time their faces drew level, he realised that his own leg had been released. He didn't have time to turn, didn't have time to do anything, except brace for what he knew was coming.

He heard the sound first, felt the pain an instant later.

Three massive blows to the middle of his back, close grouping, as the point-blank gunshots smashed into his spine.

He yelled, tasting blood, unsure if his ballistic vest had done its job.

But either way, shot through or not, with the last of his strength, he had to finish this, and he had to do it now—winded, no air getting into his body, shot, bleeding, maybe dead in the next ten seconds. Still clutching at the second agent, he rolled, pulling him in front of himself like a human shield, screwing his eyes closed against the muzzle flash as the first agent fired again. This time, hitting his partner. The man convulsed in Church's arms, howled like a kicked dog, clutching at his stomach, the blood already gushing through his hands.

The first agent stepped back, shocked, and the opening was all Church needed. He sprang from the steps, throwing a vicious elbow into the man's jaw.

A loud crack rang out, and Church wasn't sure if it was his elbow or the man's face.

Everything hurt, his whole body vibrating, his nervous system overloaded with pain.

Dazed, the agent reeled backwards, bouncing off the wall, and Church seized him by the back of the head, taking a fistful of hair, and dragged him forward, turning and lining up the steel railing above the staircase. And with the very last of his strength, drove the man's skull straight into it, hard enough that he felt the bone give out under his grip.

The agent fell limp instantly, slithering back off the bloodied steel and collapsing into a dead heap next to his friend.

Church tried to breathe, couldn't, winded, and reached up his back, trying to force his hand under the vest to assess the damage, but he couldn't get there, the vest too tight, his body too weak.

He went to a knee, putting his now reddened hand on the floor, his fingers covered in fresh blood.

He could feel it running down his back.

He coughed and spat more blood, thick globs, the red liquid running between his teeth, dripping from his lips.

'Halberg,' he squeezed out, whispering, her face swimming in the darkness in front of his eyes.

He tried to breathe again.

His body refused.

Come on, he urged himself. *Take a breath. Take a breath you coward.* The pain was so searing it almost made him black out. But air, just a trickle, wormed its way into his lungs. *Again,* he told himself. *Again. Take another breath you weak fuck.*

His body obliged. This one a little bigger.

Get up, Church, get up!

He berated himself, forcing his foot underneath him, reaching out for the rail for support. He felt it warm and slick with another man's blood under his palm, and staggered to his feet, staring upwards into the endless stairwell.

Halberg was up there, somewhere, and he needed to get to her.

He just hoped, by the time he reached the top...

It wouldn't be too late.

THIRTY-SEVEN

2010, NOBILSK

THEY WERE RUNNING on fumes by the time they reached the extraction zone.

The massive, roaring engine of the all-terrain SUV was necessary to haul its bulk through the deep snow, but despite its gargantuan fuel capacity, it still slurped down diesel with abandon.

By the time they saw the faint outlines of the herding settlement swimming on the horizon, they were on empty. A few clicks short, the vehicle ran out altogether and came to a squealing stop, the car diving into the soft snow and laying still.

Cole sighed and leaned forward on the wheel, still wearing his respirator.

They all were. For their own benefit.

Church had his right hand clamped over the throbbing entry wound on his left forearm, the skin blackened beneath it. He could taste blood in his mouth. It hurt to blink. Breathing was becoming uncomfortable and he revolved through unbearable cycles of feverish heat and cold, sweat beading inside his mask, pooling around his chin. But he dared not take it off.

The doctor and Mitch were bunched up so tightly against the other door that he might as well have been a leper.

'Right then, lads,' Cole said slowly, staring across at the settlement in the far distance, 'we're on foot from here.'

They nodded quietly and Cole looked around to stare at Church as though to appraise him, to see whether or not he'd be able to make it.

'What about you, Solomon, you still got some fight in you?' he asked, forcing a brief smile.

Church wasn't sure if his throat had swollen closed or whether simply the lump in there was precluding him from speech, but either way, all he could do was nod. Honestly, he didn't know if he had the energy or the strength to make it, but he wasn't going to sit here and die alone in that seat.

If there was any hope for him at all, in that 10% survivability range, it wasn't here, it was there.

They disembarked and sank up to their knees in the snow, all of them exchanging looks, knowing that this wasn't just going to be a slog, but a mission in itself.

Cole waved them all to set off and dug in his pack for a sat phone, unfolding it and punching in a number, dialling out as the men began their journey.

Church was struggling to lift his legs, Mitch immediately seeing it and lacing his arm under Church's shoulder, supporting him, carrying him forward.

'You know,' he said, straining under the weight, 'there's this newfangled thing called Atkins you might consider. Supposed to work wonders. You might think about giving it a try when we get home, eh?'

Church couldn't muster a laugh or even a smile—he could hear Cole's voice faintly behind him. He could have walked while he made the call, but it was apparent that he wanted some distance between himself and the men before he said his piece. Some distance between himself and Church, specifically.

'This is Cole,' his voice drifted through the frigid air, 'we're an hour from the EZ, on foot—slowly—every man accounted for. Our HVT is in good health...' He waited before continuing, waited until he thought Church was out of earshot. 'But we've got one man showing signs of infection. We're going to need a medical tent and quarantine set up when we arrive back on British soil, antivirals, the whole nine yards.'

He stopped talking and Church felt a flicker of hope deep inside himself.

'What do you mean?' Cole said then, his voice dwindling in the back of Church's periphery. 'You're fucking kidding?' he spat, his voice rising. 'Not a chance, no way,' he went on, 'we're not leaving him here in this fucking hellhole. Listen to me, if you think —' The vitriol rang across the tundra, but he was cut off abruptly.

Church assumed by the DSF, Hugh Haddon. Likely with Ros Kerr in his ear—the SIS rep.

'Yes, I understand, sir, but—' Cole said, but he was cut off once more. 'No, I hear you. Yes, I understand. Yes, a direct order, right— Sir? Sir?'

Church glanced back, could see Cole holding the phone in front of him, staring down at it as though he couldn't believe what he'd just been told before the DSF had hung up on him.

The hope died in Church's chest, the tiny flame snuffed out. It wasn't hard to tell what had just happened.

He felt the weight of his body increase on his weary legs.

'Come on,' Mitch said, 'you got to help me here a little bit, Sol.'

But Church could barely walk.

And wasn't sure if he wanted to at all anymore.

He sagged forward, putting a hand down into the snow, his whole body convulsing with shivers, the sweat, murky and grey, running up his visor now as he doubled forward.

The angle aggravated his chest, made him cough, and the first specks of blood flecked on the inside of the clear plastic.

'Leave me,' he told Mitch.

'Not a fucking chance,' Mitch replied.

'I'm not coming home with you, Mitch. Didn't you just hear Cole's conversation?'

'I didn't hear a fucking thing,' Mitch said back.

'And anyway, whoever lands that plane—they're going to be outgunned and outmanned. If you think we're leaving you here, to die in this frozen fucking wasteland, you got another thing coming.'

'If they're ordered not to take off, they won't take off,' Church said.

'Yeah, and I can fly a fucking plane, if I need to,' Mitch replied.

Before Church could respond, he felt Cole under his other arm, Church's infected wrist laying across his shoulder.

He and Mitch hoisted Church to his feet unwillingly, and dragged him forward through the snow.

'Mitch is right,' Cole said, 'fuck orders. Either we're all getting out of here, or none of us are.'

Church wanted to protest, wanted to tell him how stupid that was, but once more, he couldn't speak. All he could do, as he was hauled towards their extraction, was smile.

By the time they reached it, the distant rumble of jet engines was already washing across the white desert, a dark mass lumbering down out of the clouds that had gathered to the north, ready to land on the frozen runway.

It was a battered old cargo plane, rusted and unfit to fly by the looks of it. Its wings bobbed as it came down, its wheels touching and the whole body snaking left and right as it lifted its flaps and forced itself to decelerate.

Church and the others waited at the far end of the

runway watching it come, the men standing, Church sitting, doubled forward, on a pile of their packs.

Church wasn't sure what to expect—whether or not there'd be soldiers filing off the plane to make sure Cole's orders were followed, that Church was left here, abandoned to the cold. But it wasn't the response that he got.

The plane made an about-face and lowered its rear cargo ramp. A dozen men in white hazmat suits came running down carrying boxes and bags, four of them in the middle holding what looked like a carry case containing a giant gazebo.

They jogged towards the side of the runway, aiming for the herding settlement—just a cluster of semi-permanent shacks and yurts, lived in half the year as the reindeer herds migrated in and out of the area.

Currently empty, mercifully, Church thought.

He wouldn't infect anyone else.

His team watched in silence as the men in hazmat suits set about unfurling the structure, a white tent springing to life.

They opened the boxes they'd brought and carried equipment inside, doubling back to the plane to fetch a gurney and other medical machines.

Church pieced it together, and so did Cole, who turned back and slapped him hard on the shoulder—harder than necessary—grinning down through his mask at Church.

'Doesn't look like you're getting off that easy,' he said. 'They're rolling out the red carpet for you.'

Church looked up at Mitch.

'I told you I wasn't coming with you.'

'Yeah, but you made it sound like you were going to lie down and just sort of die in the snow like a stray cat. This is luxury, mate. Five-star treatment.'

'They're even giving you a hot shower,' Foster chimed in with what felt like his first words of the entire mission.

He grinned down at Church, gesturing to two men carrying an oversized flight case, the words *Decontamination Shower* stencilled on the side.

Church forced himself to smile, gathering what little strength he had to get to his feet, one of the men in the hazmat suit coming towards him now.

'Which of you is infected?' he called out without ceremony, his accent not British.

Church couldn't place it—European, Scandinavian, German maybe—one of the UK's allies, he thought.

How they got all this mobilised and into the country, he wasn't sure, but he was glad they did. What they'd accomplished, what they'd managed to pull off in Nobilsk could end up saving millions of lives. And it would keep a catastrophic bioweapon out of the Russians' hands just a little longer.

In fact, if anything, this was the least they could do, Church thought. Though he wasn't sure if any of this pomp and circumstance improved his 10% chance of survival.

The men parted, leaving Church an island in the middle of them, and the doctor behind the white hazmat suit—a clear screen showing his face, but a surgical mask covering his mouth and nose regardless—gestured for Church to come forward with heavy rubberised gloves, stepping back as he did, not wanting to get too close until he had to.

Dr Zorin called out then: 'Interferon. High dose. Twenty million units. Administered intravenously. Constant drip for the first twenty-four hours.'

'That'll cure him?' the doctor in the hazmat suit asked, measuring Zorin in his ill-fitting clothes.

Zorin shook his head gravely. 'No,' he said. 'But it might give him a fighting chance.'

'That's all he needs,' Cole said firmly. 'Solomon?'

Church looked back at his captain. Cole was standing there with his backpack in his outstretched hand.

'Here,' he said. 'The mission's not over for you yet, not until you make it home, alright? You beat this thing, and then you come see us.'

'No promises, Captain,' Church said softly, smiling at his friend, at his brother.

'Bollocks,' Cole said. 'I don't need your promise. That was a fucking order.'

Church smirked a little, staring down at the backpack still being held out to him. He realised then that it wasn't his.

'What's that?' he asked.

'You know what this is,' Cole replied, shaking it a little, the hard drives inside clacking together.

The team watched on silently as Church stared at it.

'Why?' Church asked him.

'Because,' Cole replied, 'when you're lying in bed in there, I don't want you thinking I'm a colossal fucking prick, alright? I'm human, Church. I am.'

Church came forward and took the bag from him, gripping the handle tightly. 'Cole... this could be filled with solid fucking gold,' Church said back, 'and I'd still think you were a colossal fucking prick.' He laughed painfully. 'But you're doing the right thing. Orders or not.'

'Yeah,' Cole sighed, 'I hope so.'

Behind them, a high-pitched whistle echoed from the plane, and the team looked over, seeing a man standing on the ramp in a grey jumpsuit and a pilot's helmet.

He waved his arm at the men frantically and then pointed to his wrist. They were on the clock. As always.

The men filed towards it one by one, not saying anything else, not saying goodbye, not accepting that as a possibility. Mitch's eyes lingered longest, and then he turned away too, the three of them escorting Zorin towards the plane.

The rear ramp swallowed them up, and they were gone what seemed like all of a sudden. The doctor in the hazmat suit pulled at Church's arm, tried to guide him towards the quarantine tent, but even in his weakened state, he wouldn't budge. Nothing could have moved him as he stood there, Cole's backpack hanging at his side, the plane's engines spooling up once more. The propellers pulled it around in a circle and it began rumbling back down the icy runway, gathering speed until it hauled itself up into the air, wingtips wobbling horribly as it climbed higher and higher, disappearing into the cloud bank, the engine noise dwindling to a low and distant hum, and then disappearing altogether.

'Please,' the doctor said, 'we have to hurry. Every second counts.'

'Yeah,' Church said, shouldering Cole's bag and turning towards what he truly believed was his death. 'It always does.'

THIRTY-EIGHT

PRESENT DAY

IT TOOK MORE than Church thought he could give, the floors rolling by in a painful haze, each one more difficult than the last.

He stopped to cough and spit blood every few steps, his breaths tiny and wheezing as he fought his way upwards, this climb harder than facing the two agents. But eventually, numbly, he reached the open fire door leading onto the roof and staggered into the quickly fading day, shielding his eyes against the low-hanging sun blaring across the rooftops of the city, his pistol hanging loosely in his hand, blood dripping from the muzzle.

He willed his eyes to adjust, assessing the scene, looking for Halberg. He spotted her in front of him, standing in the middle of the gravel-covered roof, the carrier in front of her, heels on the edge high above the promenade below.

She turned, looking back at him, her right hand outstretched towards the carrier, and gave Church a silent order not to move, to stay right where he was.

She focused on the carrier once more—his eyes sunken and bloodshot, his lips purpled, skin white, veins popping in his neck.

He was clutching the medical bag, holding it in front of him, breathing hard, searching for a way out. But from here, there was only one, and there'd be no coming back from it.

He'd said before he'd rather die than be captured. And if he took the fast way down, his body would burst like a balloon, his blood everywhere, infecting who knew how many people. It was something that couldn't happen.

'Please,' Halberg urged him, 'you don't have to do this.'

His eyes flitted from Halberg to Church and back.

'Just step down,' Halberg said, her voice soft. 'We can talk about this. It's just us. It can be just *us*.' She gestured back at Church, not taking her eyes off the carrier. 'Just me and you, we can talk about this. I work for Interpol,' she told him. 'I can help you. If you tell me everything, if you cooperate, I can make sure that you're looked after. That you get the treatment you need. That you're treated fairly. That you're not extradited. We can keep you here, in the UK. We can keep you safe. I know that's what you're afraid of—going back?'

He said nothing, but his grip tightened on the medical bag. He had threatened his own death, but now that he was staring it in the face, it seemed harder for him to make that decision.

Church knew that weight—the weight of stepping willingly into your own demise. It was a weight that he'd carried. A weight that he'd borne.

A weight that he'd buckled under.

Church's hand moved to his forearm, the pain suddenly emanating from the scar there, the memory of what he'd been through, the fate that seemed to be awaiting this man.

He rubbed furiously at his arm, scratching at it, the knotted tissue sensitive under his touch. And mercifully, as the pain emanated from beneath his hand, it seemed to fade from his back, his legs, his body.

He let out a long breath and then drew a difficult one, swallowing, assessing the situation.

He could see it in the man's eyes.

He wasn't ready to die.

He was ready to take Halberg's deal.

She had her hand out to him, offering it. 'Please,' she said again, 'take my hand. I promise you'll be safe.'

The carrier measured her, his skin shining with sweat, and Church watched as slowly, with shaking fingers, he began to reach out—taking a step forward from the ledge, foot crunching on the gravel, six feet from Halberg now.

'That's it,' she said, nodding, smiling at him.

Church watched, staring at her still outstretched hand. An invitation to safety.

An invitation to spread his disease.

Church didn't even think about it, the decision made for him the instant that thought flashed in his mind.

His hand leapt to his hip, drew his pistol like a gunfighter, and lifted it.

The carrier saw all too late, didn't even manage to turn his attention towards Church before he fired—the bullet ripping past Halberg's ear, a few inches away, no more, and hitting the man square between the eyes.

His head rocked backwards on his neck and he crumpled sideways, just inside the ledge.

Halberg gasped, a thin mist of red blood hanging above them for just a second before it dispersed, drifting away on the wind high above the city.

She stood there still, Church's muzzle still smoking, his weapon still raised, and turned towards him, her expression oscillating between confusion and fury.

'W—what—?' she began, stammering, shaking her head, unable to comprehend.

But Church said nothing. He just dropped his gun and came forward, scooping her up in his arms and holding her so tightly she couldn't say anything else.

He buried his face in her shoulder, squeezing his eyes shut, knowing she'd hate him for what he did but that it was the right thing. Maybe not for her. Maybe not for anyone else. But for him.

And though she struggled, he held on to her for as

long as he could, wondering if this might be the last time he ever did.

'What the fuck did you just do?' she managed to force out, still pinned against him.

'I wasn't going to risk it,' he said. 'I wasn't going to risk you. Not a fucking chance.'

She beat against his chest with her fists and he let her down, holding her by the shoulders.

'I made that mistake you were about to, fifteen years ago, and it very nearly killed me. I wasn't about to let you take the same risk.'

She searched his face for something to hold on to. For something to hate.

But after a moment she softened, nodding almost imperceptibly, and then encircled him in her arms, her fingers brushing across his bloodied back.

But she didn't recoil. She didn't even flinch.

She just held him, understanding, finally.

Seeing right through him, just like she always did.

EPILOGUE I

CHURCH HISSED, the pain lancing up and down his spine in bolts.

'Jesus, Mitch,' he growled, wincing away from the rag he was dabbing on his back.

'When did you get so sensitive?' Mitch replied, arching an eyebrow, the reddened cloth in his fingers just a few inches from the angry, weeping welts on Church's back.

'I don't know,' Church replied airily. 'Maybe when I got shot three times in the fucking spine?'

The ballistic vest had just about succeeded in keeping the bullets from mincing his organs. But the damage was still significant. The force of the shots from that range had been tantamount to being hit with a sledgehammer. The impact sites had destroyed the top layers of skin and the damage would leave permanent scars. The shock to the surrounding tissue had caused quickly spreading bruising the colour of plums, and the pain was a constant, radiating heat—bad when Church was still, agonising every time he moved.

Cracked ribs, torn intercostals, swollen vertebrae, internal injury too—he expected the list to be long and long-lasting.

'Well, you never used to be such a wimp. Getting soft in your old age, Church,' Mitch goaded him.

'Maybe you're just getting clumsy in yours,' Church grumbled, sitting backwards on the chair, his arms and chin on the backrest. He straightened with difficulty and rolled his lifted T-shirt down over the wounds, stifling a groan as he did. 'I wouldn't exactly describe your care as gentle, Mitchy,' he added, easing himself to his feet.

'Maybe I'm being intentionally rough,' he replied. 'So you just bite the bullet and ask the person you really want to be doing this. Instead of chickening out and getting me to do it.'

Church turned towards him, his judgemental look enough to make his blood boil.

Mitch's eyes drifted to the window, where Hallberg was visible outside the front door of his farmhouse, walking in circles, on the phone with her boss at Interpol—Paul.

Church had landed her in some seriously hot water at work. It was a miracle they weren't in a cell at that moment. But the way things had shaken out in Canary Wharf... Church had killed two MSS agents who'd opened fire in a public area, shot the carrier of a deadly disease in possibly the best location he could have, and ultimately prevented a massive epidemic.

They'd been taken into custody almost immediately afterwards, but had said nothing. Church knew the drill well: sit and wait to be bailed out. And Hallberg had done just that. Paul had sprung her after pulling some strings—or twisting some arms, more likely—at the NCA, and she'd collected him shortly afterwards. On the proviso that they were remanded to house arrest, ready to be punished later once some of the dust had settled.

And that was just fine with Church. Home was exactly where he wanted to be. The only place, in fact.

They'd stuck themselves into the middle of an NCA investigation, and defied direct orders, as well as interfering with an active investigation. The only saving grace was that they'd got the job done in the end and saved lives. Had they not been there, things might have turned out the same way. Or they might have gone a lot worse. If nothing else, for now, the virus appeared to have remained contained. And that was what mattered the most.

'Looks like she's taking the brunt for you,' Mitch sighed, wiping his hands with the clean part of the rag.

'She did drag me into this,' Church said, watching her through the window.

'Oh, right. You're completely innocent. I forgot—sorry about that.'

Church scowled at him.

'Sol,' he went on, more serious now. 'What are you going to do about this?'

'There's nothing I can do,' he said. 'This is between Hallberg and her boss.'

'No, not that,' Mitch tutted. 'What are you going to do about *this*?' He made a sort of revolving gesture with his hands, signalling to both Church and Hallberg. 'It'd take a blind man not to see the way you're looking at her. The way she's looking at you. Did something happen out there?'

'A lot of things happened,' Church muttered, voice thin. 'But nothing like that. Not really.'

'Not really?'

'What is this, a third degree?'

'Maybe if you were a little more forthcoming, I wouldn't have to interrogate you,' Mitch said lightly.

'Maybe if you got a fucking TV you wouldn't be so bored and miserable all the time and have to take an intense—and strange—interest in my love life. Or distinct lack thereof.' He shook his head, folding his arms. 'And anyway, even if there was something going on—which there isn't—it couldn't... happen. It just couldn't.'

'You telling me, or yourself?' Mitch sighed, standing up and heading towards the kitchen, the look about him of a man about to fix himself a cup of tea.

Church remained in place, looking through the window, unsure of the answer to Mitch's question.

It had been a little over twenty-four hours since they'd set off from Mitch's house to head after the carrier, and his words were still ringing in Church's head. He'd accused Hallberg of being Church's girlfriend, and when denied, he asked Church if she knew that.

As Church watched her, she turned, locking eyes with him through the window. She rolled her eyes at the phone conversation she was having, lifted her hand and knocked her thumb and fingers together in the universal *blah-blah-blah* signal.

Church smiled.

She really was something. Even now, while she was getting professionally eviscerated, she was gesturing to her back and giving Church a questioning thumbs-up— *how are you?*

Selfless. Fearless. Smart. Kind. Beautiful. And too good for him. She was well-adjusted, functional. She had a career, a future ahead of her. She'd meet someone nice, someone that hadn't killed people. Whose hands weren't as rough, as bloodied as Church's. Someone who could care for her, provide for her. Someone who'd ask her how her day was when she walked through the door. Someone who would be a good father to their children.

Church was old. Broken. Unemployed. Borderline homeless. He was barely functioning, a recovered alco-holic—barely at times, it felt like, when the thirst hurt so bad it made his throat ache. And today was one of those days. Hallberg was everything he wasn't. And she deserved more than him. A lot more.

'The longer you leave it, the worse it'll be. Make it quick. It's the best thing for both of you,' Mitch called from the kitchen, the kettle starting to whistle. 'If you keep stringing—'

'I get it,' Church practically snapped, turning to see Mitch in the doorway.

He shrugged slowly and Church knew there was only one choice.

Go out there.

Tell her the truth.

It could never happen.

They could never happen.

He let out a long breath, the pain blinding, his nerves worse now than at any point in the last day.

'You're doing the right thing, Sol,' Mitch told him.

Church heard it, but wished he hadn't. Wished Mitch wasn't right.

He moved forward, reaching for the door. The moment it opened he heard Hallberg's voice, her back now to him, her tone sweet—even angered and through gritted teeth—as she apologised over and over, trying to placate Paul, trying to save her career.

Church walked numbly, the weak sun warming his face.

Hallberg turned at the sound of his footsteps, looked up at him questioningly, sensing the apprehension in him, that something was wrong.

She lowered the phone, Paul's voice drifting tinnily from the device.

'What is it?' Hallberg asked.

How to start? What to say? So many things. He

clenched his fists at his sides, opened his mouth to speak. And failed.

Hallberg waited.

Church let out another shaky breath.

'Fuck it,' he muttered. *Make it quick. Like Mitch said.*

He didn't hesitate for another second. He just stepped forward, put his arms around her waist, lifted her towards him.

And kissed her.

EPILOGUE II

Weeks passed.

Church was healing. Slowly.

But more than that, there was something else. He was… happy. Or at least as close as he'd been for a long time.

Hallberg had been slapped with a suspension, and Church knew his body needed rest. Which meant that they both had little to do and nowhere to go. And that meant Hallberg had scarcely left the farm. Mitch was disapproving and sullen, which Hallberg didn't understand, and kept asking Church about.

'Did I do something?' she would say.

Church could only shake his head. 'No, he's just a grumpy old git. He liked living here alone, and now that he's not…'

Hallberg nodded like she sort of understood, but she didn't. Church did. It wasn't her. It was him. Mitch was angry at him for doing what he was doing. Being selfish.

He knew, deep down, that it wouldn't, couldn't last. And he thought that she did too—whether either of them would admit it aloud.

That there would be something that would come between them. Something big, he feared. Or maybe it would be something small. They'd butt heads eventually and there'd be an end to this. This curling up in his little stone cottage in front of the open fireplace, listening to the rain patter the roof. Watching as it dripped through the forest outside, the first buds forming on the trees, fighting to bring the spring, railing against the cold and the dark of the winter that finally seemed to be ending.

In those moments, Church never wanted to leave. Not the cottage. Not bed. And not Hallberg, either.

But his world couldn't remain that small, and eventually they always seemed to need something. Food. Fuel for the fire. Something.

It was past nine on a Tuesday evening when the fire began to dwindle. It would be cold in the night, and there wasn't enough wood to get them through to morning. And it'd been a particularly wet and windy few days. Church's store had run low, and the pile of logs to be split outside was soaked through.

Luckily the petrol station sold split firewood in mesh bags, along with sundries and the basics—milk, bread, eggs. Enough to survive.

Church eased his arm from under Hallberg's ear and pushed himself gently upright, her body warming the single bed in the corner of his one-room home. The small stove across the flagstone floor was aglow with dying embers, and he knew that the longer he waited, the colder the house would grow.

Hallberg rolled onto her back beneath him, looking up wordlessly.

'We need the fire.'

'We can survive.'

'It'll get freezing in here. Fast.'

She shuffled closer to him, her tanned, bare skin glowing in the soft light of the dying flames. 'We can share body heat.'

He smiled. 'Not forever.'

'Why not?'

He swallowed, looking away, and then got up, feeling her watching him.

The stone floor was already cold under his bare feet as he found his jeans and pulled them on.

The springs of his bed squeaked as she sat up, wrapped in the blanket. She reached up behind him and ran her fingers over the pronounced lumps of healing flesh on his back.

He recoiled, not expecting her touch, the pain sudden and sobering, the area still tender.

'Sorry,' she said.

'It's fine.'

'They're healing well.'

'Mm,' was all he replied. He was doing his best not to think about them. Every time they twinged or itched it reminded him who he was outside these walls. Who they both were. The life that he had no doubt would find them both soon enough. He just hoped they had a little more time. Months. Weeks, even.

'I'll be back soon,' he said, taking a heavy shearling-lined coat off the hook next to the door and throwing it around his shoulders.

'Hurry back,' she called from bed, sinking down beneath the covers once more.

He nodded to her and ducked out into the cold, squinting against the rain, regretting not zipping up the coat before he left.

Church made his way down the stone path towards the treeline and into the open. An old trail led across the meadow to Mitch's farmhouse, Church's Land Rover Defender sitting on the drive next to it. Smoke curled from the chimney above the slate roof, lights burning in Mitch's living room.

He had a sizeable woodstore. Plenty for both of them. But he'd resigned himself to near silence since Church had kissed Hallberg, his blessing far from given. So Church didn't think that pilfering his wood was a good move for their relationship. He was letting Church stay at the farm out of the goodness of his heart. And Mitch was the best friend that he had. Hell, he was practically the only friend he had. And he wasn't going to jeopardise that for some kindling.

Church unlocked the Defender, and with muddied boots climbed behind the wheel. The engine turned over instantly and the bright LED headlights carved a path through the darkness, lighting up the field he'd walked through, cutting all the way to his shepherd's hut a hundred yards up the hill.

He kept his eyes fixed on it, the tiny square of yellow light—the window above his bed—as he backed up and turned the truck around, trundling towards the gate and civilisation.

Fifteen minutes later he pulled in at the petrol garage off the side of a B-road just outside a little hamlet that already seemed to be asleep.

He was thirty minutes before closing, and the clerk behind the counter had already checked out for the night. She was a young woman, chewing gum, totally locked into her tick-tock or her instant-gram. Church didn't have a clue about either, but had been reliably informed by Hallberg that they were social media platforms people used to—mostly, by the sounds of it—post lurid pictures of themselves online for strangers to look at and then reward them with 'likes', a form of digital currency worth exactly nothing.

He was reminded every day that the world he'd fought for once upon a time had moved on in big, paradigmatic ways. He was sure he liked the new version less than the old. But fighting against that was a losing battle.

Church parked up and went inside, a bing-bong chime playing as he opened the door. The girl behind the till looked up for just a second, and then went straight back to 'doomscrolling', which was what Hallberg called it. He could see why. The girl looked dead behind the eyes, fixated on her phone.

The exuberance of youth, Church thought sardonically as he milled through the shop, visualising the inside of his fridge. Seeing as he was here, he should pick up a few things. Stuff for tea. For breakfast. Enough to keep them going.

He drifted towards the dairy fridge and opened it, feeling the cool air on his skin. Absently, thinking of the warmth of his bed and of Hallberg's body, he reached out and lifted a bottle of milk, looking at the label but not reading it while he lamented leaving after all. Maybe they could have made it to morning. Shared body heat like she'd said.

Church sighed and put back the bottle of skimmed, grimacing at the thought, reaching for the full cream instead.

The door chime rang out behind him. Bing-bong. He glanced up, seeing a woman heading towards the till.

He let the milk hang from his index finger by the handle, and moved around the end of the aisle towards the bread. He liked brown. Hallberg liked seeded. They only had white.

With a sigh, he reached out for the last, lonely loaf on the shelf.

'Don't you know that shit'll kill you?'

Church froze, bread in hand, and looked up at the source of the voice. The woman who'd just walked in. The woman he'd not looked twice at.

She was standing halfway down the aisle, wearing a cream-coloured coat with black buttons over a fitted black turtleneck, her hands in her pockets, legs parted in a strong stance.

She was in her early sixties by Church's assessment, with white hair trimmed into a neat bob, her thin lips painted rich red. It took him a moment to place her. The blonde lustre of her hair had faded, her skin more lined now than it had been the last time he'd seen her. Fifteen years ago.

'Rosalind Kerr,' he said, taking his hand off the bread so that it could hang free and empty at his side.

She smiled a little, perhaps impressed. Perhaps not. 'You've got a good memory.'

'Not easy to forget someone that signs off on your death warrant.'

She blinked and looked away, as though surprised he'd said it. 'If you're talking about not allowing you to get on that plane—what would you have done? Do you even know how hard it was to muster a biohazard response of that size in that timeframe?'

Church scowled. He'd had a long time to consider that very claim, and investigate it. He had found out where those doctors had come from. That they were already on that plane, parked up at a runway in Vorkuta, masquerading as a cargo aircraft. That they'd been instructed to set up the containment tent inside the hold initially.

He'd gotten friendly with the doctor who'd treated him for Zorin's virus. And whether the man had simply wanted to appease a dying patient in his final hours, Church didn't know. But either way, he'd shared his orders, and it was clear to Church that they'd been expecting someone to be sick—just not him.

The medical team had been briefed on their priority: keep Zorin alive by any means necessary. They'd been anticipating him to be the one to fall ill. And had been ready for that. Ready to treat him in the air, too. Ready to bring him back, sick or not.

When they found out it was Church, their priority changed. And he'd nearly frozen to death in Siberia as he fought that thing off. Days of delirium, sickness, blood and bodily fluids leaking—hell, shooting—out of every orifice.

So no, he wasn't buying that line for a second.

'What do you want?' he asked Ros Kerr bluntly. 'Because you're not here for a social call.'

'No, I'm not,' she replied. 'And I suspect I don't have to tell you who I'm here on behalf of.'

'Not unless you've changed teams.'

'I haven't.'

'Then make it fast,' Church replied. 'This isn't where I want to spend my night.'

'No, I suppose not,' Ros said, her eyes peeling the skin from his bones. 'You're keen to get back to that little hovel in the woods, I suppose. Back to her. To Julia.'

Church stiffened a little, drew a breath, felt his fists curl.

'Down, boy,' Ros said easily. 'She's not in any danger from me.'

'You just wanted to flex your muscles, hey? Let me know that you know all about me.'

'Intelligence is sort of in the name.'

A car pulled up outside and Church looked past Ros through the windows of the shop, seeing a man dressed in black walk towards it from his position outside the door and stoop to the driver's window. He said a few words, showed them some credentials of some kind, and then sent them away.

He noticed then that the girl behind the counter was gone, too.

They were alone in the shop.

'What do you want?' Church asked again, hoping they could skip the preamble, the peacocking, the intimidation tactics.

'Straight to the quick,' Ros smiled. 'I like that. You know, Solomon, you and the boys did a bang-up job in Siberia. I'm sorry I never got to tell you that in person. Zorin has been an excellent addition for us through the years. You have no idea the impact that mission had on national security.'

'So mail me a fucking medal,' Church said. 'Can I go now?'

She held a hand up to signal the answer was a big fucking no.

'It was a shame—what happened in the DRC. As you can imagine, we had a hand in that whole… thing.' She waved her still-raised hand in a circle and sighed. 'To hear of the death of any service members is always difficult. But it's what we sign up for, isn't it.'

'Is there a point to this?' Church asked. 'My milk is getting warm.'

'It'll keep,' Ros said. 'We watched closely—what happened after, what happened with Blackthorn. I never liked the man. The opposite, in fact. And I never thought we could trust him. But, high up on the branches as I am… I'm not at the top of the tree. Yet. And those with more clout than I seemed to want him to succeed. They wanted him in Number Ten. For their own machinations, I suppose. Who even knows.' She laughed a little, red lips puckering.

It was clear she loved what she did. The chess. The cloak and dagger of it all.

'I'm sure someone had something on him. Lots of things. Thought they could control him. It's all conjecture, isn't it. But nothing happens in my world without a reason. It's all just shades of grey. Shadow games. You know the sort of thing, don't you.'

'I can imagine,' Church said through gritted teeth.

'But you, Solomon Church, Mister back-from-the-dead. You operate in a world of black and white, don't you. Blackthorn was a piece of shit. And he deserved to die by your judgement. So you made that happen.'

'I don't know what you're talking about.'

Ros smiled. 'Right. Don't incriminate yourself. They never did catch the killer, did they?' She shrugged. 'Nasty business, that. Though after the story broke about his misdeeds, there was no love lost there. Few mourned.'

'Colour me shocked.'

'But you didn't stop there, did you? And your crusade hasn't just bloodied British soil, either. France, Germany, Czechia, Serbia… You do get around, Solomon. Friends in high places makes that easier, doesn't it?' She hooked her thumb over her shoulder. 'Funny number plate, passport registered to—what is it —John McCallister? Come up with that one on your own?' She chuckled. 'Don't worry. I'm not here to burst the little bubble you've created for yourself. You and your friend out there playing house in the country, enough unregistered guns between you to put up quite the fight if anyone unwelcome comes knocking…'

'You can find out for yourself if you want.'

'Oh, I value my life too highly to make an enemy of you. I'd much rather a friend, Solomon. What do you think? Do you want to be friends?'

Church's grip on the milk tightened. 'Less than anything in the world.'

'Well, I thought I'd offer the old-fashioned way first. See if you still bleed red and white.'

'Just red these days,' Church replied. 'Trust me. I've seen plenty of it lately.'

'You have been busy. And your skills remain undulled with the years.'

Here it comes, Church thought.

'I suspect if I was to draw attention to your growing list of indiscretions—not least of all what you did at Oxford University—and told you that I could make them a very real problem for you once again—'

'I'd tell you to shove it up your arse?' Church replied.

'Took the words out of my mouth.'

'Intelligence is in the name, isn't it?'

She was amused by that. 'Threatening a man like you is pointless. It just stokes ire. And I don't need you angry at me. I need you focused. And I believe that the carrot works far better than the stick.'

'I don't like carrots.'

'You'd like the stick even less.' She took a step closer. 'Your little girlfriend—Julia Hallberg.'

Church's heart beat harder.

'She's very good at what she does—taste in men notwithstanding—but on this last sojourn, her judgement was compromised. Clouded, I suspect.'

Church said nothing.

'Her job hangs by a thread—' She cut herself off. 'Let me rephrase that. Her career is in pieces. And Paul Salinger—current Director of Operations for Interpol UK, her boss—is selling her down the river. Or at least making an attempt to. She's suspended, and under the impression that Paul's fighting her corner while the internal investigation develops over her actions. I can tell you right now that the only reason she hasn't been sacked and formally charged with something is because I've got the heel of my Louboutins on Paul's testicles.'

She let that sink in.

But Church didn't need time to understand it. 'And if I don't do something for you, you're going to remove your foot from his balls and let him gut Julia—ruin her to save himself?'

She stared at him. 'No,' she replied evenly. 'That is indeed the stick. But one I don't want to use. Not that it's even me using it. I'd simply be letting things run their natural course. Letting a guilty woman face the consequences of her actions.'

'So what's the carrot?'

'The carrot is me blowing the Interpol investigation clean out of the water altogether, allowing Paul to step away from his position as Director of Operations without so much as a shadow hanging over his impeccable career—with a sizeable severance bonus. And then putting Julia Hallberg in his chair before it even goes cold.'

The words hung in the silence of the shop, the only sound the faint buzz of electricity moving through the halogen lights above them.

'You want to give Hallberg a promotion?' Church asked, making sure he had this right.

'I don't want to do anything,' Ros said, removing her hands from her pockets and turning one of her many rings around her wrinkled fingers. 'I'm just putting this out there. There's something I need. Something that you can do for me. Something that… we can't officially be involved with, if you catch my meaning.'

'I do.'

'But I have other options. And I can do a lot of things for a lot of people. Quite frankly, if I wanted to nail you to the wall, Solomon, I could. Ten times over. If I wanted, with one phone call, you could be in a three-by-three standing cell in Guantanamo Bay before the sun comes up, unable to sit or bend, shitting down the insides of your legs, begging for the cold hose just to wash away the feeling of your own hot shit caking between your toes.'

'Guantanamo Bay is the CIA,' Church said, albeit a little stiltedly.

'And I've got a lot of friends in high places.' Her gaze bored into him. 'I could do that, but it does nothing for me. And frankly, while you're doing what you're doing—which seems to have a net-good effect, messy as your methods are—I've got no desire to hamstring you. But I can help. You don't need anything, or want anything, from me. But your friend Hallberg is in a very precarious position. She's cosied up in your bed right now, sleeping soundly, blissfully unaware that there's a shotgun against the back of her head—metaphorically, of course—before you go running off to save her. Again.' She chuckled. 'But, like I said, I can fix that. I can do better than fix that.'

'And all I have to do is say yes?'

'You do something for me. I'll do something for her. And you do want good things for her, don't you?'

His silence was the answer she already knew.

'I'll take that as confirmation, then,' Ros replied, nodding. 'Good. I'm glad we could catch up. I'll get the ball rolling and call when I need you.'

She turned and began walking towards the door.

'And Julia?' Church called as she moved around the far end of the aisle.

'Consider it done,' Ros said back, nearing the door.

'And she won't know it was me?'

'She won't know a thing. You can go right back to playing house. And come the morning, she'll have the phone call she's been waiting for. Do try and act surprised, won't you? Let's not give the game away. Because you know what else is in the name, don't you, Church?'

'Secret,' he muttered, narrowing his eyes at her.

'Good boy.' She smiled at him once more, and then with another door chime, she was gone.

Church looked down at the crushed handle of the milk bottle in his hand, feeling a little sick. He'd hoped never to see Ros Kerr again. But now… who knew what awaited him getting into bed with the SIS.

Something we—the agency—couldn't be officially involved in. Something messy. Something bloody. Something overseas. Where the British had a vested interest and no jurisdiction. His mind whirled with the possibilities, his body aching with the fight already.

His phone started buzzing then.

He reached into his pocket. Hallberg, he figured, asking where he'd got to.

He'd have to start lying to her, he thought grimly as he lifted it out. The lies start here. The end starts here. He swallowed, thinking about that. How could it be anything else? He was messing with her life without her knowing—for the best—but she'd still never forgive him. Not for doing it without telling her. Not for protecting her without her asking. Not for making a deal behind her back. And not for trading a favour for a promotion. If she knew the real reason she was getting that job, she wouldn't take it. She'd take the punishment instead. She was honest like that. Stupid like that, maybe. He was probably the same.

Either way, he was waiting for the other shoe to drop. For the thing that would end them before they began. And this was it. He knew it. Every time he looked at her now, he'd think of this. Of how he was lying, keeping this secret.

Fuck.

He looked at the phone. Still ringing.

Not Hallberg though.

Blocked number.

He answered and pulled it to his ear, expecting Ros Kerr's voice. Making sure he knew how to answer it— and would—if she called.

'That was fast,' Church said without ceremony.

But there was no immediate reply, just a dim crackle of static.

The hair on Church's neck stood up. 'Who is this?'

'It's time,' a dark voice said in his ear, the accent immediately apparent. Russian.

Church froze in place, holding his breath.

'Your debt is being called in, Mr Church,' the voice droned on, a little tinge of what Church thought was sadistic pleasure laced between the words. 'I hope you're ready.'

AUTHOR'S NOTE

Hello, readers!

I hope you enjoyed this one. It was definitely a departure from the last two war-centric books, and I wanted to make that jump to ensure the series wasn't going to become one-dimensional as it progressed. And as for the subject matter itself... I went back and forth on it, honestly. The idea of writing a pandemic book was something I wasn't wholly sure about simply because of recent history. But I was also struck by this frustrating notion that history, however terrible, should be able to be claimed and reclaimed by storytelling. So many books and movies come out about wars and atrocities (my stories included), so why should the pandemic that swept the globe in 2020 suddenly put all stories of this kind off-limits?

I think it's a frightening concept, and always has been—the idea of an epidemic taking fierce hold of a city. It's why viral and zombie media has always had such a stranglehold on audiences. There's something exciting about an unseen antagonist. Something exhilarating about that. Or at least that's how I've always felt about these kinds of stories.

Ultimately, I wanted to craft a book in this genre, but without the *what-comes-after* part. So many of these stories take place after the initial contagion stage, but I felt there was more to explore before that happened. And getting to contrast Church's usual stalwart courage with an indomitable foe—one that wobbles him more than we've seen before—that was also something I wanted to explore.

These types of books have a way of painting heroes as superhuman. And when that happens, characters become caricatures, which is something I was determined to avoid with Church. That's part of the reason I chose this story now. We didn't have a big, named antagonist lording over the plot here, which allowed the focus to fall on Church's reactions to the enemy, rather than the enemy themselves. Narratively speaking, the conflict shifts from external to internal. It's not about Church defeating the bad guy—it's about him defeating something inside himself.

I'm not going to summarise and ram the plot you just read back down your throat, don't worry! I just wanted to touch base briefly to give you some insight into why I chose this story and why I set it out this way. For the next one, we're diving back into the explosive, conflict-centric story the Church series is becoming known for, taking a tour of both Europe and the Georgian Caucasus Mountains as Church does battle with the Russian mob.

This author's note isn't going to be as long as the others, as there's no big history I want to unpack and explore for you all. Not so much context surrounding this book as the last few. But maybe that's okay, and instead I can take a beat to give you some insight into what writing these books has looked like over the last two years.

Church was first introduced in one of my Jamie Johansson novels, *The Mark of the Dead*, in October 2023. Chronologically, that book takes place after the next Church book (number five, in case you were wondering about overarching series order), but after I finished writing it, I felt a real connection to Solomon Church as a character, and didn't think he could be allowed to simply exist as a floating side character in Jamie's world.

Flash forward a few more Jamie books, and Church just wouldn't go away. By that point, I had already finished *The Devil in the Dark*, and I was beginning to feel like the Jamie series was going to reach its natural conclusion after the next few books (sixteen in total!). Readership was really consistent, but when you're that deep into a series, readers often begin to look for something new. And for an indie author like myself, that means each new book—which takes the same amount of work and time to write—returns a little less than the last in terms of sales.

And, unfortunately, as this is my career and the thing

that pays my mortgage (just barely, alongside my day job!), I needed to look for ideas for a new series. And the only thing that came to mind was Solomon Church. Readers really took to him in the Jamie books, and I wanted to do something peripheral to—but outside of—crime. It seemed the perfect fit to give Solomon his own adventures.

I put together the first outline for *The Exile* way back in, I think, January 2024, but didn't put pen to paper until later that year, putting up the pre-order in December 2024. I knew I had something readers would enjoy even before I finished the book, and I was excited to get it out there! By the time it dropped, I already had *The Fury* practically written, and the next book after that planned too. By the time *The Widow* comes out, that'll be five books in the series released in nine months. And when we're talking about 2025 as a year, it brings my total number of book releases up to 10!

These are—*The Exile, The Fury, The Outcast, The Carrier, The Widow* (to be released), *The Blood We Share, The First Snow of Winter...* and a trilogy of sci-fi novels I published under another pen name. These weren't all written this year, but it definitely makes 2025 my busiest release year to date. Still, I have written six novels in the last ten months, and that certainly takes its toll.

I'm working and writing relentlessly to try to make this something I can do full time, and I can't express how thankful I am to the readers of this series for helping make that happen. With each new release I can put a little more into my marketing and continue to reach new readers. I'm always pushing to try to make the most of my books, and to try and always do something different—something that pushes the envelope even just a little. And I always dedicate my all to ensuring each one is something I'm proud to put out in the world.

And I hope that shows through every page, and that this book, *The Carrier*, is no different.

Thank you for coming on this ride with me. And be sure that the next Solomon Church adventure is always right around the corner. So long as readers keep buying them, I'm sure as heck going to keep writing them!

Until next time—

Dan

PS. If you'd like to help me make a success of this series, please recommend it to other readers! Lend a paperback, gift a Kindle copy, tell your friends, your neighbours—anyone who'll listen. Word of mouth is still the most powerful tool for getting books out into the world, and I appreciate every single one of my readers who steps up to make that happen! But, of course, if you're not the chatty type, I still appreciate you taking the time to read the series, and I hope you might take a minute to leave me a quick rating or review on Amazon or Goodreads. It really helps Amazon recognise books that people love and is the simplest way to support authors you enjoy.

THANKS FOR READING

Reviews are the best way to support authors you like. They help other readers discover new writers, and they tell Amazon that books are worth reading! Just leaving a rating or a few words is immensely helpful to indie authors like myself, so if you enjoyed *The Outcast,* please consider leaving me a rating or review when you have a second.

And if you'd like to reach out to me to let me know what you thought of this book, please do! I respond to all reader emails and messages when I can and I love hearing from you.

To stay up to date with all things Solomon Church and Morgan Greene, find me on Facebook as Morgan Greene Author, or head to my website: *morgangreene. co.uk*

SOLOMON CHURCH WILL RETURN

A promise has been made. And it's written in blood.

When Church receives the phone call he's been dreading, one of his bad decisions comes calling. The daughter of a Russian mob boss is being held by a rival in order to force his hand in a business deal that will reshape the European criminal underworld. Church, a debt of blood owed to these men, is dragged into the middle of it, his goal singular: a deadly and explosive extraction mission, delivering the kidnapped girl safely back to her father. Complete the job and his debt is forgiven. Fail, and he'll pay for her life with his own.

As Church begins to understand the scope of the war he's been thrust into the middle of, he relives the last brush with the Russian mafia he experienced while on mission in Georgia. Tracking jihadist cells working with the Russians to traffic both arms and drugs through Georgia and into Turkey, Armenia, and Iran, Church's troop faced resistance with every step. What is supposed to be a covert surveillance op quickly turns bloody, transforming the remote villages of the high Georgian peaks of the Caucasus Mountains into a fierce battleground.

As he runs through fire in both his past and present, the only thing he's sure of is that the Russians deal in a type of violence unmatched by anyone else. And if Church hopes to get out alive, he's going to have to sacrifice everything he's tried so hard to hold onto.

The Widow is available now. Secure your copy today!

Printed in Dunstable, United Kingdom